Off to the East Fork

By HL Miller

Copyright 2022 HL Miller

All Rights Reserved

Without limiting the rights under copyright reserved above, no part of this publication may be reproduced, stored in or introduced into a retrieval system, or transmitted, in any form, or by any means without the prior written permission of the author of this book, except for the use of brief quotations in a book review.

Thank you for respecting the work of this author.

This is a work of fiction. Names, characters, businesses, brands, media, places, events, and incidents are the products of the author's imagination or are used in a fictitious manner.

Author's Note

This adventure unfolds in the little town of Darby, Montana and the East Fork of the Bitterroot River. One rule of writing is to write what you know and while today I am a stranger in Darby, in my youth, I knew everything that happened there. I couldn't have asked for a better place on God's Earth to come of age and routinely made sure my parents knew how thankful I was we lived along the East Fork and not in some shithole city. All the main characters are fictitious, but I've used family names, businesses, and places true to the period to give the story a solid background. I have nothing but respect for those folks who raised their families around Darby. As my dad said, there are East Forkers and West Forkers, and all the rest are Mother Forkers.

Please keep in mind, everything that follows is fiction until "The End."

Introduction

As a writer, successful or not, you have acquaintances tell you that they too want to write a book and a few of them will hand you a manuscript to read.

In the case of this book, a good friend handed me a dozen Mead notebooks of handwritten chicken scratch asking me to turn it into a book. First, the narrative was in first person. I dislike writing in first person. Second, the story needed a lot of work. Third, it spent pages discussing the boring topics of fencing and hiking. I wanted to wait a few months, return the notebooks, and make the excuse that I just didn't have the time.

But the friend had always been a great friend. To honor our friendship, I aspired to rewrite the story in the third person, delete the extraneous nonsense, and produce a tight, fast-paced, action-filled tale. Converting the text to third person consumed large amounts of my time and proved beyond the scope of my writing abilities. Since I grew up in the same area as the author, I got sucked into his descriptions of people and places and added my own observations. Instead of trimming out the fat, I spooned more bacon grease into the skillet. Halfway through the rewrite, I realized I couldn't hear my friend's voice in my head as I read the draft manuscript.

I deleted my rewrite files and went back to the notebooks. I left the narrative in first person and added a few little tricks to try to make the plot more interesting. Instead of weaving my comments in with the author's, I added notes along the way. If you are reading this on an ebook, you should have handy links to jump back and forth from the main story to my comments. If you're reading this in old-fashioned paper form, employ bookmarks to help you keep your place. Or better yet, ignore my ego-driven comments and enjoy the story.

I'm not sure how the final product turned out. I like it, but if this tale were a river, it would ox-bow slowly across the plains, completely unlike the East Fork of the Bitterroot during high water. I hope you enjoy.

HL Miller

Chapter One

I stumbled away from the campfire, leaving its light behind and wiping away the tears in my eyes. I'd never seen my father cry and even here in the middle of nowhere, I didn't want to cry. The branches of a fir tree scratched my face as I blundered into it in the dark. I spun away from the branch blindly fleeing until I tripped and fell, grabbing wildly for anything to help me keep my balance. I slammed into something, not a tree trunk but softer. Arms wrapped around me and slammed me on my butt. I thought Pete had followed me from the campfire and I pushed away from him telling him to leave me alone. A strong hand covered my mouth pushing my head into the bear grass. Whoever I had run into now sat on my chest cutting off my air. The quarter moon waxed, or maybe it waned, in the sky to the left. I could never remember which was which, but the light it gave off was sufficient to tell it wasn't Pete sitting on my chest.

There he was, the fugitive we had been scouring the forest for sat on my chest, clamping my mouth shut with one hand with a pistol in the other. Even in the low light, I could see him forming the shush sign by holding the muzzle perpendicular to his lips.

I guess I should have been scared, but I wasn't, which surprised me. Every Louis L'Amour book I'd read said that the opening in the end of a gun barrel appeared huge when the gun was pointed at you, but I could plainly see the barrel was almost a half an inch in diameter, which meant a .45 was pointed at my head not a 9mm.

After the surprise, shock set in as I realized my life had become a story. Last winter, one of my mom's clients had recommended the book *A River Run's Through It* to her. Mom had told the guy how I always read before going to bed and he suggested Mom buy Norman Maclean's book for me. This was back before Brad Pitt met Louise and Thelma and went on to tell everyone how fly-fishing was for the cool kids. Back when people fly-fished because they wanted to catch more fish to eat, not release.

Besides the fly-fishing story, the book had two more stories in it. I had wondered why the guy recommended the book to my mom because the second story featured a tough logger who liked to screw fat women. What kind of guy recommends that story to a lady's impressionable fifteen-year-old? I'm not sure which story, probably the last story about the Forest Service ranger who played cribbage, but one of the stories talked about how sometimes your life becomes a story.

Well, when I read that, I was disappointed because my life had never been a story and I was eager for the day something would happen to make my life a story. I tried hard to fashion everything I did into a legend, but it wasn't until the kidnapper stuck a gun in my face that I knew, right then, my life had become a story. In fact, my life had been a story for a while, but I just hadn't known it. If this man killed me, then I hadn't figured out I was in a story until the last page of the last chapter.

His hand eased the pressure on my mouth as I quit struggling. He hissed, "Yell, and so help me, I'll put a bullet in your brain."

I wiggled my head against his hand letting him know I wouldn't scream for help. That was the last thing on my mind. When did my life become a story? When did this start? When I agreed to go with Pete to look for the kidnapper? No. Earlier, when I agreed to build the fence for Cherylann?

The fugitive shifted the muzzle of the gun to the side of my head and leaned forward. His black eyes were wide in the pale moonlight and his breath was hot compared to the damp air. "What the fuck are you doing? Why did you run into me?"

I blinked, feeling the dried tears in the corners of my eyes, then looked past the muzzle of the gun at the kidnapper's face. I didn't run into him. He'd tackled me. I tried to speak but only stuttered nonsense about getting away from the fire.

"Did you hurt the girl with you?" His words searing like a hot cast-iron skillet.

I found my voice, replying in a whisper only he and the half-dozen mosquitoes circling our warm breath could hear. "No."

"What was all the yelling?"

How do I explain to a man holding a gun to my head that my best friend had just destroyed my life then tried to kick my ass? "We had an argument."

His leaned back a hair, giving me room to breathe. His whispered voice turned nonchalant as if we were discussing the weather while waiting in the checkout line at People's Market. "Do you have any guns?"

I thought of the revolver buried inside my backpack. If I told the kidnapper about the gun, I would lose the chance to use it. If I didn't tell him and he found it, it would anger him. If only I had it strapped to my belt right now.

That line of thought flitted away like a mosquito, my mind drawn back to the question of when had my life become a story. Graduation day when Jenny, Pete, and I stood around in the parking lot talking after the ceremony sprang to mind.

The gun pushed into the side of my temple. "Boy, you don't answer me, and I may not shoot you, but I will choke the ever-livin' shit out of you." His hand gripped my throat to emphasize his point.

I thought about it. Yeah, that was exactly when my life became a story.

Chapter Two

I waved at Jenny, caught her eye, then pointed to her parked car indicating I would meet her there. She looked cute in a long black skirt and red top with her brown hair in a French braid. I lost sight of her as she exited the gym since everybody was wearing some combination of Darby High School colors.

Jenny and I had been seeing each other steady since the start of our junior year. This would be our first summer together to enjoy each other without schoolwork or sports getting in the way. I was looking forward to spending time at Lake Como and hoping to convince her folks to let me take her on an overnight camping trip to Horse Creek Hot Springs.

I eased through the parents talking in the sunshine outside the door to the gym while waiting for their kids to claim their diplomas. Darby High School didn't hand out the real diplomas during the ceremony. Not since Rusty Carter had grabbed his diploma, knocked the principal down with a short hook to the chin, then ripped off his gown, and ran stark naked out of the gym to the applause of all the students in attendance and a few of the moms. Now they handed out the leather cover, but you had to go to the principal's office after the ceremony where he and the football coach gave one student at a time their diploma.

I heard snatches of conversation as I made my way through the parking lot—timber sales, summer plans, and the grass for summer range was coming in good, but it needed to rain soon. I had heard the same talk every spring for as long as I could remember. I glanced at the sky. A wall of stringy clouds was to the south. Maybe there would be a rain shower this evening.

I stepped past Diana Varner and gave her a quick smile and a wave. She waved back but didn't smile. I didn't take offense since Diana rarely smiled. She seemed self-conscious in her red dress rather than her customary blue jeans. Her family lived near mine up the East Fork and although we didn't hang out in high school, our folks had played cards together when we were younger and Diana's mother had often babysat me. Diana had graduated from school last year then stayed around Darby working for her dad. Diana's father ran an outfitting business specializing in bowhunters with hunting camps in the Big Hole and in the Selway Wilderness. They didn't use horses. They packed the camps in on their backs. Since junior high, Diana had worked for her dad packing in supplies and packing out game.

My best friend Pete, future starting quarterback of the Darby Tigers, appeared next to Jenny, making her look even shorter than her five foot three compared to his six foot two.

Pete laughed as I approached. "Hey, Scabs, nice tie." I grinned. My neck was starting to sweat in the afternoon heat and I loosened the tie my father made me wear to any social gathering where praying occurred.

My nickname had been Scabs since the fourth grade when I wrecked my bike. I was at Pete's house for a weekend sleepover. We rode bikes around his ranch, and when we came back to his house, Pete rode onto the slab of concrete in front of their garage from the side. Pete popped a wheelie as the front tire approached the concrete that was six inches above the dirt and rolled onto the pad with practiced ease. I popped my wheelie too early causing my front tire to slam into the ground right in front of the curb. The bike rocked forward, throwing me over the handlebars. My head hit the concrete then slid across it, scratching my face.

By the time I went to school on Monday, my face resembled a spiderweb of scabs. Infected scabs because of the dirty gravel trapped under my skin. First thing in the morning, a group of kids asked about my face. Before I could say anything, Pete barged into the group and said, "Hey, Scabs, before you spend the night again, learn to ride a bike."

Like a bad rash, the nickname had spread. Even after my face healed, everybody except my parents called me Scabs. Most kids dreamed about scoring the winning touchdown in the big game, but I dreamed of everybody calling me by my real name.

"He looks cute in a tie," Jenny said then stood on tiptoe to give me a quick peck on the cheek.

Pete ignored her public display of affection. "You two going to the party up Chaffin Creek tonight? I hear Matt's bringin'..."

Pete's voice trailed off as he stared over my shoulder. I shifted to my left so I could see what he was looking at and spotted Kristi Harm getting into her Toyota Celica. Kristi had on a black pleated skirt similar to her cheerleading outfit only shorter. She wore a red sweater that would have been tight on a girl half her age.

"Take a picture, Pete, that might be slightly less obvious," Jenny chastised.

The Celica's engine began to purr and music poured out the window as Kristi cranked it down while looking at Pete the whole time. She drove off, flipping Pete the bird out the window while John Cougar sang about small towns.

"Skank." Jenny stated giving Pete a dirty look.

"You're just jealous because Kristi has a better ass," Pete teased. "Right, Scabs?" he added, putting me on the receiving end of Jenny's glare.

I'd gotten to see Jenny's ass a couple of times in nothing but her panties and while I hadn't seen Kristi Harm's bare ass, I knew that it didn't matter what I really thought. As Jenny's boyfriend, there was only one right answer. "I'd have to say Jenny's ass is nicer and she's got bigger ta-tas."

Pete laughed. "Oh, so you have seen Jenny naked. Dude, you're not supposed to play strip poker and tell."

Jenny punched me in the shoulder and I tried to disarm her anger by grinning. "What do you want me to say?"

Pete's laughter died away, his face taking on his "I'm serious" look. Anyone who knew Pete knew he was being anything but serious. "You kids haven't been breaking The Oath, have you?" Pete said in the same tone I'd once heard Pete's mom ask if we had been drinking his dad's beer.

Before Jenny and I started dating, she'd asked me to an after-school meeting at the Conner Church. I didn't go to church much, usually only on Christmas when my mom made me dress in my pajamas to play one of the wise men because they didn't have enough kids to do the Christmas pageant. I went with Jenny because when the girl you've had a crush on since eighth grade asks you do to something, you do it. I told Pete I was going with Jenny and he decided to come along.

Instead of a biblical play, they had a couple of kids, Darby alumni, who talked about how great it had been to wait until after high school to have sex. The guy, Todd Harley, said how fantastic it had been to focus on sports and not have to worry about getting his girlfriend pregnant and having to quit school and get a job to support a family. The girl went on and on about how it was better to be more mature and know what you wanted out of life and not worry about your reputation at school. At the end of the night, they handed out forms with a long, complicated oath written on it that basically said you wouldn't have sex until you graduated high school. If someone broke The Oath, they condemned their soul and their parents' souls to hell. I was a little shocked when Jenny signed hers, and I figured if Jenny wasn't having sex and I wanted to be with Jenny then in a way I'd already signed the oath, so I signed it. What was really shocking was seeing Pete sign his.

Before I could respond to Pete's jest about The Oath, Jenny squeezed my hand, letting me know to keep my mouth shut. Pete chuckled. "I'll tell you guys one thing. I'd break my oath in a minute to be with Kristi Harm. Maybe thirty seconds if I already had my pants off."

"If you like that skank so much, maybe you should go hang out with her and her dirthead friends." Jenny sounded a little bit like her dad when she was mad.

Pete stopped laughing. "Hey. No need to get ornery. You know I like hanging around you guys."

Awkward silence followed then Pete asked, "Soooo. Going to the party up Chaffin Creek?"

"I have to get up early in the morning for my job interview," I reminded Pete. "I can't be out late. By the time we drive all the way up Chaffin and then I drive Jenny home then back to my house, it'll be too late."

"That's right. Tomorrow's the big interview with Cherylann." Pete turned to Jenny. "You sure you trust him around Cherylann? She hired Randy last summer and he hinted she had him doing more than ranch chores."

Jenny pulled me into a tight hug looking around my shoulder at Pete. "Randy's a liar, and if by some miracle something did happen, Randy should just be happy and keep his mouth shut." She pulled away from me. "What is this anyway? Pick on Jenny day?"

Pete's smile left his face. "Sorry, Jenny, I get carried away sometimes." His face took on his contemplative look. "Scabs, how about I give Jenny a ride home from the party. Then you don't have to drive from Chaffin Creek out to Lost Horse and then back up the East Fork."

It was a pretty good idea. It would save me an hour of driving. I'd have enough time at the party to make going worthwhile and be in bed on time so I could get up early for my job interview. Pete lived on the flat near Cooper's Post and Pole just north of Jenny's house. While it wouldn't be that far out of Pete's way to take Jenny home, it was super nice of him to offer.

"Are you sure you don't mind?" I asked.

Pete shook his head. "Not a problem, dude." Pete stepped back and gave a funny bow to Jenny. "As long as the lady doesn't mind."

I eyed Jenny waiting for her answer.

"Sure," she said. "Sounds like fun."

That was the thing about Pete. He could be obnoxious with his rough teasing, but if not for him, Jenny and I would miss the graduation party. My dad called to me, getting chuckles from the nearby kids who didn't know my real name. Dad pointed to his watch as he waited for Mom to get in the truck so he could close her door. Without another look, he walked around the front of the truck to leave. That was his signal I needed to leave so I could meet him out at my fake grandpa's to shoot rifles.

I said goodbye to Jenny and gave her a kiss full on the lips. Pete gave a disgusted grunt, complained we were grossing him out, and left saying he would meet us up Chaffin Creek.

I had parked in front of the school and after watching Jenny drive off, I headed into the gym, fighting against the tide of people streaming out. The talk I heard now centered on jobs for the graduating class. Maybe I tuned into those conversations since I had been wondering about my own employment future. Some lucky kids would adopt the family trade of logging or outfitting. More than a few hoped for a job at one of the local lumber mills. Some would continue working the family ranch. I heard one kid mention getting a job with the Forest Service fighting fires for the summer then maybe working plowing roads during the winter.

My family didn't have a ranch or logging operation. My dad worked odd jobs involving carpentry or home construction. He sometimes guided in the fall and last summer, he had worked for WLH Surveying on a job near Gird Point. He didn't have a business I could take to make a living at, since he barely made a living. My mom worked as a masseuse, rubbing kinks out of cowboys, loggers, and board turners at the mill. It wasn't a lot of money, but combined with what Dad made, they did okay.

I didn't have a family path to a career and we didn't have the money for me to go to college, which was what I really wanted to do after high school. I wanted to do something to get out of Darby. I didn't want to leave because I disliked the town or the people. The people who lived around Darby were the best folks on the face of the earth. Everybody waved to each other when they passed on the highway. If someone's truck broke down, the first person who came along would stop to give you a ride or a tow. Wanting to leave made me feel a little weird and it upset Jenny and Pete whenever I talked about it. I just had this crazy idea that the world was a big place, and while Darby might be one of the best places, I still wanted to see more of the world, good and bad. The only way I could afford college was if I secured a good-paying job this summer and worked again the following summer while saving all my earnings. The guidance counselor at Darby, a real cool guy, said he would help me apply for scholarships. With my savings and a small scholarship, I might have enough for the first year of college. That was as far as I could look ahead — just make it through one year of college. That goal seemed like a long shot, but it all started with me doing well at tomorrow's interview.

Cherylann might have the reputation of being odd, but she paid well. My dad had done a few carpentry jobs for her and she liked his work, which had led to my interview with her to be her handyman for the summer. I didn't have any other interviews for summer jobs. There weren't that many jobs for kids my age in Darby. If I didn't get the handyman job, I'd end up doing something like washing dishes at the Rocky Knob Lodge or sucking farts out of seat covers in the used car lot for Milken Motors.

Pete planned to go to college at Montana State University but only, as he put it, "to get an associates in party hardyin'." He said it like it was spelled hardy, but I had always thought the saying was party hearty. Then Pete would come back home to the family ranch. Jenny wasn't going to college, but she planned to take over her mom's video rental store in a couple of years when her dad retired from the highway department.

I made it through the halls of the high school and pushed open the red doors leading to the school's front parking lot. I waved at Cowboy Bob as he drove out of the parking lot in his old station wagon. Bob lived up the East Fork and often gave the kids who lived closer to town a ride to school, offering them a brief reprieve from the drudgery of riding the school bus. Since Cowboy Bob's family wagon didn't have a radio, he required that his passengers sing to pay for the ride.

My shadow walked to my right as I crossed the lot to my truck. I opened the door to my 1975 Ford Courier and slid behind the wheel. The starter clicked and stuck on the first turn of the key, but on the second, it spun the engine to life. I needed to hurry to meet Dad. The sooner we shot our rifles, the sooner I could go pick up Jenny and head to Chaffin Creek. [HL-20]

I met Dad at my fake grandpa's place off the East Fork Road north of Conner right on the East Fork of the Bitterroot River. He wasn't my real grandpa, but since my real grandpas were dead before I was born and he was old, I called him my fake grandpa. Dad knew him from his time in the Marines and we spent every Easter, Thanksgiving, and Fourth of July at his house on his sixty acres along the river. Fake Grandpa grew hay on half of it and Dad and I sometimes helped him hay in July stacking the bales in a large building he used as a garage and hay barn.

I met Dad in the attic area above the garage part, carefully keeping my head from hitting the dusty rafters of the low ceiling. I'd grown a lot in the last few years, but Dad still had an inch or two on me. I outweighed him by a few pounds since his profile resembled a rail. Dad said he had grown another two inches after high school, so there was still hope I might be as tall as him. He smiled instead of saying hi, typical of him since he never said much.

A large window with its wood shutters pulled open revealed a hayfield and three hundred yards away, a three-foot-square piece of plywood was nailed upright on a post with two rifle targets tacked to it. Sandbags lay across a picnic table facing the window so a shooter could sit on one side of the table, lean across, and rest their rifle on the sandbags. During hunting season, the whitetail came out of the river bottom to feed in the hayfield just before dark and we ambushed them.

The other guys from school teased me that shooting animals from the barn wasn't hunting and I guess my dad agreed with them. He didn't think it was hunting either. It was a way to fill our freezer with venison and it allowed us to make clean kills. The reason we shot so well was we shot once a week, every week, so we knew exactly where our guns were sighted in when hunting season rolled around.

Most kids at school waited until the week before hunting season then went out and sighted in their rifles. I didn't complain about having to shoot every week. I liked shooting, enjoyed the time with my dad, and after shooting, we'd visit with my fake grandpa and do little chores he needed done around the house. Afterward,

Fake Grandpa would often mix me a drink when he made one for Dad.

Dad had our Winchester Model 70s on the picnic table. Both rifles were chambered for .30-06 with his rifle a few years older than mine and with a lot more rounds through the barrel. Dad liked to let the rifles sit outside the gun case for fifteen or twenty minutes so they would adjust to the temperature in the attic. The attic wasn't heated, and the window wasn't glass, but a section of the wall had been made into shutters. With the shutters open, the attic cooled to the temperature outside. Letting the guns adjust to the temperature must have been something Dad learned in the military.

Dad had been a Marine during the Vietnam War and didn't talk about his time in the service. He hadn't spent any time in Vietnam. Instead, he'd worked undercover in Canada tracking down deserters and draft dodgers. I'd heard a few of the older folks in town make snide comments about him being in Canada during the War. I guessed they thought he should have left the draft dodgers alone.

"You going out with Jenny tonight?" Dad asked.

"Yah," I answered. Dad wouldn't approve of me going to the party up Chaffin Creek, so I kept quiet on exactly what we had planned.

"Doing anything fun?"

I stuck with being vague. "I thought I'd let her pick what we do."

Dad paused in the act of putting on his earmuffs, holding them in front of his chest. "Don't stay out too late.

I did those jobs for Cherylann last fall as cheap as I could to create a little goodwill and get you an interview."

Dad slipped his earmuffs over his head after his long speech. When he spoke again, he returned to his normal briefness and raised his voice slightly higher than normal. "Don't mess it up."

He eased into the bench seat on the picnic table, fed a single round into the magazine, and closed the bolt. He eased the forestock of the Winchester across the sandbags, nestling it into place. His logbook sat on the table and I picked it up along with the pencil beside it. He'd already entered in the date, time, air pressure, temperature, and distance. I watched his chest rise and fall as he took a couple of deep breaths. He thumbed the safety off and I brought my hands to the sides of my head, plugging my ears with my index fingers while holding the pencil and logbook with my other fingers. The gun roared extra loud in the confining space of the attic. Dad worked the bolt on the rifle, ejecting the brass and catching it before it hit the floor.

He smiled at me, "A little right, an inch."

I made the notation in the logbook then swapped him the book and pencil for the earmuffs. Sitting at the picnic bench wasn't exactly comfortable, as I always felt too upright. I loaded a single round into the chamber and closed the bolt, making sure the safety was on. I shifted the rifle on the sandbags pushing on the bags in places to compact the sand until I finally got the crosshairs in the scope to settle on the target while letting the gun rest completely on the sandbags. I molded myself to the gun, applying a little forward push with my shoulder to hold the butt of the rifle tight to my shoulder. My left hand rested on top of the scope holding everything steady.

I flipped the safety off and focused on my breathing. Since I fired only one shot each week, I wanted to make it count. If I rushed this shot, then I would have to wait a whole week before I could redeem myself. I drew in slow, steady breaths. I pushed harder with my shoulder to bring the crosshairs down to the center of the target. I let out my next breath and then it happened.

It was a funny thing, something I hadn't talked to even my dad about. At times, I had the power to slow time. Well, I couldn't control when it happened, but at weird moments, time slowed for me. It happened the most when I shot, especially when shooting at deer. Time had slowed for a few other things, like when Mom and I slid off the road in a spring blizzard. It felt like it had taken three minutes for the old Chevy truck to slide into the willows near Robbins Gulch, but it had really only been three seconds.

With time slowed, the crosshairs vibrated with each beat of my heart, but each beat seemed to have three seconds between them. After the next heartbeat, I eased an extra half pound of pressure onto the trigger.

Time returned to normal as I worked the bolt after the shot, flipping the spent cartridge through the air, which my Dad expertly caught. I smiled at him. "Felt good. It went dead center."

Dad made the notation in the logbook as I removed the bolt and opened our small gun cleaning kit we kept in the attic. "You know, Pete and his dad sight in by doing three-shot groups then adjust the scope to be on at a hundred yards." I tried to make my tone sound like I wasn't complaining as I added, "And they only sight in once a year, right before hunting season."

"I am sure that works for how Pete hunts," Dad said.

I cleaned my bolt and then used a cotton swab to clean around the extractor.

"Pete's dad hunts by hiking through the woods and his shots are a hundred yards or less at deer that probably have been spooked. So that method of sighting in works for them."

Dad paused for a second like using so many words had tired him. He inspected his rifle barrel then grabbed another cotton patch for his cleaning rod. "They're not shooting like we do. They usually don't have a rest and they need to shoot quicker, not necessarily jerking the trigger, but not a slow squeeze. Like shooting ducks with a shotgun, you have to make the trigger break at a precise moment, not wait and slowly keep adding pressure until the gun goes off like we do."

Satisfied with the cleanliness of his rifle bore, Dad began wiping the entire rifle with an old cloth diaper. "We're shooting a long way at deer that don't know we are around. I need to know exactly where my bullet will land for any weather at that distance. That's why we sight in the way we do."

We finished cleaning our guns, which didn't take long since we cleaned them each week after shooting. Dad wanted the barrel clean before each shot because that was how the barrel would be when we shot at the deer.

I tucked my rifle into its case feeling I needed to let Dad know I was okay with his way of sighting in rifles. "Sounds good to me. I like shooting. I was just thinking maybe some nights when we don't have anything going on we could shoot more."

Dad gave me a look, a funny grin on his face. "But not today?"

I smiled at him. "Yeah. I was hoping you'd let me skip out on checking the targets so I could get over to Jenny's a little earlier. You know, since I need to be home early."

He waved me off with a flick of his hand. "Get."

Chapter Three

Cherylann had told me to be at her house at sunrise for the interview. Sunrise seemed a simple time, but as I slowed down to turn left on Conner Cutoff Road, I peered out the window to the east at the mountains and realized it wasn't simple. I knew from hunting it was light enough a half an hour before sunrise to see to shoot. That varied depending on cloud cover and if you were at the bottom of a steep valley. Also, even if the sun was technically up, the sun might not shine on Cherylann's house until long after sunrise. The sun didn't hit our house in the summer until after ten in the morning. When did Cherylann want me to show up? At light enough to see to shoot, sunrise, or when the sun started shining on her house? I decided to time my arrival for a half hour after I could see to shoot, closest to actual sunrise and hope Cherylann hadn't meant when the sun's rays first hit her house.

Two other kids from school also had interviews with Cherylann, so it wasn't a done deal I would get the job. If I didn't get this job, I wasn't sure what I would do for the summer. I could make okay wages changing sprinkler pipes for a couple of ranchers trying to grow hay. I could pick up more work stacking hay bales, but none of those jobs would bring in the amount of money I needed for my college fund.

I'd already put a backup plan in motion by filling out a form letting the Marine recruiter know I was interested in any college programs they offered. I didn't want to join the military, but I didn't want to stay in Darby struggling to find work to make ends meet. I guess in my head I wanted to go off to college, graduate, find a great job, and then return to Darby with a bank account full of money and start a business, like my own Foto Hut.

I broke free from my worrying as I saw a Ford Escort pulled off the side of the road by the Conner Store. A tall man stood on the edge of the road waving at me. I hit the brakes and flipped the wheel around making a tight turn to pull alongside the Escort. It was a pain to roll down the window on the Courier, so I put the truck in neutral and opened the door.

"Need help?" I called out.

The guy, wearing a dark sweatshirt with the hood up, came around the front of the Courier. "I need a jump start. I've got jumper cables. If you can pull closer and pop your hood, I'll hook them up."

I didn't recognize him as being anyone local. The license plate on the car started with a four, so the car was from Missoula. What could he be doing here in the valley this earlier in the morning?

He stepped out of the way into the road as I closed the door then pulled up to the hood of the Escort, leaving a couple feet between the vehicles. The stranger already had the hood open on the Escort. I put the Courier in neutral, set the parking brake, and got out to open the hood.

If this guy's battery had went bad or if his alternator had gone out, jump starting wasn't going to help him for very long. Worried that being a good Samaritan might delay my arrival at the job interview, I asked, "What happened to your car? Will a jump start work?"

"Battery terminals were all corroded. I cleaned them while I was waiting for someone to come by. I think if we can get it started we'll be fine."

He stepped between the cars and hooked the cables to the posts on the batteries instead of hooking the negative cable to a metal bolt on his Escort. I didn't say anything. It was his car and cables. He half jogged around the car to the driver's side and as he slid into the driver's seat, I thought I saw a kid looking at me from the back seat of the car, but in the dark, I couldn't tell for sure.

I revved the Courier's engine to create more juice. Sure enough, I heard the Escort starter turn over a few times then the little engine sputtered to life. The stranger hurried from his car and began unhooking the cables. Sparks flew when he accidentally let the clamps touch. He seemed to be in more of a hurry than me.

As I stepped out of the Courier, he wrapped the cables around his arm. "Hey, you know how to get to the Mash Lake Trailhead?"

That made sense. Just some guy from Missoula going fishing.

"Sure. Keep going the way you're headed and take a right on 93. Then just before the Sula Post Office, turn left onto the East Fork Road. A few miles after the pavement ends, the dirt road splits near the Wolverine Creek

Campground. I think there's a sign that will point you in the right direction."

Without a thank-you, he got into his car and drove by me, heading on his way. I realized I could pick out individual trees down the road a hundred yards or see a deer if one were to come out on the road. I slammed the door on the Courier, made a 180, and sped toward the West Fork Road. It would be just my luck to get home early from the graduation party but then end up late to the interview because I stopped to help some goofball from Missoula. I made a left turn onto the West Fork Road and ran the little Courier as fast as I could, hoping no deer or Job Corp kids jumped out in the road in front of me, until I turned onto Cherylann's driveway.

Cherylann, never Cheryl, she'd made that clear enough times the word had spread around Darby, was a newcomer to the valley. She'd bought two houses on adjoining property near Triple Creek Ranch eight years ago, burned them to the ground, and built a new house. That had gotten her labeled a little crazy. I mean you could burn down one perfectly good house to build a house of your own design and maybe get away with it. Destroying two perfectly good houses, in a place where you were blessed to have one house, well that got people calling you crazy. Cherylann didn't spend winters in Montana but showed up during the summer months and kept to herself. Sometimes she could be spotted at Medicine Hot Springs or Dotson's Bar arousing interest in the men with her sexy clothes and a pang of jealousy in the women. The last half dozen summers, she stayed from May to October and had hired a high-school kid to do chores around her property.

She spent most of her time at her house, a beautiful Neville log home on the west side of the valley, overlooking the West Fork River. [HL-30] I parked in front of the garage but back enough I wouldn't block anyone inside. A giant deck ran around the house above me with huge windows running to the peak of the roof. I found a note at the base of the stairs to the deck telling me to go around front and come on in to the living room.

I opened the door feeling self-conscious about letting myself into the house. "Hello the house," I called in a loud voice as I shut the door behind me. People got shot in the Bitterroot for entering people's houses unannounced. I saw a row of shoes along one wall and realize Cherylann must prefer people leave their shoes off when in her house. I heard a responding call down the hall, and after setting my shoes by the door, I headed toward the voice. Hunting photos from Africa graced the hallway walls, but I didn't stop until I walked sock footed into a giant living room. The room was so big my folks' entire house could have fit in it. A love seat and a projection TV filled one corner and a four-person bar was in another. The middle of the room held a large sectional couch that faced the floor-to-ceiling windows that looked out over the large deck to the valley below.

Cherylann stood near the top of a long ladder positioned in front of the windows, a bottle of Windex and paper towels in her hands. She glanced over her shoulder, nodding at the stone fireplace hearth. "Your timing is good. That's one point in your favor." She turned to the window, spraying more cleaner, then rubbed vigorously with the paper towels. The sunlight peeking between the mountains to the east hit the widow at an angle revealing the slightest smudge on the glass.

Cherylann wore blue shorts and a white t-shirt. Her black hair was pulled into a clipped ponytail. From the gossip mill, I knew Cherylann was probably older than my mom, but revealing glimpses of the bottom of her butt cheeks as she leaned forward to scrub the window made me realize she didn't look anything like my mother. She turned sideways on the ladder, and the sunlight not only revealed smudges on the window, but it also penetrated the thin material of her t-shirt, showing she wasn't wearing any bra. Cherylann looked like a thirty-year-old dark-haired Kristi Harm who had aged extremely well.

"Why does everyone call you Scabs?"

It was an odd first question to a job interview, but then I'd never been interviewed by a woman cleaning windows before. I hadn't even been interviewed before. "I wrecked my bike and got road rash on my face. The scabs took a while to heal."

That seemed to satisfy her and she stepped up one rung on the ladder and sprayed more Windex. "Have you built any fence?"

I tried to keep my eyes off her as she worked choosing to stare straight ahead. "I helped my Dad fence our place and I've repaired fence for a family friend."

She stopped wiping and looked back over her shoulder. I made eye contact with her.

"What kind of fence?" she asked then went back to wiping the window.

I couldn't answer right away as I had to concentrate to force my eyes away from her shorts to the bottom of the ladder. "Uhh," I said clearly.

She stopped wiping, turned her shoulders, and looked at me, drawing my eyes to hers. "Wood rails, barbed wire, chain link?" she questioned in an exasperated tone.

I held the eye contact even though the intensity of her gaze made me want to look at my feet while another part of me wanted to stare at the outline of her breast shining through the t-shirt. "Wood posts and five-strand barbed wire," I managed before breaking eye contact and looking at my feet.

Fortunately for me, Cherylann worked her way down the ladder, getting out of the sun spotlight. Unfortunately, she tugged the ladder a few feet then climbed back up it. "Your dad did some work for me last summer. He did a great job. But I have to say, you seem a little slow on the uptake."

"Hell, Cherylann," a man said to my right, startling me. "You're half naked in front of a seventeen-year-old boy and you expect him to sound intelligent?"

An old guy leaned against the wall by the stairs to the basement. I'd been so fixated on Cherylann I hadn't heard him approach. He was a little taller than my dad and at least ten years older with gray hair and skinny but with a noticeable beer gut. Was he Cherylann's father or her boyfriend?

Cherylann didn't turn around. "You ever work with metal fence posts and barbwire?"

I kept my eyes on the old man. "No," I answered. "But I can learn quick and I'm a hard worker like my dad."

"You know the difference between fencing in and fencing out?"

"Sure," I replied.

Cherylann turned around, giving me a dirty look and I realized she wanted me to explain the difference, which I did, trying to sound intelligent explaining the obvious.

Cherylann backed down the ladder carrying the paper towels and Windex. "While I'm putting these away, you can take the ladder out to the garage for me and I will meet you out by the horseshoe pits." Cherylann disappeared into the kitchen while I stood up.

The old guy held out his hand. "Name's Irwin. Nice to meet ya, Scabs."

I started to correct him and tell him to call me by my real name, but then thought better of it. A job interview was not the time to start making a stink about using my real name, even an interview this weird.

We wrangled the ladder through the house, managing not to bump the walls or any of the numerous knickknacks. With the ladder hung on the garage wall, I went back to the house to get my shoes then hurried back to Irwin in the garage. I glanced over the organized garage and the dirt-coated blue Toyota 4x4 with a roll bar parked inside it. Irwin led the way out to the horseshoe pits where Cherylann waited. She hadn't put on a jacket and the cool morning air made it clear she hadn't put on a bra either. I diverted my eyes to the metal fence post she held upright with the bottom stuck slightly in the sand of the horseshoe pit.

Irwin gave an exaggerated shiver. "It's a bit nipply this morning."

Cherylann didn't appear self-conscious in the least. She frowned at Irwin. "Could you at least try to act half your age?"

Irwin chuckled. "I am."

I decided Irwin must be Cherylann's boyfriend, or at least I hoped he wasn't her father after his nipply comment. I tried to ignore them as they continued to banter. The fence post was all green except for maybe the top eight inches that was white. It was made in the shape of a "T" with little nobs running down the flat side, and near the bottom was a shovel-shaped wing of metal.

Finished chastising Irwin for being juvenile, Cherylann faced me. "Put this in two feet." She shoved the top of the post at me. Irwin gave a snort and Cherylann gave him a look that told him to stop it.

I caught the top of the post as it swung toward me then studied the fencing tools on the ground near the edge of the pit. I'd never used a fence-post pounder, but I'd seen them before. The one lying on Cherylann's lawn had apparently come from Russia after a training camp with Ivan Drago. The black tube of metal had two large handles that came off the tube at an angle, ran parallel to the tube for eighteen inches, and, with a ninety-degree turn, went back to the tube. I leaned the post over so I could reach the pounder. Lifting the pounder, I realized it weighed even more than I thought. I struggled getting the end of the tube over the post and realized I needed to tip the seven-foot post until the top was hip height to wrangle the pounder over the top of it. I stood the post up straight and grabbed the handles of the pounder with both hands. I couldn't get much height lifting the pounder since the fence post was almost as high off the ground as my arms could reach. I pulled the pounder down onto the fence post. The resulting smash of metal on metal sent a shrill clang into the quiet morning air. I kept at it, trying to keep the post straight as I lifted up then pulled down on the pounder.

I hated the noise—the scraping sound of the pounder sliding along the post and the clang as the pounder smashed into the top of the post. As the post sank into the ground a half inch at a time, I could lift higher with the pounder getting more distance on my pull and more force, ramming the post faster into the ground. I stopped when I thought I had driven the post two feet into the ground and lifted the pounder off the post. I could feel the beginnings of blisters on both of my palms. If Cherylann wanted another post pounded into the ground, I was going to have to ask for a pair of gloves or get some serious blisters. I wondered which action would hurt my chances of getting the job.

Cherylann ran her hand up and down the post. "A little crooked, but not too bad," she commented causing Irwin to chuckle again. She ignored him and walk out into the short cut lawn, stopped with her right foot out and pushed her big toe into the grass. "Dig a fence-post hole right here," she instructed.

I happily set the pounder down and grabbed the post-hole digger. I was back on familiar territory as I had dug dozens of holes with a post-hole digger when helping my dad.

As I approached, Cherylann added, "Two feet straight down."

I shoved the two attached spades into the grass in front of her toe, noticing she was barefoot and had a gold ring around her little toe. I made a mental note to ask Jenny if she had ever heard of anyone wearing a toe ring. I shifted ninety degrees and stabbed the digger into the turf. This time, I pulled the handles apart, pinching the sod between the spades, and lifted a neat circle of grass from the lawn. I didn't have gloves and even though the wood handles were easier on my skin than the pounder, blisters formed on my palms. A foot deep, I ran into a rock and switched to using a long black metal bar that for some reason is also called a post-hole digger. The metal bar had one pointed end and the other was flattened like a slotted screwdriver and it weighed about twenty pounds. Using the pointed end, I rammed the bar into the rock until it cracked. Then I continued with the other post-hole digger. Sweat broke out on my forehead despite the cool morning air as I forced the cracked rock from the hole. Thankfully, I hit decomposed granite after the rock and the rest of the hole almost dug itself. HL-31

Cherylann seemed duly impressed with my hole-digging ability although she didn't make any comments to me. She turned to Irwin. "Show him the project. I'm going to shower while you're doing that and then you can take me into Bud and Shirley's for breakfast."

She walked toward the house and I watched Irwin watch her walk away. When he saw my look, he said, "That woman has got the best poop chute on the planet."

I succeeded in not laughing but couldn't keep from smiling.

Irwin nodded at the Courier. "Grab your truck and follow me."

He started walking around the garage and I turned to my truck wondering if I should offer him a ride. The interview wasn't what I had expected as everything seemed like a test. After a minute, Irwin came into view riding a Honda Big Red three-wheeler and I followed him down the driveway. He waved for me to follow him as we reached the gate at the property entrance. He turned off the road and followed the four-rail fence heading uphill. Near the tree line by a wooden shed, he stopped the three-wheeler and waved at me to stop.

"Trail is too narrow for your truck." He pointed at a patch of brown dirt by the shed. "Park there then hop on."

I swung around Irwin onto the back of the wheeler, making sure to keep my legs out away from the tires. Pete's dad had bought a yellow three-wheeler a few years ago. His dad had ridden a motorcycle all his life and had the habit of putting his foot off the pegs near the ground when he made a turn. When he did that with the three-wheeler, the back tire on that side grabbed his foot, pulled him off the machine, and ran over him. That had happened about four times and on the last time, he broke his arm. Pete's dad had sold the wheeler and made a point of telling everyone just how damn dangerous they were.

I kept my feet out and my hands behind me on the metal rack so I didn't have to hug Irwin. He drove alongside the fence that turned into barbed wire with metal fence posts after the shed. After a half mile, he stopped and pointed where the fence made a ninety-degree turn through the trees. "Bit of a mix-up with the property line. This is where we thought the property ended, but it really doesn't."

Before I could make any comment expressing amazement that someone could make such a mistake, Irwin revved the engine on the three-wheeler, jerking me backward, as we headed up the hill. He stopped at a survey stake and shutting off the wheeler, he leaned forward to give me room to unload. He walked over to a survey stake and swatted at the pink flagging streaming from it.

"Cherylann wants the fence moved from down below to up here." He took long strides in the direction the new fence should run pointing to another survey stake in the ground ahead of us. "The guy from WHL Surveying marked off the property line. Him and his daughter—" Irwin paused abruptly and looked at me. "You know his daughter?"

That was a stupid question. Everyone in Darby knew everybody else. "Yeah, she's older than me, going to college. She works for her dad and tends bar at the Sportsman's Saloon."

Irwin absorbed that information. "Tends bar at the Sportsman's...you don't say. She's a looker, boy, you ever get the chance, you should try to cozy up to her."

I didn't know how to respond to Irwin's interest in a woman less than half his age, so I kept silent and didn't mention that said woman had a younger sister.

"Anyhow," he said, starting to walk toward the next survey stake. "The fence line is already brushed out and these stakes have been put in every hundred and fifty feet. All you need to do is put in a metal fence post every twenty feet and string the wire. Wire's stored at the shed along with the fence posts. You can use the three-wheeler to haul everything up here. Just make sure to keep it parked in the shed at night. Fence line will run for a mile across the side of the ridge here then drop into a valley. You need to run posts and wire from the end of the previous fence. And when you get the new fence done, you need to take down the wire from the lower fence line, roll it up, and put it in the shed."

Irwin turned and faced me, giving me a deliberate up-and-down look. I pictured in my mind what Irwin saw. A young, short-haired, blond kid, a few inches short of six feet tall with a little extra weight. Not extra in the belly like Irwin, more spread out over my body so it wasn't too noticeable until compared to my dad.

"Think you could handle that chore?"

I made an effort to look like I was sizing up the job, trying to appear confident in my answer. "Sure, no problem."

Irwin pulled his ragged ball cap off and rubbed his

short patch of gray hair while he studied me like he was trying to figure out just by looking at me if I could do the job. He slapped the hat on his head and, with a wave to follow him, and headed to the three-wheeler.

On the ride, I felt a hot breeze blowing uphill. Not even a wisp of a cloud graced the blue sky. Today was going to get hot, maybe even break ninety degrees, probably a record for this time of year. He dropped me off at my truck with instructions to head to the ranch. The starter on the Courier spun three times before finally catching, jerking the four-banger to life. I drove slowly feeling weird with Irwin bird-dogging behind me on the three-wheeler. I definitely got the feeling Irwin didn't think I could build a fence.

Cherylann stood in the yard, her hands on her hips, waiting for us. Her damp black hair reached the Doobie Brothers concert t-shirt she wore. She wore black cowboy boots with the squared-off toes, something I'd only seen dudes who didn't ride horses wear, with her jeans tucked into the tops of the boots.

She ignored Irwin and pointed her finger at my chest as I approached. "Tell me what the job is?"

I stumbled through everything Irwin had told me forgetting at first needing to pull the wire from the old fence on the wrong property line, but remembered before I quit talking and added it in quickly.

Cherylann looked over my shoulder at Irwin after I finished. I resisted the urge to look at him to see if he was giving her a thumbs-up or more likely a thumbs-down.

Cherylann's black eyes bored into mine. "I figure the

job at two hundred and forty hours. That's a fence post every twenty feet, so two hundred and ninety-four fence posts. Should take you twenty minutes per post. Then another twenty minutes per post to stretch and hang the wire, fencing out not in. I need the wire tight but not so damn tight the elk snap it when they run into it. I want a little give. That's two hundred hours of work plus another forty hours to roll up the wire from the old fence. You can leave the posts. Irwin needs something to do around here to earn his keep."

She paused and I realized I should say something, but the numbers she threw out of her mouth seemed small for the size of the job. I needed time to work through her math.

"At ten dollars an hour, that's two thousand four hundred dollars for the job." She paused letting that amount sink in and I realized she was talking about paying me for the job, not by the hour and that made me really wish I had time to do my own figuring. I didn't want to agree to do a job that would take longer than Cherylann estimated and end up making only a few bucks an hour.

Cherylann gave me a little smile. "I'll bump that up to five thousand, but you have to have the job done by August first."

I tried to do some quick math in my head. At forty hours a week, I could finish the fence in six weeks if Cherylann's estimate was accurate. I had some of June and all of July. That gave me seven weeks for a six-week job. I could build the fence and since two-a-day football practices didn't start until the middle of August, I could do a few jobs with my dad after building the fence. I could end up making around five and half to six grand for the summer.

I couldn't keep from smiling. "Sure, I can have the fence done before August."

Cherylann approached me and I could feel Irwin pressing in from behind me. Cherylann's little smile disappeared. "You can work from sunrise until eight at night any day but Sunday. I don't want to see you here on Sundays. In fact, I don't want to see you at this house at all. Drive to the shed and park there. Don't come to the house. If you need more tools or supplies, call me and leave a message. Nobody helps you with the fence. No friends on my property. If you don't finish by August, I only pay you twenty-four hundred and you don't get paid until the fence is completely done." She stuck her hand out for me to shake. "Do you agree to the terms?"

My mind raced with plans to bust ass on the fence putting in twelve-hour days, six days a week, then getting another job after I finished the fence. Things were looking up for me. I could make good money this summer. My dream of going to college and buying Jenny something special for her birthday was just a handshake away.

I gripped Cherylann's hand firmly, surprised at the strength of her grip. She continued to hold my hand even after our shake. "One more thing. Anybody asks what you're doing here for me, you tell them mowing lawn and taking care of the garden. You don't tell anyone about building fence." She let go of my hand with a little push. I had no doubt in my mind that, despite her age and being a woman, Cherylann could and would kick my ass if I didn't follow through on my part of the agreement.

I swallowed hard. "Sure thing, boss."

Cherylann walked away toward her open garage door and the late-model Toyota pickup calling for Irwin to get his ass in gear. Irwin stopped to shake my hand. He slipped a twenty-dollar bill into it. "For gas for the wheeler. There's a gas can or two in the shed you can fill."

I mumbled, "Not necessary."

He physically waved off my protests. "Just don't fuck it up." He hurried toward the garage, breaking into a trot. "Tell your mother I said hi," he called over his shoulder.

Chapter Four

Jenny dropped the Lionel Richie cassette into the tray, closed it, pushed play on her Sony boom box, and leaned back against her bed. For the size of Jenny's house, her room wasn't much bigger than mine. Her single bed ran along the wall I faced, a large shelf she used as a desk was under her window on the wall to my left, posters of Madonna and Sting framed a movie poster for *Purple Rain* on the wall behind me, and the hallway door was to my right. I sat on the rectangle patch of brown carpet facing Jenny, wondering if I should leave early to give us more time for a goodbye kissing by the Courier.

I put the dub tape I had just made of *Synchronicity* by The Police in my fake leather case. Jenny had a membership to Columbia House, so she had tons of music, and with her new dual cassette player, she let me copy any tape I wanted. Although most of her tapes, like Billy Joel and Lionel Richie, I didn't want. I had made a copy of The Police not because I thought they were great but Jenny thought they were great. That way I'd have a copy of it if something happened to hers.

Jenny's folks were visiting the Jones family on the other side of Darby playing pinochle for the evening. I had timed my arrival for right after they left and planned on leaving before they returned. If Jenny's parents came home early, I planned to tell them I had just stopped by to let Jenny know I got the job as handyman for Cherylann. But the odds were they wouldn't be home until after I left since Jenny's dad wouldn't leave until they'd consumed the half rack of beer he'd brought for the evening. ^{HL-40}

Jenny eased next to me as I put the case away pushing me onto the floor. She tousled my hair then kissed my neck and with a gentle yank of my hair, began to kiss me deeply. That continued until I finally worked up the nerve to start unbuttoning her blouse. Jenny helped me out by rolling up her jean skirt so she could straddle my body. She let her shirt dangle in front of my hands as I fumbled through the buttons with nervous anticipation.

With her blouse open, Jenny leaned forward, crushing my hands between our chests kissing me playfully on my nose then attacked me with her tongue. For my part, I tried to push my hands around to reach her bra clasp. We'd fooled around like this before, but Jenny usually stopped me from unhooking her bra. I had a feeling I might get past that point tonight.

I kept one ear tuned for the sound of her parents' truck outside. Jenny's dad seemed pretty cool, but if he caught me with his half-naked daughter in her bedroom, he'd probably kick my ass out the door—or her bedroom window.

Jenny sat upright and with a wicked smile, she reached around and unhooked her bra for me. I resisted the urge to say "Bomb bay doors open" as Jenny shrugged forward, letting the bra drop around her waist. I stared, speechless, as her gorgeous breasts came into view. She leaned forward putting them in my face. I didn't know what to do with a woman's breasts. Sucking on the nipples seemed weird, like a baby nursing. I bit her nipples softly with my lips then kissed them. Jenny shifted lower on my body, kissing me and rubbing her body against mine in the right places. I let my hands roam around her body, rubbing her ass at times, but mostly trying to cup her firm breasts.

Jenny moaned softly and putting her hands on my chest rose, pushing her breasts together between her arms. She looked so damn beautiful with her long hair hanging around her face and ending at her breasts. I closed my eyes to keep from making a mess in my pants.

Jenny stopped grinding, reached down, and grabbed the top button on my Levi's 501 jeans. With a deliberate tug, she popped the button open. I took ahold of her hands before she could tug any more.

"What are we doing?" I asked, my voice horse.

Jenny tugged again, despite my hands interfering, another button popped open. With a shy smile, she said, "I thought we could do this without our clothes on. Not doing it, just sliding together."

A thousand thoughts flew through my head in an instant. I would never be able to contain myself and since that had never happened before, I didn't know how Jenny would react. Would she be grossed out? What if I lost control and slipped inside, breaking not only my oath but Jenny's?

When I didn't answer, Jenny's smile disappeared. "It will feel good for me too. You'll rub against my clit."

I had been about to answer, but when Jenny said clit,

it shocked me silent. I wasn't even sure what a clit was or why rubbing against it would feel good. I wondered how Jenny knew what it was and that it felt good to rub.

Weirdly, my brain, operating on a different tangent, suddenly made sense of why Pete catcalled "Here, clitty, clitty" to the cheerleaders. I could never understand before now why he mispronounced kitty.

Jenny pushed against my chest, her eyes telling me my silence upset her. "What about the oath?" I managed to squeak out.

"We won't be breaking it, just having fun. We'll only slide."

I grabbed her hands to stop her from tugging on my fly. "Jenny, I don't think I could stop…"

She leaned forward. "Whatever happens, I'm okay with it." She gave me a gentle kiss that quickly turned rough.

That threw me for another loop around inside my head. It sounded like Jenny had said she wanted to go all the way. I wanted to do exactly what she wanted, but I knew it would ruin our first time together. I scrambled away from her. I wasn't sure I was ready. I mean, I was ready, but I didn't want Jenny to break her oath.

Jenny ended up sitting on her butt, her legs out in front of her and her hands still holding my knees as I scrunched across the floor. "I don't want you to break your vow."

Tears formed in the corners of her eyes. "You know I'm not a slut." Jenny wiped at the tears to keep them from spilling down her cheeks. "I didn't want to go all the way. I'm a senior now. It's okay for me to have some fun. Is that so bad?"

I didn't have the slightest clue what to say in response, but my mouth spewed out whatever it thought needed to be said to keep Jenny from crying. "I don't think you're a slut. You surprised me." I rolled forward on the carpet and pulled her into a hug. "I don't want to do anything unless we plan it. That way, we won't regret it."

Jenny pushed me away. "Sliding around with me is something you would regret?"

I'd managed to vanquish her tears, but I had replaced them with anger. "No. I want to make sure we're both ready in case something more happens." I leaned into her.

She scooted away from me, grabbing her blouse and pulling it across her chest. Suddenly, she opened her blouse showing me her breasts. "Take a good look. It'll be a while before you see them again."

I did take a good look, it would have been impossible not to and I willed time to freeze. Unable to slow time, a groan escaped me as she buttoned her blouse. Unfortunately, before I could say something to ease the mood, I heard the front door to Jenny's house open. Jenny's mother called out, "You kids all right?"

I scrambled to button the fly on my 501s while Jenny dashed to the chair at her cubby desk, furiously buttoning her blouse. I grabbed a cassette to look like I was busy labeling tapes.

"We're upstairs listening to music," Jenny called out. Right on cue, Lionel finished singing the last song on the cassette and the play button popped, making it sound like we weren't listening to music at all. I hit the eject button, flipped the tape over, and pushed play. Jenny's mom appeared in the bedroom doorway just as Lionel crooned the first line of the next song. "Thank God, you're safe, Jenny, there's a maniac on the loose," Jenny's mom said. Her eyes, looking small in her round face, swept the room going between my face and Jenny's.

I hit the stop button on the boom box. "What maniac, Mrs. Peck?" I asked, hoping to keep her from asking any questions about what Jenny and I were doing.

"A kidnapper is on the loose. He was last spotted in Stevensville heading toward Darby. I was worried something had happened to my baby girl the house was so quiet when we got home."

Jenny's dad materialized behind her mom, standing in the hallway outside the bedroom. I couldn't help but take a quick look at Jenny and even though she held her shoulders shrugged forward, I could easily see her loose bra pushing against her blouse. If I could see it, I worried her father could see it.

Mr. Peck put a hand on Mrs. Peck's shoulder and spoke in his deep voice. "We heard on the radio that a man who kidnapped a boy had been spotted getting gas in Stevensville and that he headed south yesterday evening. The police think he might be hiding out somewhere near Darby. They asked everyone to keep an eye out for him." He gave a slight eye roll toward Mrs. Peck. "I'm sure you kids are safe."

His gaze settled on Jenny and his bearded face

molded into a frown. "I didn't know Scabs was coming over to visit."

Mrs. Peck ignored the comment about my presence in the house. "The radio said he was armed and not to approach him."

Mr. Peck turned sideways and eased past his wife's pear-shaped figure into the room, his frown now directed at me. "Just to be on the safe side, I'll walk you to your truck, Scabs."

"Yeah, uh, sure," I responded eloquently. I grabbed my cassette carrying case as I said goodbye to Jenny. She barely glanced at me when she said see you later. I went through the bedroom door, turning sideways to slide past Mrs. Peck's round figure.

She turned with me as I went by. "Scabs, son, you missed a button."

I looked down to see the middle button on my fly sticking out like a silver doorknob. Heat raced up my cheeks. I mumbled something about missing it when I went to the bathroom and quickly hurried to the front door.

Mr. Peck caught up to me on the front porch. Laying his large hand on my shoulder, he walked slightly behind me to the Courier. As I reached the truck, the hand gripped my shoulder and turned me around. I looked up into Mr. Peck's bearded face.

"You mess around with my daughter, have the decency to do it somewhere other than my house."

I wasn't sure how to respond to that. Seemed like anything I said would be admitting I had fooled around with his daughter and yet the look on Mr. Peck's face told me I had better not try to deny messing around with his daughter. The Courier was a rock, Mr. Peck a hard spot, and I was right between them. Luckily, the rock had a door.

Shrugging out from under his hand, I opened the truck door and slid behind the wheel. Mr. Peck held the door open when I tried to close it. "Do me a favor, Scabs. Don't let me see you for two weeks."

"Uh, sure." I turned the key, silently begging the starter to work. When the engine sputtered to life, I tugged at the door letting the clutch out at the same time, pulling the door out of Mr. Peck's grasp. I stopped at the end of the driveway, shut the door so it latched correctly, and put on my lap belt.

Halfway home, I remembered the face of the kid inside the Escort of the angler from Missoula I'd helped that morning. Did Mrs. Peck say what kind of car the kidnapper had been driving?

Chapter Five

I parked the Courier in front of the shed, set the worn parking brake, and left it running with the headlights on so I could see inside the shed in the morning twilight. My arms ached making everything I lifted feel like twice its actual weight. I didn't have to lift the fence-post pounder as I had left it strapped to the tiny front rack of the three-wheeler. I started the wheeler and drove it out of the shed until the front tire struck the Courier's bumper. The brakes on the wheeler barely worked, but I didn't want to complain to Cherylann. I didn't know how to fix them myself, so I had decided to learn how to drive the Honda without using the brakes.

The shed contained everything a shed on a ranch should have, rolls of barbwire, stacks of metal fence posts, and a pile of assorted rough-cut timbers. In the corner, a Stihl chainsaw sat on a shelf with a plastic dishwashing soap bottle filled with chain oil tied to a gallon Wesson oil jug filled with saw gas. A half bundle of survey stakes lay on the floor. The shed also contained a few oddities. A wooden tripod with a transit mounted to the top of it leaned in the corner and a section of wall had two dozen coiled climbing ropes hanging from pegs along with about five hundred feet of two-inch-diameter rope in a huge pile on the floor. I couldn't picture Irwin doing any mountain climbing and guessed it must be one of

Cherylann's hobbies. On top of a giant white cooler was a large box of leather gloves exactly like the kind they gave to forest firefighters to wear. And when I say exactly, I mean exactly because they had the same FSS stamp on the cuff. I'd already snatched a pair to wear to keep the pounder from shredding my palms.

After a couple of trips into the shed, I had a mound of metal fence post laid across the back rack of the wheeler. With three pieces of rope and trucker's hitches as tight as I could make them, I secured the fence posts to the rack. Experience told me the posts would shift as I drove up the hill to the property line, forcing me to stop at least once to tie everything down again. I had a good idea Cherylann hadn't included the time it took to secure the fence posts to the damn wheeler in her assessment of time needed to complete the fence.

When I reached the fence line, I didn't need the headlight on the Honda to see, which put off hardly any light anyway with the pounder strapped to the front rack. I weaved around trees trying to keep the long fence posts on the back of the wheeler from hitting anything. I turned too sharp, hooked a tree, and rotated half the posts off the rack.

I killed the engine on the wheeler and sat on the seat for a few minutes watching the light grow stronger until I could pick out the spot on the horizon where the sun would eventually rise over the mountains. A slight breeze whispered that the clear sky promised the day was going to be a hot one, but in the early morning, I shrugged off the chill as I dismounted the wheeler.

I pulled a post from out of the mess on the rack, the metal scraping on metal disrupting the sounds of the birds and squirrels. I carried the post along the line until I reached the last post I put in the ground less than twelve hours earlier. I had found some twine-like cord in the shed and tied it between the wooden stakes set in the ground marking the property line to keep the posts in a nice straight line.

I'd rigged another piece of twine to the required twenty-foot length and tied loops in both ends so I could hook it on the last fence post then stretch it to the next post to be put in the ground until the cord went taut. It made me think of referees stretching out the chains at a football game to determine if the team had made a first down. I hooked the bottom of the post in the loop and stretched it out, finding the right distance from the last post. I pulled the cord on the ground off to the side so I wouldn't cut it, pinning it out of the way with a large nail from the shed.

Tipping the top of the post toward the ground, I swung the pounder up with effort, settled it over the top of the post, and walked the post upright. I grabbed the handles of the pounder tight in both hands then remembered I had forgotten my gloves on the wheeler. Shit. To get the gloves, I'd have to lay the post with pounder on the ground, walk back to the wheeler, then walk all the way back, and lift the damn pounder.

Screw it. One post wouldn't make my hands hurt any worse than they already did. I slid the pounder up the post. Then pulling my body weight into it, I slammed it down. The clang of the pounder hitting the top of the post shattered the idyllic calm of the morning hurting my ears. Each clang deepened my hate of the pounder.

My arms gave out with the post only a foot in the ground. I rested, holding the pounder in place drawing in deep breaths. I had thought I was in pretty good shape, but pounding in posts the last two days had torn up the muscles in my shoulders and arms. I enjoyed the quiet of the forest, prepped myself mentally for the return of clanging metal, and told my arms they could do it. The post sunk a quarter inch at a time with each blow. As it lowered into the ground, I threw my weight into the downward yank on the pounder. Concentrating on keeping the post straight, I lifted the pounder off the top of the post accidently and when I yanked the pounder down, it caught on the edge of the post and came crashing into the side of my face. I stumbled away from the post, letting the pounder drop to the ground, cussing at the pain in my temple.

I pressed a hand to my face then looked at it. No blood, no harm, no foul. I wrestled the pounder off the ground and back over the top of the fence post. This time, I focused on the top of the fence post as I tugged the pounder up and down and discovered why the tops of the green metal posts were painted white. The white paint warned you the pounder was reaching the top of the post, allowing you to reverse direction before the pounder came off the top. I wasn't sure who the guy was who came up with the idea, but I was pretty sure he had a few bruised body parts, a knot on his head, and hadn't been compensated nearly enough for his idea.

When I heaved down one last time, sinking the post the last quarter inch into the ground, my arms came up with a new plan for the day.

I left the pounder on top of the post, walked to the wheeler, and took off my jacket. I jostled the wheeler around and reorganized the posts on the rack. By putting up the fence posts, I was blocking my path through the trees and making it hard to drive the wheeler and avoid hitting the posts, either the ones on the wheeler or the ones hammered into the ground. The smart thing to do would be to set out all the posts first. I drove the wheeler carefully around the last few posts then stopped every twenty feet and pulled a post out of the bundle on the back of the wheeler. It worked pretty slick and with the wheeler empty, I headed to the shed for another load.

I had another idea at the shed and finding an old bent fence post, I wedged it in the front rack so it stuck out to the side a couple of feet. I lashed it to the rack with about a hundred feet of rope. I found another bent post and lashed it to the back rack. Now I had a way to carry the fence posts parallel to the wheeler instead of crosswise, which would make it a ton easier to navigate around obstacles. I loaded fence posts until I thought the wheeler might tip over from their weight hanging off to the side and started driving up the fence line. Since the front wheel was secured to the front rack, the front rack secured to the fence posts, and the fence post secured to the back rack, turning the front wheel was impossible.

I stopped not ten yards from the Courier saying a few

choice words about how stupid my brilliant idea had been. Pity party over, I unloaded everything from the wheeler. Using the bent fence posts created a rack on the back of the wheeler to help hold the fence posts in place. I loaded fence posts on the back rack until the front tire lifted off the ground. Climbing on and leaning forward, I piloted the Honda up the hill.

The day wore away into a hot blister. The cool breeze turned into a dry shimmer as I hauled load after load of fence posts, distributing them along the property line. I brought my lunch with me on one trip, eating it in the shade alongside the tiny creek that flowed at the end of the property line, quenching my thirst with its cold water. In another week or two, the creek would dry up if we didn't get any rain. I would need to start bringing a water jug with me. I managed to lay out all the fence posts along the fence line. After wrestling with the handlebars on the three-wheeler all day my shoulders had loosened up. I pounded a few more posts into the ground then decided to call it a day a little early. Tomorrow, I could hit it hard, start driving one post in after another and get back on schedule.

As I came down the fence line to the shed, I saw Pete sitting on the hood of his giant boat of a car, a 1970s Cadillac. Pete's dad had taken the car in trade then given it to Pete to drive. Since the car was built like a tank, he figured Pete would survive any crash. He hadn't realized the car had a giant engine and even though it leaked oil and took two miles to get up to speed, the old boat could do over a hundred miles an hour. Pete often reached those speeds on the straight stretch between Rye Creek and Conner Cutoff.

I waved as I drove the wheeler into the shed. Pete slid off the hood and approached, offering me a Coors Light. A cold Coors Light I realized as I grabbed it.

"I thought the working man might want to have a cold beer after a day of hard work." Pete said with a grin.

I chugged down half the can in a couple of swallows then handed the can to Pete so I could close the shed. Pete finished the beer, licked the side of the can, crushed the can flat against his forehead, counted the seconds it took until it slipped off, then deftly caught it before it hit the ground. Grinning, he tossed the can into the bed of the Courier.

"Thanks for the beer, but I told you Cherylann doesn't want anyone with me on her property while I work."

Pete smirked as if I was the biggest worrywart on the planet. His voice became his best Spicoli imitation. "Relax, dude, you're messing with my cool buzz. I'm here looking for some tasty waves."

I had to laugh at his impersonation even though it was bad. His voice returned to normal. "Besides you can't see the road from the house, so they don't know I'm here."

"Where'd you get the beer?" I asked, wondering if he had any more.

"Snuck it out of Dad's fridge in the garage. He won't be able to remember if he drank eight or nine from the half rack last night."

Well, that answered that question.

"So, have you seen Jenny, or have you spent all your

time working?" Pete asked.

"Mr. Peck caught me and Jenny making out and told me to stay away for a couple of weeks." I filled him in on all the details. "The worst part," I finished, "was hoping the damn starter would work on the Courier so I could get the hell out of there."

"You know what I would have done," Pete said. "I'd have looked him right in the eye and said, 'Mr. Peck, since Jenny won't be able to suck my dick for the next couple of weeks, are you volunteering?'" Pete chuckled.

"Yeah, and then he would have beat my ass and told me to never see Jenny again."

Pete hit me on the forehead by shaking his hand causing his middle finger to flick into my forehead. "That's for being a dumbass." He eased his butt onto the hood of the Caddy. "Peck knows he can't stop you and Jenny from boinking. He can't hit you, or that would turn you into a bad boy, and all high-school girls want a bad boy. He knows punching you or telling Jenny not to see you anymore guarantees Jenny spreads her legs for you."

Pete had a point, and I decided I would only wait a few more days before seeing if Jenny wanted to go do something after work, away from her house.

Pete slapped his hands on the hood of the car behind him. "Hey, did you hear about the kidnapper that's on the loose?"

I quickly told Pete about jumping the battery for the guy stranded at the Conner Store.

When I finished, Pete exploded. "Fuckin' A, E I, O, U, Scabs. You're shittin' me."

Pete had come up with the idea of adding the rest of the vowels after saying fuckin' A. He thought it was funny since if you cut out the middle, you were also saying fuck you.

"That's not even the best part. I swear, I totally saw a kid hiding in the back seat of the car," I added.

"That is major, Scabs. Fucking major." Pete kicked at a knapweed growing on the edge of the road scuffing the dirt around its base and tearing the plant away from its roots. "We should go up there and take a look around for him. Catch him and we're not only saving a kid—they've got a fifty-thousand-dollar reward for the piece of shit."

That mentally rocked me back on my heels. Fifty thousand. That kind of money would definitely get me to college. Hell, half that would get me through college. "Jenny's mom said he was armed and dangerous."

Pete kicked harder at the knapweed, completely separating the green from the root. "We don't have to arrest him. We just have to be able to bring the cops to him. We find him, take the cops to him, they arrest him, and we get the reward."

I couldn't believe it. I mean the odds of us finding the kidnapper had to be one in a million, but it would be worth a weekend trip for the chance. Besides, I was supposed to stay away from Jenny, and this would give me an excuse so I didn't look like I was afraid of Mr. Peck. Plus, maybe I could talk Pete into camping overnight at Mash Lake and doing some fishing. Pete hadn't had a better idea in his entire life. It even topped his idea to drive Jenny home from the graduation kegger.

"I'm in. We should go this weekend. Head out first thing Saturday morning," I suggested.

"Sounds good," Pete said. "I'm stoked. I'm gonna grab a bite to eat at home before heading to the gym. You want to come eat at my house and we can get our plan set before we go lift."

I'd forgotten Wednesdays were weightlifting days. The football coach opened the weight room at the school each Wednesday night during the summer break. He expected his football players to be there lifting to keep up their strength in the off season. My arms felt like limp noodles and I dreaded lifting anything with them. If I did any lifting with my arms, I wouldn't be able to lift the pounder tomorrow, let alone ram fifty posts into the ground. I could go and only work my legs, but I felt wore out. All I really wanted to do was go home, eat something, maybe watch *Hardcastle and McCormick*, then go to bed.

Before I could tell Pete I wasn't going to lift weights, he slid away from the Caddy while nodding his head at the hill behind me. I turned and there was Irwin jogging down the hillside wearing funky knee-length shorts and a three-quarter-sleeved April Wine concert t-shirt that pouched out tight around his beer gut. So much for Cherylann not knowing about Pete coming to see me.

"You've got to go," I said to Pete quickly before Irwin came to stop beside us.

Despite his gut, he didn't have much of a sweat going. Irwin stuck out his hand to Pete. "Irwin."

Pete shook hands introducing himself. The handshake

done, Irwin turned to me. "Cherylann said no friends on the property visiting you. He needs to leave and never come back."

Pete drew himself up to his full height, eye level with Irwin and definitely wider in the shoulders. "Scabs asked me to check into the cost of getting a new starter for his truck. I stopped by to give him the news and make sure his truck starts."

A thin smile spread across Irwin's face revealing an upper row of crooked teeth. I got the feeling nothing would make him happier than for Pete to take a swing at him.

"Leave," Irwin said, calmly jabbing his left index finger at Pete's face.

Pete must have sensed the same thing I had about Irwin because he walked to the driver's door of the Caddy. "Bill at the Parts House said he'd have to order the starter and it costs forty-five bucks." He swung the heavy door open on the Caddy glaring at Irwin. "You going to make sure he gets home if his truck doesn't start?"

"Get the fuck off the property, you lying piece of shit," Irwin spat.

I cringed at the words and spoke before Pete could do anything stupid. "Thanks, Pete, I'm okay. Please go."

Pete backed away from us, pulling off the dirt road into the grass, then spun the tires for a good thirty yards, throwing dirt into the air.

Irwin fixed his cold eyes on me. "He comes back, I tell Cherylann, she fires you."

I muttered that I understood and headed for the

Courier trying to escape his gaze.

Irwin stopped me before I could get in the truck. "I ran the new fence line. I counted only twenty-five fence posts in the ground. Now, I'm not as good at math as Cherylann, but after three days, that seems like you're taking three times too long to get those posts in the ground."

I opened the door then looked at Irwin over the top of the truck cab. "I got the posts laid out today so I plan on getting back on schedule tomorrow."

Irwin cocked his head to the side as if he was considering the effectiveness of my plan. "Let's just hope nobody comes along and steals those posts or the pounder you left out on the ground, instead of in the shed."

I hadn't thought about that when I was laying out the fence posts, but now that Irwin mentioned it, I worried for a second. I decided I didn't have much to worry about. No one in their right mind would sneak all the way around to the end of Cherylann's property just to steal metal fence posts.

I didn't know what to say, so I slid inside the Courier. For the first time ever, I hoped the starter wouldn't work. Thankfully, it clicked and whirred. I let off the key, thanking God for small favors, while waiting for the starter to quit spinning. The point made that the Courier did have a bad starter, I hoped it would now work so I could get the hell out of there. I turned the key and the little four-banger coughed into life. I waved to Irwin then gave him a thumbs-up that he didn't answer. I backed the

Courier into the grass then slowly pulled away.

Pete waited, the Caddy pulled off to the side of the road, just outside of the wooden gateposts that marked the beginning of Cherylann's driveway. I pulled the Courier alongside, then leaned across, and rolled down the passenger window.

"You comin' to dinner?" Pete asked.

"No. I'm beat, been busting ass. I'm going to go home and to bed early. I'll give you a call tomorrow evening after work so we can make a plan for looking for the kidnapper."

Pete's head jerked back almost like I'd physically shoved him. "You're not going to lift. C'mon, dude, couch potatoes don't start."

Our football coach had a rule about open gym. If someone didn't show during the summer at open gym, then they didn't start on the football team. They might get to play if they were really good, but they wouldn't start.

"I'll be in next week. Besides, it's not like I'm starter material anyway." I justified.

"Okay, Scabs, just don't turn into a dirtbag." HL-50

"Chill, Pete, I've had a long couple of days. I've done more working out with my arms the last three days than I did all last summer at open gym."

The opening guitar riffs to "Photograph" escaped out Pete's window and he turned up the volume on the Alpine stereo in the Caddy. Ten speakers responded by pumping out the opening line letting everyone know Joe Elliott was out of love.

Pete came around the front of the Courier then leaned

on the cab of the little truck, talking down to me through the window. "You seeing Jenny tonight, or are you going to wait a day or two before you start sniffing around again?" Pete yelled into the window over the roar of the rock music emanating from the Caddy.

I shook my head smiling. "I'm going to give it a day or two."

"Cool. If I see her at open gym, I'll tell her you're missing her and you told me her dad's an insufferable prick."

Before I could say anything, Pete jogged to the Caddy, hopped in, and pulled out onto the road in front of me. When the back tires hit the gravel road, he must have mashed down on the gas because a hail of little rocks peppered my windshield. Over the wave of gravel, I heard the bass thumping.

I headed home, choking Pete's dust for the first mile. I turned left on the West Fork Road and headed toward Conner. My mind kept wrestling with the reward they were offering for the kidnapper. That much money could completely change my life. It seemed like a pretty small chance two high-school kids could find the kidnapper, but man, if we did. I might have to rethink my trip to Horse Creek Hot Springs with Jenny. I'd need to get caught up at Cherylann's first. Then I could take a few days off. I'd give Pete a call tomorrow night to see how open gym went, remind him to never visit me while I was working on the fence, and get a plan together about searching for the kidnapper.

Chapter Six

Work on Thursday went awesome. My shoulders felt great as I hammered the posts into the ground one after another. I took a half-hour break in the shade by the creek to eat lunch and then went back to it. By the end of day, I had worked for ten hours and put thirty-five posts in the ground, jumping my total posts to around sixty, which meant I had one-fifth of the posts done. If I accomplished the same amount tomorrow, I'd be ready for a weekend of hiking, fishing, and making a citizen's arrest of a perverted kidnapper.

I parked the three-wheeler in the shed with the pounder strapped to the back rack. The Courier felt like a furnace after sitting in the hot sun all day, even though I had left both windows rolled down. I had to turn the key on the Courier three times for the starter to catch. I hadn't seen Irwin jog by along the fence line, and it made me wonder if he had spotted Pete on the property then came jogging by as an excuse. I remembered the funny little grin that made me think he hoped Pete took a swing at him and I decided Irwin didn't pretend. If he had seen Pete drive up the road, he would have followed him.

Mom had left a plate of food for me in the refrigerator. I sat on the couch with her watching *Simon & Simon* on TV. Dad sat in his oversized recliner and his eyes slipped closed before the show ended. Dad had been doing remodeling work at the Shining Mountain Ranch in French Basin. The long days were wearing him out.

I called Pete's house after the show and Pete's mom answered. Always cheerful, she told me Pete wasn't home but she expected him real soon. She promised to have him call me as soon as he got home.

I wondered what Pete could be up to and debated taking a shower now before he called back or waiting until after he called. If he didn't call soon, I ran the risk of violating the phone rules. My dad had a rule about the phone ringing after ten o'clock and Pete had already broken the rule a few times. Dad didn't look at it as Pete breaking the rule. Since he was calling me, I was breaking the rule and I didn't want Dad taking away my phone privileges. Luckily, Pete called after five minutes. He didn't waste any time in crushing my dream of getting a fifty-grand reward. HL-60

"Dude, sorry. Something came up, so I can't go backpacking this weekend."

What in the hell could have come up to change Pete's mind? He'd seemed so psyched about it yesterday. "Everything all right, Pete? Hope nothing bad happened."

Pete's voice came through the phone in a mumble.

I realized he was talking to someone else in the room and must have his hand over the phone. "You okay?" I asked.

"Yeah, Scabs, I'm great, just can't make it this weekend. Tell you what though. How about we go next week? Go first thing Thursday morning, and stay through the weekend camping."

That didn't sound good to me. I had fence to build and I didn't feel comfortable taking two days off work for the long shot chance of finding the kidnapper. I also wanted to take Jenny to Horse Creek Hot Springs that weekend and as much as I liked Pete, Jenny looked much better in a bikini. "I thought we were just going for the weekend?"

"C'mon, Scabs." Pete's tone turned harsh. "Do you want to go camping or not? That's when I can go and if we're going to do this, we might as well take enough time to do it right."

I almost hung up the phone to give Pete a day to get out of his funk. Maybe something had come up with his folks. Word around town was their marriage wasn't doing well.

When I didn't answer, Pete asked. "You gonna fish or cut bait?"

So much for soaking in a natural rock pool of hot water with Jenny. "Yeah, Pete. Sounds good. We leave next Thursday and return Sunday evening."

"Good," Pete said and hung up.

I held the phone in my hand for a minute, wondering what the hell happened to change Pete's mind about going this weekend. I sat the phone in its cradle. What was I going to do this weekend other than staying away from Jenny? Since I was going to miss next Thursday and Friday of work, I should probably work this weekend, but I could only work Saturday since Cherylann didn't want me on the property on Sundays.

I decided to call Jenny to feel out if I might be able to

see her on Sunday. Mr. Peck had only said to stay away not that I couldn't call. I pulled the phone out of the cradle and dialed Jenny's number. Mrs. Peck picked up on the second ring answering the phone with her cheery "Peck residence."

"Hi, Mrs. Peck, is Jenny there?" I didn't hear anything for so long I thought she might have hung up the phone. "Mrs. Peck?"

"Oh, yes, sweetie, I'm here. Jenny's over at a friend's. I don't think she'll be back until late. Is it okay if I have her call you tomorrow?"

I wondered about the long pause. Did she not know who was calling? "Mrs. Peck, it's me, Scabs, could Jenny give me a call tonight before ten o'clock?"

Again, there was a long pause on the phone and I wondered if maybe there was some issue with the connection. Mrs. Peck answered, her tone a little gruff, "When Jenny gets home, I'll let her know you called."

The line went dead and I put the phone back on the wall. Something was definitely up at the Peck residence. Maybe Mrs. and Mr. Peck were having a little disagreement about keeping me away from Jenny. Mrs. Peck was always inviting me to stay for dinner when I came to visit. Maybe I had the women of the Peck household on my side working for me to keep Mr. Peck calmed down.

I found a book, *Fair Blows the Wind* by Louis L'Amour, from the family bookshelf and sat reading in the hallway to be close by the phone if Jenny called. At nine o'clock, Jenny hadn't called and I'd already head-bobbed to sleep once. I brushed my teeth then went to bed looking forward to Friday and getting ahead of schedule on the fence.

~ ~ ~ ~ ~

The first fence post went into the ground like a hot knife through a can of butter-flavored Crisco—for the first nine inches. Then it stopped sinking into the ground but not with the distinctive sound of a metal fence post hitting a rock. I gave the pounder another half a dozen heaves before pulling it off the post and letting it fall to the ground. Much to my surprise, the post wouldn't come out of the ground. I wobbled it back and forth but succeeded in only bending the damn thing. I hustled down the fence line to retrieve the pry bar digging tool at the wheeler. I stabbed the pointy end into the ground loosening the dirt around the post. Dropping to my knees, I dug the dirt away from the fence post with my gloved hands. A root. I'd driven the post into the center of a large tree root until the little spade on the bottom of the post hit the root.

I calculated in my head how long it would take to run to the shed and get the axe stored there. I compared that estimate with how long I thought it would take me to free the post using only the pry bar. I opted for the pry bar, making a mental note to bring the axe back on my next trip to the shed. I began stabbing at the edges of the root trying to rip it apart. A half hour later, soaked in sweat, I wrestled the post out of the root. I carried the post to the three-wheeler. Using the back rack, I placed the bent post in such a way that when I pulled down on the end of the post I straightened out the curve in the bottom. A somewhat straight post in my hands, I placed it a foot farther down the property line from the root, tipped it to the side, and slipped the pounder over the top of it.

I'd determined that putting a metal fence post in the ground involved muscle converted into energy. Getting the post out after you put them in halfway required grit and a little anger. I was positive Cherylann hadn't taken into account hitting rocks and roots when figuring how long it took to put a post in the ground.

I made it eight inches before I hit a rock. At least the post came out of the ground easier as the fin at the bottom of the post was barely underground. I shifted to the opposite side of the root and started pounding again. I made it almost the required two feet before I hit a rock. I tried to smash my way through by throwing all my weight into the pounder. The post shifted under the blows, tweaking to the right, but finally sank in the required distance. I pulled the pounder off and studied the post leaning out away from the property line at a thirty-degree angle. I dropped the pounder, walked around the post, and pushed on the top until I bent the post upright. Good enough. I checked my watch. One fence post in the ground and it had taken me an hour, but I still had the rest of the day to catch up

I carried the pounder to the spot for the next post. This one made it eighteen inches before hitting a rock and try as I might, I couldn't get the damn thing to come out of the ground. I took a break to catch my breath. I hadn't quite spaced the fence posts properly when I laid them out on the ground, or maybe someone had stolen a post here and there so the missing posts wouldn't be noticed. Someone like Irwin trying to teach me a lesson. Either way, I needed a few extra fence posts to fill in the gaps. If I made a run to the shed for the extra posts, I could also bring the axe in case I hit another root. Maybe the shed of miscellaneous ranch supplies contained something to help me dig up the damn stuck fence posts.

I returned to the fence line an hour later with a dozen new fence posts, a short length of chain, an old floor jack, and a block of wood. I used the chain wrapped around the knobs on the fence post and the pry bar to keep it from slipping. I kept the chain close to the ground and let the pry bar stick out from the post about half a foot. With the other end of the pry bar against the ground, I sat the jack on the block of wood under the short end. Then I pumped the jack to raise the pry bar and lift the post out of the ground.

I shifted the post another foot down the fence line and started pounding. This time the post made it to within a couple inches of the required two feet before coming to a stop. Root or rock, I couldn't tell and I figured it was close enough. It wasn't like Cherylann was going to walk up here in her fancy clothes and put a tape measure to every post.

I wiped the sweat from my forehead and put my Dotson's Bar ball cap back on my head. Four hours and two fence posts. Cherylann had screwed me over. At this rate, I might not get the job finished by the deadline, forfeiting my bonus. I felt like sitting down in the shade and crying over this miserable fucking job. I ate my lunch right there not bothering to walk to the cool shade of the little creek. Less than a half hour later, I lifted the pounder over the top of another fence post. This post didn't go into the dirt any better than the first two.

I worked longer than I planned, trying to get in one more post, and managed ten posts in nine hours. My shoulders were sore but not in that stiff, painful way, just the "too tired to do anything more" way. I idled the three-wheeler down the hill to the shed enjoying the little breeze it created. Cherylann's Toyota pickup was parked beside the shed and Irwin had his head under the hood of the Courier.

He turned around from the engine block when I rolled the wheeler to a stop behind him. "Well, I was hopin' to finish before you got here, but it took me a little longer than I thought it would." He gave a knowing leer. "Plus, some unexpected afternoon delight happened, so I got started a little later than I planned."

While I didn't want to picture Irwin having sex in the middle of the afternoon, I did let my mind picture Cherylann for a moment before I asked, "What are you doing with my truck?"

Irwin, a box wrench in his hand, waved me toward the driver's side of the Courier. "Get in and turn the key. Let's see if I got this in right."

I did what he said and the Courier's little engine sprang to life as soon as I turned the key.

Irwin closed the hood and came around to my side so

he could talk to me through the open door. "Had an old starter in the garage. Thought it might be a fit for your rig. Looks like she's going to work. Turn her off and try again."

I did as told. The engine fired right up, the newly installed starter working perfectly. I turned the truck off and swung my feet out, facing Irwin. "Thanks," I said, wondering what to call him. I didn't know his last name, so I could call him mister or Irwin. I hoped he wasn't expecting me to pay for something I hadn't asked him to do, but I felt obligated.

He must have read my thoughts by the look on my face. "Don't worry about it. Happy to do it. Now you won't have to have your friend come and rescue you." He turned away then looked back at me over his shoulder. "It's Friday and long past five o'clock. Time for a beer after a hard day's work."

Irwin went around to the Toyota, grabbed a petite blue cooler out of the cab and pulled not one but two Miller Lites from it. He tossed one can to me. With his newly freed hand, he dropped the tailgate on the Toyota and sat down. The beer felt cold in my hand, but it seemed odd having a beer with a stranger.

"How's the job going?" he asked then took a drink of his beer. After swallowing, he added, "Less filling."

I caught on and popped the top on my beer. The cold liquid felt great going down my throat and the taste wasn't horrible. "Tastes great," I said.

After another sip, I answered his question about building the fence. "A little harder than I thought it was going to be," I admitted.

"Well, you still got plenty of time." He pronounced well as if it was whale-ell, dragging it out into two syllables.

I thought now was as good a time as any to let him know I wouldn't be working next Thursday or Friday. "I'm going to work tomorrow since I plan to take next Thursday and Friday off. I'm a little worried about getting behind schedule."

Irwin just stared at the beer in my hand. I got the message and took a sip.

He drank then asked, "What you got planned next week? Hanging out with some young filly?"

"'You heard about that kidnapper that's hiding around Darby?" I'm not sure why I asked that. Maybe the beer was already loosening my tongue, or maybe I just wanted to have a more important reason for missing work than going camping with a friend.

Irwin tipped his head forward, acknowledging he had. "I think I ran into him the day I interviewed with Cherylann, and you." I took a full drink of beer this time. "I think he might have told me where he was headed to in the mountains, so a buddy and me, we're going to hike in there and check it out."

Irwin stretched his legs out in front of him then let them drop, the heels of his boots scuffing the dirt. His eyes were down underneath the brim of the straw cowboy hat looking at the ground. "What kind of hardware are you taking into the woods?"

Hardware. I didn't have any idea what Irwin meant

by hardware. "We're taking a couple of sleeping bags, maybe some Visqueen to sleep under if it rains, some dried soup, and a fishing pole with a couple lures and some dry flies. That's what I take when I go camping with my dad. Enough for a few days."

Irwin looked at me, a slight grin twisting his lips but not enough to show his teeth. "That redhead on the news said this guy is a bit of a badass." He took a drink of beer then added, "Armed and dangerous."

"There will be two of us. And we aren't planning on hog-tying the guy and dragging him out of the hills." At least, I wasn't planning on doing that, but I realized I wasn't sure what Pete planned on doing. Irwin went back to studying the toes of his boots saying nothing. I figured he was waiting for me to tell him what we did have planned, so I opened my mouth. "One of us will keep an eye on the guy while the other one gets the cops. The reward is for information leading to his arrest."

Irwin repeated his leg-kick thing, elongating the scuff marks his heels made in the dirt. His eyes made contact with mine over the top of his beer as he took a drink. "When you head out the door into the wilderness, well, the world can be a dangerous place. You thinking about taking a gun with you?"

I hadn't thought about taking a gun. While working on the fence, I'd spent most of my time thinking about the fence or wondering why Jenny hadn't called me back. The only gun I had was my Winchester rifle, and even though Dad referred to it as my gun, if I pulled it out of my closet to take it with me, Dad's eyebrows would raise in disapproval. When Dad and I went camping, he didn't bring a rifle. He always said bears were more afraid of us than we were of them. I said as much to Irwin.

He slid forward off the tailgate and set his empty beer can on the ground. He stomped it flat then threw the white biscuit of aluminum into the bed of the Toyota. He wrangled the little cooler around, pulled out another beer, and gave me a questioning look.

"Still working on this one," I replied.

Irwin resumed his position on the tailgate, complete with letting his heels scuff the ground, before taking a drink of his beer. "Heard some local gossip that the problem grizzly bears in Yellowstone Park, the ones getting aggressive with the tourists, are being tranqed then turned loose in the Selway or way up the head of the East Fork."

I'd heard the stories too. The bears were subdued with massive amounts of PCP, and before the park removed a bear, it had been darted three times, which had hooked them on PCP. Then this drug-crazed bear that wasn't afraid of humans was turned loose in remote areas of the Bitterroot. People wondered what would happen if the bears ran into people and why the Park Service worried about tourists but not the people who lived in Montana.

"I've never heard of anyone seeing a grizzly bear up the East Fork. We should be okay."

Irwin picked up his pace of swinging his legs, scuffing the ground twice in a minute. "Well," he said, taking another drink of beer, "I'd recommend you take a weapon with you for self-defense reasons just in case the varmint you're looking for tries anything." He scuffed the ground a couple times then added, "Something lightweight that can handle a man."

Irwin seemed to be really hung up on us taking a gun. I took a big drink of my beer thinking the sooner I finished the beer, the sooner I could make an excuse to leave. "I'll talk to Pete. His dad has lots of guns."

"That's a good idea. They did a study on shoot-outs involving cops a few years back. Cops shooting bad guys, bad guys shooting cops, and they looked at not only the caliber of the gun but the type of bullet that was used. They discovered that the best combination was the .357 magnum using a 125-grain hollow-point bullet. Ninety-five percent one-shot knockdown." [HL-61]

I drained my beer can then stomped it flat and tossed it into the back of the Toyota. "That's good to know. I'll let Pete know about that when I ask him about bringing a gun." Since I didn't know what to do next, I rubbed my left shoulder to work out a kink. "Thanks for the starter. I really appreciated it. And the beer, but I need to be heading home. I'll be back tomorrow."

"No problem, that old starter was just taking up space in the garage. You off to see some pretty little filly?"

I thought again about Jenny not returning my phone call and wondered if I should call her house again tonight. Would it be pushing my luck to detour all the way into Darby on my drive home to see if she was working at the video store? Mr. Peck couldn't get too mad at me for renting a movie on a Friday night.

"Yep," I replied to Irwin. "I'm off to see to see a filly."

I walked around to the Courier and nodded goodbye to Irwin as I sat in the driver's seat. The little engine sparked with barely a turn of the key. I drove down the dirt road with my mind filled with questions. Why was Irwin being so helpful? Was it really worth going with Pete to look for the kidnapper? Why did Cherylann have to have the fence done by September? Why hadn't Jenny called me back? Mr. Peck and his command to stay away from his daughter for a while was starting to wear on my nerves. I wondered if he had told Jenny to dump me.

Chapter Seven

By next Wednesday, I'd revised my fence completion date to the Sunday right before the Monday when two-a-day football practices started. If I kept running into roots and rocks and it began to look like I couldn't get it done before football, then I'd have to ask Cherylann if I could bring a friend to help me finish on time. Since she wouldn't have to pay the bonus if I didn't finish on time and part of the deal had been just me doing the fence, I didn't have much hope she would agree. I could always work for a few hours in the evening after the second practice, but I was stiff, sore, and tired the first week of two-a-day practices and I doubted I'd have enough gumption to work on the damn fence.

I loaded the tools on the rear rack of the Honda, securing them with what felt like a mile of rope. The only things left on the hillside were the fence posts I hadn't pounded into the ground. A lot of fence posts since apparently the entire mountain was created out of slabs of rock hidden a half foot under the dirt held together by bull pine roots. My shoulders no longer ached when I finished the day, finally adapting to the daily beating of using the pounder and the other pounder. I had begun to think of bar pounder as a pry bar to keep the two pounders straight in my head.

On the ride to the shed, I debated running into Darby

to see Jenny again at the video store. I hadn't seen or heard from her since last Friday. She had been annoyed at me for bothering her at work. She'd told me to leave after a half an hour, saying customers were leaving because of my sweat stink. She did tell me her dad hadn't told her to break up with me, so that had been good news.

Pete wanted to meet at Wolverine Creek Campground tonight, which didn't leave me much time to visit with Jenny, and I decided not to call the store from my house before I left. I might score some brownie points for not bugging her at work and maybe not hearing from me would make her appreciate me. She had given me a hesitant maybe about going to Horse Creek Hot Springs, just for the day, the Sunday after the camping trip.

I parked the wheeler in the shed and made sure to close the door securely since I didn't plan on being back for five days. When I slid behind the wheel of the Courier, I found a handgun in a red leather holster in the middle of the bench seat. A half sheet of paper sat on top of the gun with a message scrawled across it. "I want it back after your trip. Irwin."

I slipped the Colt .357 magnum from the holster and worked the cylinder open, ejecting the bullets, jacketed hollow points, into my palm. I'd bet a week's work on the fence they weighed 125 grains. I didn't see any other bullets other than the six in the gun. Enough bullets if I really needed it, but not enough to screw around shooting the gun for fun. I reloaded the Colt and slipped it into the holster.

I pulled into our driveway looking at the sunlight on

the open hillside behind the house. Along the top of a ridge, the sun lit up a standing dead tree that grew out of a rocky outcropping making it resemble a cross. The gun Irwin gave me stuck out like a sore thumb on the seat of the Courier and I hid it under the seat on the passenger side. Dad wasn't home from the bathroom remodel job in the main house on Shining Mountain Ranch, but I didn't want Mom to see it.

Mom fluttered around me as I gathered my camping equipment. I'd organized my backpack the last few evenings, so I didn't have much to do other than change into clean jeans and a t-shirt then grab my backpack out of my room. Mom made me sit at the dinner table and I wolfed down six flour tortillas cover in pizza sauce and pepperoni she had broiled in the oven.

Mom wore a pretty black dress that came down to just above her knees and I could smell perfume. "You and Dad going out to dinner when he gets home?" I asked between bites.

"No, I have a client scheduled, so I'm running into town, but maybe I'll meet your dad later at the Knob for hamburgers."

Mom kept an office in Darby for her massage therapy. The motel in town, Bud and Shirley's, let Mom rent a room cheap as an office.

She followed me out to the Courier, making me feel smart for hiding the gun under the seat. She gave me one last hug before I got in the truck then said through the open window, "I sure hope it's just you and Pete going on this trip. You're a little too young to be sneaking off on a camping trip with Jenny."

I smiled at Mom trying to reassure her. "Just me and Pete, Mom, no girls. You can always stop by the video store and check with Jenny's mom or Jenny herself."

I drove off before she could ask any more questions, pausing at the end of the driveway for a logging truck to roar past before turning south heading for Sula. I watched Mom pull onto Highway 93 in the rearview mirror heading for Darby in the opposite direction.

I kept my speed at fifty-five around the next few lazy turns the highway made as it followed the river then shot over a bridge crossing the East Fork just as the sun dipped behind the steep mountains letting the fir and bull pine draw in a deep cool breath after the long hot summer day.

I slowed for the narrow turn in the road before Laird Creek and the Rocky Knob Lodge. The Knob had been a bar and restaurant for about a hundred years and I figured it would be a bar and restaurant for another hundred. It had a great pinball machine. When you won a free game, you also won a half-price dinner from the Mexican food menu. I saw the green WLH Surveying truck with its large metal box instead of a truck bed in the parking lot as I went by.

The speedometer on the little Courier crawled to sixty-five in the straight stretch before The Rock Shop by the Medicine Hot Springs turnoff. I had my foot on the brake as I went by the turn for Spring Gulch slowing for the curves ahead as Highway 93 clung to the curves of the river for the next few miles. The road to Spring Gulch took you north on the other side of the Bitterroot River to Coyote Gulch where ancient Native American petroglyphs were on some rocks. At least that was what I had been told and having looked at the rocks, I'd seen the markings, but it was hard to believe they were hundreds of years old. HL-70

The narrow river ran alongside the road at an equal depth all the way across, and here and there, a large boulder lay in the middle of the stream. I'd been told Fish and Game had hired a guy with a backhoe to place those rocks in the river to create habitat for trout. Halfway through the turn at Jim Hell Rock, I mashed the gas pedal to the floorboard, picking up speed through the next few turns.

I slowed and hit my blinker, taking the fork in the road to the left, leaving Highway 93 and turning onto the East Fork Road.

I followed the curvy road with grassy mountains to my left, leading to Sula Peak Lookout, and open hayfields to my right. The road turned into the center of the valley, putting hayfields on either side of me. I went past the turn to French Basin Road and the Shining Mountain Ranch. Since I hadn't passed my dad going the other way, the bathroom remodel must not have been going too well. I passed the bridge leading to Wetzsteon Ranch, remembering the pavement had ended here a few years ago.

After a few more miles, timbered mountains encroached on both sides of the road. I braked to avoid tailgating a Buick Skylark turning into the Broad Axe

Lodge. The Broad Axe served exceptional dinners and at each table sat a pair of binoculars, or field glasses if you prefer, so the dinner guests could look at the wild animals roaming the open hillsides across the valley.

The Courier barely reached the speed limit then I mashed on the brakes hard to make it around a thirty-mph turn. Right after the turn, I came to an abrupt stop in front of a dozen bighorn ewes and lambs. They were crossing the road heading uphill into the rocks, no doubt heading back to the ridge tops of Shirley Mountain after coming to the river to drink their fill. One lamb kicked its heels at the grill of the Courier and I hit the horn, spooking them enough I could ease through the dusty brown sheep. I accelerated to the speed limit plus a little more, dodging a few rocks in the road near the turnoff to Guide Creek.

I kept my speed along this section of the road with lodgepole-covered mountains to my left and the East Fork River, now a tumbling brook, to my right. I mashed the accelerator to the floor at the turn to Meadow Creek and watched the speedometer creep to seventy-five miles an hour as the Courier ran alongside the airstrip by Fred Wetzsteon's ranch. I managed to hit eighty before the slight turn to the left and the bridge taking me down the straight stretch of road past Bonanza Land and Springer Memorial.

I let off the accelerator and eased on the brake, slowing the Courier to dirt-road speeds as I left the pavement behind at the turnoff into Springer. I went past the East Fork Guard Station—I never have understood what it's guarding—and drove through the thick stands of lodgepole on either side of the road. I turned to the right to pull into the loop for the Wolverine Creek Campground. The sun slipped behind the mountains as I idled into the campground, but I knew that this deep in the canyon the twilight would last for more than an hour. Only Pete's Cadillac was parked in the campground and he had strategically taken the spot farthest from and upwind of the stinky Forest Service outhouse.

Pete greeted me with a "Hey Scabs, you made it," and a high five. He had a fire going in the cut-off barrel fire ring. The massive trunk of the Caddy was open and half filled with sixteen-inch rounds of lodgepole pine.

Pete laughed. "Fuck cutting firewood. I just took some from the wood porch."

Pete's dad had a reputation for being extremely fussy about what kind of firewood he burned. He only cut down standing dead lodgepole pine that all the bark had weathered off. This often involved Pete and I having to carry or throw blocks of wood down the mountain past other dead trees with their bark still on when getting wood with his dad. I figured Pete's dad wouldn't mind since we had helped get the wood. Pete pulled a five-gallon bucket holding a block of ice in it out of the trunk. He squeezed a hand past the ice and pulled a Coors Light out of the bottom of the bucket.

He tossed it to me with a grin. "I took the old man's whole six-pack. Safer than just taking a couple because the old fart will probably think he forget to buy beer."

I smiled at Pete's humor, but Pete's dad would never

forget how much beer he had in his fridge, as it seemed to be an important matter to him every time I visited Pete. He said the beer helped relax the muscles in his lower back so they didn't hurt. The beer must not have completely killed the pain because last winter he began seeing my Mom weekly for a massage. Pete grabbed a beer for himself and we sat on the bumper of the Caddy drinking and acting grown-up by talking about the weather and the weather that might be coming. Pete asked about the fence and I asked how the hayfields were doing and who Pete had gotten to change sprinkler pipes for him while he was gone.

Our first beer done, we set Pete's orange, triangular, two-man tent up on the flat spot across the fire from the Caddy. The tent had an aluminum pole at the front and another in the back of the tent to keep the center of the roof in the required triangle shape. The back pole had a habit of getting knocked over in the middle of the night if you shifted around in your sleeping bag and you'd wake up in the morning with the tent around your face.

I crawled into the tent to put the center pole in place when Pete called, "Scabs, car coming out from the trailhead. Is it the kidnappers?"

I bear-crawled out of the tent in time to catch sight of a car as it disappeared in the dark.

"So?" Pete asked.

"I don't know, Pete, hard to tell in the dark. The color seemed different." I shook my head and shrugged. "Could have been, I guess."

"That totally sucks the big one." Pete tossed his rolled-up sleeping bag into the tent. "We might have missed him by a half a day."

I wanted to point out to Pete that if we had gone on the trip when we were supposed to we wouldn't have missed him, but maybe it wasn't the kidnapper's car. "Probably not even him. We'll see in the morning if any cars are at the trailhead." I stopped talking, wondering why we hadn't thought to drive to the trailhead earlier in the week to see if the car had been parked there. Well, I had been working, so that was why I hadn't, but maybe Pete could have.

"Whatever," Pete said. "He might not even leave his car at the trailhead. Maybe he hitched a ride with someone. Let's not worry about it." He reached into the bucket of beer and produced a packet of hot dogs. "I'm jonesing for some campfire dogs."

We cut willow sticks by the creek to roast the dogs. I used a forked stick and stabbed the dog in two places while Pete went with the straight stick method and speared his dog lengthwise through the middle of the dog. We roasted the dogs over the fire and ate them straight from the sticks since we didn't have any buns or ketchup.

A truck appeared, its headlights picking out the dirt road in front of it. We watched in silence waiting to see if it would turn into the campground. The truck drove past the campground toward the trailhead.

"Wonder where they're going," I mused as the sound of the truck faded away. There weren't any campgrounds up the road, only the large turnaround spot at the trailhead into the lakes.

"Maybe someone spotlighting rabbits," Pete suggested. "I guess we'll see if they come back after a bit." Pete grabbed another set of beers from the bucket and we resumed our positions on the bumper of the Caddy. After a few minutes of staring into the campfire and a few swallows of beer, Pete asked, "Jenny mad at you for staying away from her?"

I hadn't been able to talk to Jenny enough to determine if she was mad at me or not. "We've both been busy working. She can't visit me at Cherylann's and she told me not to bug her at the video store, but we might be going to Horse Creek Hot Springs next weekend."

Pete sat his empty beer can on top of some red coals bracketed by two logs in the fire. I had three-quarters of my beer left and declined when Pete asked if I was ready for another.

Pete downed a large gulp of his new beer, his third. "Yeah, don't get me wrong, Scabs, but I don't think you and Jenny are going to last. Might be better if you broke things off with her."

It felt like Pete had slapped me. What did he mean Jenny and I weren't going to work out? Sure, Jenny's father didn't like me much, but he wouldn't like any boy hanging around his daughter. It wasn't that he personally disliked me. "Why would you say that?" I asked.

"You're going to leave and go to college and Jenny is going to stay here in town and work the video store. You guys are going to break up when that happens, so why put yourself through the torture of dating all senior year knowing you're just going to split up."

Pete took another gulp of beer. "Sally Parker is always telling anyone who will listen how she's going to Bozo for college. You should try hooking up with her. That way, the two of you could go to college together if things work out."

"Yeah, but I don't like Sally. I like Jenny."

"Sally's brother Perry told me the other day that Sally has a crush on you. We were both trying to figure out how in the hell that could be."

I thought through the interactions I'd had with Sally during the last year of school. It was easy since there hadn't been very many. We'd had government class together but probably only talked a half dozen times during the year and for half the year, she'd been dating a wrestler before she broke up with him. As far as I could tell, she'd never shown any interest in me.

Pete continued, "I heard from Sally's old boyfriend she gave him a BJ once a week. That's why he was crying in the hallways at school after they broke up."

I didn't know what to say and didn't understand why Pete seemed to think I should dump Jenny for Sally Parker. "If she's so great, maybe you should ask her out."

Pete dropped another empty beer can into the dwindling fire, mostly coals and charcoal logs. He fished another can out of the bucket without asking me if I wanted another.

"Maybe we should save those for tomorrow night," I suggested. "I'll pack them into the lake." I didn't want Pete getting so drunk he wouldn't be able to start early in the morning.

"Not to worry, Scabs. I snuck a flask out of my dad's liquor cabinet. We'll have that to drink." He opened his new beer and stared at me. "Think I've had too much to drink, Scabs?"

The tone in his voice made it clear that if I hinted he should stop drinking it would lead to an argument, so I didn't say anything. At least, Pete had stopped talking about Sally. In order to keep Pete from returning to that subject, I commented, "That truck hasn't come back down the road. They must be staying the night."

"Yeah, that's not cool. We might have some competition for the fish," Pete said.

I didn't say anything else, letting the sounds of the fire and the night around us ease the tension. Pete drank his beer while staring into the fire. I drank the last swallow of my beer. I wanted to crush it into a silver biscuit like Irwin did and put it in the bed of my pickup, but I couldn't afford for my folks to find a beer can in my truck, so I dropped it into the coals where Pete's cans had partially melted away. "I'm brushing my teeth and then crawling into my bag." I walked to the Courier to get my toothbrush from my backpack.

"Always the Boy Scout, aren't you, Scabs. You don't need to brush your teeth. Your folks aren't around."

Pete had seemed in a good mood when I arrived, but something had sure turned his mood ugly. Maybe it was the beer. When I finished brushing my teeth, I crawled into Pete's tent then zipped up my sleeping bag around me. I hoped Pete's mood improved on the trip. Otherwise,

I should have stayed and worked. The long week of work and the beer took their toll on me. The last thing I heard before falling asleep was Pete getting the last beer out of the bucket. The last thing I thought was that hiking into the lakes with a hangover wasn't going to improve Pete's mood.

Chapter Eight

Pete rolled out of his sleeping bag and dressed as I stretched inside my Coleman bag trying to wake up. As he left the tent, he ripped a loud fart then called over his shoulder, "Good morning, Sleeping Beauty, have an air biscuit for breakfast."

The tent reeked of night sweats, charcoal hotdogs, and light beer. I grabbed my clothes and dressed outside the tent despite the morning chill. I pulled my sleeping bag out of the tent, stuffed it in its bag then strapped it to my pack. I helped Pete take down the little tent then I waited in the Courier while Pete parked the Caddy off the side of the road. He'd moved it in case the campground filled up during the weekend while we were gone. The damp early morning coated the trees around the creek in a wispy fog. It hadn't frosted and the clear sky indicated the sun would soon evaporate the fog. The day promised to be a scorcher.

I drove along the dirt road toward the trailhead, Pete and I munching on Pop-tarts. The road switched back up the mountainside. At shooting light, we reached the trailhead, a wide oval area for parking and turning around.

The pickup from the night before was parked on the edge of the turnaround spot. I backed into a spot beside the truck, facing out, as my dad had taught me to park.

Pete exclaimed from the passenger seat, "Shit, it's Diana. She's sleeping in her truck. Wonder what the hell she's doing here."

I shut the truck off, got out, found a rock to chock the back tire of the Courier, and hid the keys to the truck under it as Pete rapped on the window of Diana's pickup. The last time I had seen Diana was at graduation. I guessed she must be here doing something for her dad, like scouting for hunting spots.

Diana waved but didn't smile. After a minute, she slid out of the cab of the pickup with clothes on and her hiking boots in her hands.

"You slept in your truck?" Pete asked even though it was obvious based on the sleeping bag across the seat.

"Yeah," she responded in her slow, steady way of talking. "I got here after dark and didn't feel like sleeping on the ground." Diana brushed a few long strands of brown hair out of her face. "I was afraid some dumbass would drive over me turning their truck around."

"What are you doing up here? You hiking the trail?" Pete continued to ask questions when his eyes knew the answer.

Diana had on a brown shirt and a pair of blue jean cutoffs. Not the sexy type of jean cutoffs, these had been cut around the knees. The dangling white threads gave the appearance the bottom half of the legs had worn off instead of being cut. She sat on the ground and leaned forward to put her boots on. For the first time ever, I noticed that Diana, from what I could see down the neck of her shirt, had breasts and nice ones.

"Dad wants me to cache some gear at Trout Lake, so I'm taking a load in today then hiking back out to the truck to sleep for tonight. Then tomorrow, I'm taking another load of gear to cache by Myth Lake. What are you boys up to?"

Diana's slow and steady way of talking was hypnotic, but it didn't slow Pete down. He kept talking just as fast as always. "We're going into the lakes to do some fishing, spending a couple of nights." He said as he pulled his fishing pole out of the bed of the Courier.

Diana looked up from putting on her boots totally catching me looking down her shirt. I averted my eyes away from her dark-green eyes but not before I saw the tiniest movement of her lips. I couldn't tell if it was a smile or a frown, but considering she didn't hit me after she stood up, I decided to call it a smile. Diana pulled a rubber band out of her pocket, ran her fingers through her hair, and put it up into a ponytail.

"Maybe I'll see you guys in there." She walked around to her dented old Ford. She lowered the tailgate and reached in for her backpack.

I said something about her having a nice trip as I gathered my gear out of the bed of the Courier. Diana wouldn't be at the lakes very long if she had to hike in and out of the lakes each day. She wouldn't be around enough to interfere with our searching for the kidnapper. If Pete and I hurried, we could maybe get to Trout Lake before her and then while she hiked out for more gear, we could check Mash and Myth Lakes beating her to all three lakes.

I realized Pete was still talking fast and then I realized I didn't like what he was saying.

"How about we all hike together? How much gear do you got? Scabs and I don't have much to carry. Maybe if we divided everything up between us, you could just hike to Trout Lake today, spend the night, then we could help you get the rest of the gear to Myth Lake. No need to make two trips."

I tried to give Pete a look telling him I thought his idea was horrible, but he never looked at me just at Diana and that's when I realized I wasn't the only one who had noticed Diana's breasts. If Diana had any brains in her head, she would politely decline then wait an hour for us to get down the trail and out of her way.

"Sure," she said slowly. "Let's divvy up the gear and see if we can carry it."

I sat my pack down by the driver side door of the Courier and began making room to put Diana's supplies in on top. For some reason, I didn't feel comfortable wearing the revolver Irwin had given me. I had planned on putting on the shoulder holster and wearing it while we hiked into the lake. I knew Pete would think it pretty badass, but I didn't feel comfortable wearing it around Diana. I had an idea Pete might ask me who I was afraid of, Bigfoot or the boogeyman, making me look wimpy.

The bottom of the main compartment of my pack stacked on top of a smaller bottom compartment. The two cloth layers had a small piece of corrugated cardboard between them to help keep the pack wide open. My dad had cut the seam on one side and pulled out the cardboard insisting that it didn't need to be there and would get wet and rot. Leaving the holster under the seat, I wrapped the gun in an empty bread sack I'd brought along to keep my extra shirt dry then stuffed the gun into the slot at the bottom of the compartment.

Diana distributed items to us and I had trouble closing the drawstring at the top of my pack when she finished. I dropped the tailgate on the Courier and hefted my pack near the edge then sat on the tailgate in front of it. I slipped into my backpack straps and then stood up, stumbling at the weight of the pack. No way would Pete want to carry this much weight for six miles and I doubted Diana could carry that much for a mile.

Diana slung her pack over her shoulders, putting her arms into the straps without any help from Pete or me. I thought I saw Pete hesitate when the weight of his pack settled on his back, but he smiled at Diana. We all walked across the turnaround toward the start of the trail.

At the trailhead sign, Pete stopped. "We should get a picture."

Fifteen minutes later, Pete had managed to rummage his Kodak out of his pack. We rotated who ran the camera to get pictures of everybody, Diana and Pete, Pete and me, and Diana and me. Pete had his pack off the whole time, but I kept mine on, and by the time we started hiking, I needed a break. Pete had kept up a conversation with Diana the entire picture-taking time, complimenting Diana on how much she looked like an outdoor model. Diana handled his flirting, but not easily, and I wondered how Pete couldn't see she wasn't interested.

The trail gained elevation at first and I hiked last in line, not talking to save my breath for sucking in as much oxygen as I could. Pete continued to talk until Diana increased her pace, striding past him. That upset me for two reasons. One, I could no longer look at Diana in her cutoffs, and two, I really had to struggle to keep pace. Pete shut up, so I figured he must be having difficulty also.

Diana stopped in a flat spot along the trail and pointed out where the old road, the one that was gated at the trailhead, used to run into the saddle. Stumps lined the edges of the old road now filled with bear grass and young Douglas fir. Diana explained that in the old days a person could drive all the way to the high saddle above the lakes. I didn't bother looking around at what she pointed out. I was too busy finding a log to sit on so I could lean back to take the weight of the pack off my shoulders. Diana resumed hiking much sooner than I wanted. That's when I realized my decision to not bring a canteen of water for the hike had been foolish. [HL-80]

I kept my head down with my arms at my side lifting the bottom of my pack to take some weight off my shoulders. I kept plodding forward one step at a time trying not to look stressed. Diana started talking now, like she was walking in a park with no pack. She pointed out deer and elk tracks in the trail and a coil of bobcat poop. She gave a lecture on how external pack frames were much better for packing heavy loads than internal pack frames. That squirrels are born blind and that their front teeth never stop growing. She explained that if they didn't wear them down, their teeth would grow six inches in a year.

Diana pulled ahead of me until I couldn't hear what she said. She stopped for a break and I quickened my pace to reach her so I could take my own much-needed rest. As soon as I stopped beside her with a smile, she started up the trail, leaving me with the choice to stand there and get farther behind or to forgo resting. Pete made the choice for us. He mumbled something about being in shape for two-a-day practices as he hustled after Diana. I waited for a count of five then chased after Pete.

That process repeated several times until I decided I wouldn't get to rest until I fell over from heatstroke or we got to the lake. I bet a day's worth of work on the fence it would be heatstroke. It would have been less work to build fence. Finally, Diana stopped and removed her pack at a spot where the trail climbed the cut bank of the old road. She pulled a pint canteen from her pack, and by the time Pete and I reached her, she had already drunk her fill and put it away in her pack. The old road in front of us dropped down then climbed steeply in a series of rolling hills overgrown with alder bushes. My dad called the series of steep bumps Kelly humps. They were designed to keep trucks from continuing to drive on roads after the Forest Service gated them, as sometimes people could find a way around the gate. These Kelly humps had been strategically created on a steep grade of the hillside, making it really tough for an adventurous person to find a route around them.

Diana pointed out the humps while I sat against the

cut bank of the old road, taking the weight off my back and giving my feet a rest. "I heard that the Forest Service contracted with a local guy who owned a backhoe to dig out the road. When he got done making the humps, he drove the backhoe up to the saddle on the ridge above the lakes and found out there was a half dozen pickups parked up there." Diana laughed. "He had to round everybody up and have them follow him out. Then he had to smooth out the humps, let everyone go by, then remake them. I bet he didn't make any money on that contract."

I chuckled along with Diana to be polite. I wondered if this was the same guy who had dropped the rocks in the river with his backhoe. How many people had owned a backhoe in those days in the East Fork?

Diana didn't let us rest for long. Way before I was ready, she hefted her pack, made a comment about getting to the lake before the sun got hot, and left Pete and I sitting there looking at each other. I beat Pete to standing then scrambled up the bank and down the trail winding through the trees. If I had to hike until I passed out, I might as well have Diana's backside to look at. Pete ran right up on my heels and when the trail cut downhill to the old road, he gave me a push before I could turn, forcing me on through the trees. He shot down the trail into the spot behind Diana. I grabbed at a skinny lodgepole pine to stop myself then hurried down the hill onto the old road. Pete had a good ten yards on me and I leaned forward into my pack straps, determined to wrestle the coveted second-place spot from him before we reached the lake.

I managed to get right on Pete's heels, but I couldn't find the extra burst of speed needed to get around him. The trail narrowed down to a footpath running straight up the side of a ridge. I lifted my head from staring at the ground in front of my feet. Diana was taking a shortcut off the old road by going up the ridge instead of following the road as it contoured around the hillside then switched back. I dropped farther behind Pete, giving up on my goal to be second. It took all my concentration to keep putting one foot in front of the other.

From that point on, the trail seemed the same. Tan dirt with white rocks was all I saw. Every time I thought I couldn't take another step and would be forced to call out to the others to wait for me, Diana would stop for a minute. She'd smile at us as I spent my time wiping sweat off my face while holding my ball cap in my hand to let the breeze cool my head. After a minute, Diana would take off up the trail without even the courtesy of asking if we were ready.

We stopped once to look out across the forested hills stretching across the western horizon to the rocky peaks that rose against the big sky. I spotted Trapper's Peak among them. My dad and I had climbed it once. The trail to the peak was steep and straight up. Dad and I had made the hike like turtles, slow and sure. I made a mental note to never hike Trapper's Peak with Diana. We finally reached the top of the main ridge with Trout Lake to the southeast, Mash Lake to the northeast, and a long ridge separating the two lakes to the east. Trout Lake drained south into Beard Creek, but Mash Lake drained north at first then curved around to the south into Elk Creek.

Diana called over her shoulder, "Let's take a break at the spring in the saddle."

A high mountain meadow filled with yellow bells and purple flowers nestled among the white pines on the top of the ridge. Bear grass, with their long stalks beginning to open their white flowers, dotted the skunk cabbage growing near the spring, giving away its location. I eased my pack off my shoulders and laid it in the grass near the spring in the shade of a grand fir. I felt so light I thought I might spring into the air with each step. I briefly wondered if that was how astronauts felt when they walked on the moon.

Diana filled her canteen in the rock-lined spring, but Pete and I knelt on the wet ground and cupped handfuls of water to our mouths. The cool, wet ground around the spring felt good. I drank more of the clear, cold water than I should have. Diana pulled out a candy bar from her pack. Pete fished a stick of jerky from his and I got a sandwich bag of raisins from mine. I traded some raisins for a bite of jerky from Pete then sat on the ground leaning against my backpack, happy to be off my feet.

"The CCC dug this spring," Diana commented. "I'm not sure, but I think they're the ones that built the road in this far and then dug the spring."

"If the CCC built the road in, then why did the Forest Service gate it?" Pete asked.

Diana shrugged. "The Forest Service is always changing things. If they didn't change the rules on how people can get to the forest they wouldn't have anything to do."

She tucked her candy bar wrapper into her pack. "The lakes used to be called Wrath, Envy, and Lust, but somebody at the Forest Service decided those names were too religious, so they renamed them Mash, Myth, and Rain."

I'd already heard this story from my dad and thought maybe I could add something to the conversation. "Yeah, but was Trout Lake still called Trout, or did it used to be called Wrath?"

Diana and Pete looked at me like they didn't understand what I was saying, so I tried again. "The lakes from south to north are called Trout, Mash, Myth, and Rain. But did they used to be called Wrath, Envy, Lust, and Rain or were they called Trout, Wrath, Envy and Lust?"

I wasn't sure Pete understood me, but Diana's eyes lit up. "I never thought of that." She appeared thoughtful for a minute. "Nope. Trout Lake has always been Trout Lake. My dad has an old USGS map of the area, and I remember seeing Trout Lake on it. So, they used to be Trout, Wrath, Envy, and Lust. I guess it doesn't really matter though. The Forest Service will just change the names again in the future." [HL-81]

My pulse rate finally returned to normal while the sun dried the sweat on my back. Diana must have sensed I was starting to recover from the exertion of the hike because she rose gracefully to her feet, barely using her hands. She lifted her backpack to her shoulders. "C'mon, boys, it's all downhill from here."

We walked back across the meadow and picked up the trail to Trout Lake as it descended off the ridge, the white pine giving way to fir and spruce. We dropped straight to the lake, and just before we plunged into a rocky, narrow chute, the trail side hilled out above the lake into a steep bear grass meadow. The sunlight glanced off the ripples blowing on the lake, the water so clear you could see the bottom in all but the deepest areas of the lake. We couldn't see any fish, but here and there, a ring of ripples revealed where one had jumped.

I studied the lake, looking for any signs of someone camped around it. There wasn't any smoke lingering on the water from a campfire and I couldn't see any tents around the lake. If the kidnapper was around, he was being careful to hide his presence.

Diana didn't follow the trail as it curved, descending slowly to the lake, instead she left the trail heading straight down the near vertical meadow to the lake. I fell on my ass twice slipping on the dew-covered bear grass. Diana headed to a large campsite to our right near a foot-wide creek that tumbled out of a narrow gorge into the lake. The deepest part of the lake lay right in front of the campsite. A giant fir tree protected the area from the sky along with some smaller spruce and fir trees. An ancient rock ring with a log and a couple of stumps for seats surrounded the campfire pit. [HL-82]

I dropped my pack near a spruce tree with a flat spot near the base and planned to spend the night there in my sleeping bag. I found a place to lay down to suck a drink of water out of the little creek. My thirst quenched, I made my way to the edge of the lake. A large spruce tree had fallen into the lake years ago, its root crown anchoring it to the shore. The tree's bark-free trunk stuck out into the lake like a skinny round dock. I made my way out onto the log, careful not to slip into the water.

The log ran out into the water right beside the deepest part of the lake. A fish rose near the tip of the log, a large cutthroat trout, coming completely out of the water. I held on to a branch to steady myself and carefully studied the lake shore but didn't see any sign of the kidnapper. I wondered if the guy whose car I jump-started had even been the kidnapper. If he was the kidnapper, had he asked about the lake just to throw me off track? He had mentioned Mash Lake not Trout Lake, so maybe tomorrow, we'd find him there. If he wasn't around Mash Lake, then Pete and I could relax and enjoy a couple days of fishing. I could maybe even talk him into leaving earlier so I could visit with Jenny on Sunday before getting back to work on the fence on Monday.

The log wiggled under my feet. I turned to see Diana walking out on the log with a slight smile tugging at the corners of her mouth.

She made her way to me, the slight grin turning into a full smile. "How's the water, Scabs?" She asked in her slow steady way of talking.

I started to reply that it looked like the fish were jumping when Diana shoved me between the shoulder blades. I tried to grab her to get my balance, but she stepped out of reach. Time slowed for me, enough that I watched in slow motion as my flailing hand swept past her shoulder, the tip of my middle finger sliding across an inch of fabric on her shirt. I felt the exact moment when my center of gravity angled too far away from the log for me to remain on it. I fell, slowly tipping sideways, watching Diana's mouth blossom into a giant grin as I got closer to the water. My shoulder hit first, then my head went under, and the cold water took my breath away. Time returned to normal as I frantically paddled to get my head above water.

Chapter Nine

Water splashed everywhere as I smacked the surface with my hands with enough force to pop my head out of the water. I didn't know how to tread water and as my head slipped under the surface, I reached out, dog-paddling toward the log, until my left hand crashed into a branch, which I immediately gripped with all my strength. I quit floundering and concentrated on making my diaphragm flex so I could breathe.

Over the beating of my heart, I could hear Pete laughing from the shore. Diana didn't laugh. She smiled at me then did a graceful headfirst dive off the log past me into the water.

She surfaced out in the deep part of the lake, treading water. "C'mon, Scabs. Race you to the shore." She pointed across the lake to where the sunshine fell on the bear grass around a large stump at the bottom of the hillside fifty yards away. HL-90

I wanted to pull my wet ass onto the log, drip water to the campfire ring, and then start a fire to dry off. But I also didn't want Diana to think I was afraid of the water and I certainly didn't want Pete to tease me. I let go of the branch, reaching out with cupped hands while kicking hard with my feet. I surged past Diana and kept in front of her until I realized I needed to breathe. Discarding my Mark Spitz imitation, I began to noisily dog-paddle while

I sucked in gulps of air.

Diana slid past me using nice even strokes. She reached the shore before me and gave me a hand getting out of the water. Water drained off my jeans and shirt. Diana handed me my hat, which she had acquired somehow, her smile stretching from ear to ear. My hiking boots squished each time I stepped and I realized I was laughing. I also realized Diana's shirt clung tightly to her body.

Pete came jogging out of the trees at the edge of the lake coming to check on us. He stopped a few yards away watching us laugh. "I take it you guys are all right."

"Just a little sw—" I started to answer but stopped when Diana pulled her wet shirt off and draped it on two bear grass stalks. She gave Pete a stern look and before she faced me, I closed my mouth.

"Put your eyeballs in your skulls, boys. It's a bra. Doesn't show any more skin than a bikini top." She pulled her hair out of her ponytail then ran her fingers through it. She looked at Pete. "Go catch some fish while Scabs and I dry off. You catch, and I'll cook."

Pete glanced quickly at me then slowly turned away without a word. Diana watched him go then settled onto the ground after finding a spot between clumps of bear grass. She lay on her back in the sun. "Scabs, don't make me feel weird by leaving your shirt on."

I quickly stripped out of my shirt, wrung the lake from it, and spread it across a clump of bear grass. I found a spot near Diana and set my wet butt down. Pulling off my boots, I sat them upside down to drain. I peeled my socks off by turning them inside out, wrung the water from them, tossed them on top of the boots, and then slowly leaned back to keep the bear grass blades from cutting my back.

"Why do you hang out with Pete?" Diana asked.

The sun felt great on my bare skin while a slight breeze wicked the water from it. "He's been my friend since first grade. He's a good guy."

"He's a bit of a dick, not just to you but to everybody."

Diana's response surprised me. I knew Pete could be rough to take at times because he liked to tease people. It was just his way. He didn't mean any harm.

Thankfully, Diana changed the subject. "I hear you're working for Cherylann as her handyman this summer. How's that going? She putting the moves on you like Randy claimed she did to him last year?"

"She's not making any moves on me, and I doubt she did on Randy. She's got a boyfriend named Irwin living with her."

"What are you doing for her? Everybody gossips about it because no one can believe she needs a full-time ranch hand on a ranch that's got no cows."

I clearly remembered Cherylann's warning not to tell anyone about building fence. "Oh, mowing lawn, fixing the chicken coop, and cleaning out her shed." I tried to sound bored with the whole subject.

From my position, I could barely see the opposite shore of the lake. To my left, the outlet creek, Beard Creek dropped away from the lake in a nasty thicket of spruce. To the right, the hillside rose from the lake, the sun reflecting off the needles of the trees in a blinding ray of green. I closed my eyes enjoying the warmth of the sun and the smell of the trees. My pants were almost dry. I felt like I could take a deep breath, let it out slowly, and fall asleep.

"You still dating Jenny?"

"Yeah, but I haven't seen her much lately. Her dad told me to stay away from her for a while, so I'm trying not to piss him off too much. I'm hoping to take her to Horse Creek Hot Springs next weekend."

Diana shifted onto her side, facing me, and looked at me through the thick blades of bear grass. "Jenny will like that. Road right to the springs, other people around, it seems adventurous, but it's really safe."

I didn't know how to respond as it slighted Jenny, but at the same time, I understood Diana's point of view. She spent her time hiking out to the middle of nowhere all by herself. Nobody would ever catch Jenny a hundred yards from a vehicle alone in the woods.

I realized a good conversation went both ways. "So, what are you up to this summer? More trips like this?" I asked.

"Dad wants me to make another cache at our hunting spot in the Selway but later this summer. Other than this trip, I've been over with Dad in the Big Hole guiding fly fishermen on the river between Divide and Melrose. If the people have kids, I take them fishing from shore about halfway down the river. That way, Dad can pull the raft out and the family can have lunch together."

I tried to imagine being so rich I could pay someone to

take me fishing. Even if I had that kind of cash, why would anyone waste it on that? Wasn't part of fishing finding where to fish?

"What are you doing this fall? You heading to college, or will you be busy helping your dad with hunting season?" Last year, Diana only went to winter quarter of college. She'd helped her dad with elk and deer season during fall quarter and with bear season during spring quarter. Of course, the local gossip was she didn't do well at school, or she didn't have the money to go, or both.

"I don't think college is for me, Scabs. I plan to work for my dad until a rich dude falls in love with me and wants to marry me and let me spend his money."

"Don't most of your dad's clients come from some big city? You think you're going to enjoy living there?"

Diana gave a short laugh. "Yes, most of them are from the city, but they all seem to like the outdoors. And you're right." She waved a hand out toward the lake. "I'll miss all of this. I think that's why I'm so set on enjoying my time in the wild before I leave it." She sighed. "What about you, Scabs, you sticking arou—"

"Fish on," Pete called from the lake right at the edge of the timber. "It's a hawg. Somebody come help land him."

I pushed myself to a sitting position, grabbing my shirt as I did. Diana grabbed her shirt, slipped it on, and stepped in front of me. Our torsos bumped together, and it felt like a static electric shock ran through my body as Diana brushed against me. Diana stood only an inch shorter than me, and her green eyes stared straight into mine. "You blew your chance there, Scabs. If you'd made a move, I wouldn't have blocked it."

She headed toward Pete before I could say anything, calling out, "Keep the rod tip up. Make him fight the pole not the line."

Leaving my boots and socks to continue drying, I gingerly followed carefully avoiding sharp rocks. Diana continued to yell at Pete. "Quit horsing him in. Play him a little bit. You're going to rip his lips off. Do you not have a drag on that reel?"

She turned to me, flashing a smile. She was giving Pete shit to make catching the fish more stressful for him. I joined in and yelled, "Keep your rod tip up." Diana waded into the edge of the water as Pete brought the cutthroat along the shore, she expertly ran her hands along the back of the fish, gripped it by the gills, and lifted it out of the water.

The trout had to go at least sixteen inches. Easily the biggest fish I'd ever seen caught in the lake. A pocket knife appeared in Diana's hand as she squatted at the edge of the lake to begin gutting the fish. "Nice fish, Pete."

"Pete that is the biggest fish I've ever seen in this lake," I said.

Pete smiled at me. "Got him on a silver Mepps. I lobbed it into the deepest part of the lake and let it sink to the bottom before I started to retrieve it. Thought I was hooked on the bottom at first."

Diana looked up from the fish. Her pocketknife stuck though the back of its gills. "My uncle caught a twenty-three-incher up at Myth Lake."

"There's no fish in Myth Lake." The smile on Pete's

face faded.

Diana went back to cleaning the fish, not looking at Pete. "My dad says there's only a few fish in the lake. Brought up from Mash Lake by bucket biologists. For some reason, the fish have a hard time reproducing in Myth. Since no one thinks there are fish in the lake, the fish survive and grow big until they die." [HL-91]

Diana stood and favored Pete with a smile. "But I have to agree with Scabs. This is the biggest fish I've ever seen caught in Trout Lake. I'm going to get a fire going and start prepping dinner." She swiveled her head between me and Pete. "Think you boys could catch two or three more fish while I do that?"

Pete and I watched Diana make her way around the lake until she vanished into the trees by the campsite.

When she disappeared, Pete turned to me. "Damn. I don't ever remember her being that hot when she was in school. What the hell was that about her wanting to hang out with you with her shirt off?"

"Nothing. Our families know each other. I guess she just feels comfortable with me."

"So," Pete said as he scratched the end of his nose, "if something does happen between you two, it's not like the first thing I'm gonna do when we get out of here is run tell Jenny."

"That's nice of you but not needed. Nothing's going on between me and Diana."

Pete gave me an exaggerated wink. "Sure, Scabs, women hang out with guys all the time with only their bra on because nothing is going on." He put extra emphasis on the last four words.

I mumbled a protest, thinking about Diana's earlier comment, then changed the subject. "Hey," I said, reaching for Pete's fishing pole, "you got one. Let me take a couple of casts."

Pete handed me the pole with a broad grin on his face. "I got first fish and it will be the biggest fish. Bet you can't beat it. I'll give you three casts. Then my turn."

I opened the bail on the reel and aimed for the end of a sunken log off to my right, a nice spot for a fish to be hiding out. I enjoyed good-mood Pete much better. Although I hated that Diana had to leave tomorrow, her presence definitely added a weird vibration to how Pete and I got along. After we packed Diana's cache of gear to Myth Lake, Pete and I could focus on the real reason for our trip and do some serious scouting for signs of the kidnapper. In fact, before dark, I was going to make a trip around Trout Lake looking for any evidence of other campers.

Chapter Ten

While Pete gathered dry sticks for campfire fuel and Diana prepared the fish, I made my way around the lake. The east side of Trout Lake, the side away from the trail to the saddle, was shallow enough I could see the bottom out from shore farther than I could cast a #1 Mepps. I studied the signs left along the edge of the lake, a few cigarette butts in one spot and old boot prints in a marshy area. Nothing suggested someone had been at the lake in the last week. I spotted a set of moose tracks, a few deer tracks, and a place where a herd of about twenty elk had come to the water's edge. If the man whose car I jumped really had been the kidnapper and if he really had been honest when he asked about the trailhead, he wasn't at Trout Lake. He had to be at Mash Lake.

I walked into the campfire as twilight darkened to the point I needed a flashlight. As I dropped the cigarette butts into the campfire, I saw Diana's pack leaning against a tree next to my pack in the dim light. Her sleeping bag was rolled out in a flat spot five feet from mine. Sitting down on one of the old campfire logs, I pulled my boots off, propped them near the fire to dry, and positioned my feet near the flames. My boots were still damp from Diana pushing me into the lake. I hoped that overnight they would dry completely, but first I wanted to dry my socks.

Diana cooked the six trout Pete and I caught by wrapping them in tinfoil and placing them under the campfire coals. She'd made flat bread in a frying pan then coated the bread with peanut butter. For dessert, I produced a Snickers bar from my pack for us to share.

Pete came out of the darkness with a flask in his hand. "I rolled my bag out under that downed spruce tree. That way, if dinner gives me the farts, I won't gross anybody out."

The distance between Pete and where Diana and I would sleep provided us privacy in addition to protection from Pete's bodily functions. It felt like Pete wanted me to do something with Diana. I wondered if I should suggest he sleep closer or if that would set me up for being teased about being scared of the dark. I didn't say anything, deciding Diana had been pulling my leg with her comment about not blocking me if I made a move on her. I wasn't going to make a move, so everything would be hunky-dory.

Pete sat on a log by the fire and sipped from his flask then handed it to Diana. At her questioning look, Pete said, "Blackberry brandy."

Diana took a sip, gave a little shudder then said, "More like ass berry brandy."

She handed the bottle to me. Based on Diana's warning, I only let a teaspoon of the purple liquid hit my tongue. I agreed with Diana. The taste didn't match the delicious-sounding name.

Pete and I handed the flask back and forth with each of my sips getting smaller as the taste of the brandy worsened with each drink. Diana refused to drink after her first sip, which I considered a smart move.

Diana suggested that since she had help, she wanted to cache all of her Dad's gear by Myth Lake and would we mind carrying the extra weight to Mash Lake. Then she would pack it all up to Myth. I didn't have any problem with it and spoke up before Pete could saying that it was all right with me.

Pete shrugged and started regaling us with a story of playing floor hockey after school and checking Mr. Eaton into the rolled-up bleachers. Pete described how Mr. Eaton tried not to let on that the body check hurt him but had left for a meeting less than ten minutes later. We all had a good laugh at how macho Mr. Eaton would never admit a student could rough him up.

We watched the fire burn after Pete finished his story. Diana added two bigger sticks, kicking up a stream of sparks that reached for the clear sky filled with pinpricks of star light. The little bit of brandy warmed me from the inside as the fire warmed me from the outside. At least the front of me was warm, but the cool night air had begun to sink its claws into my back. I eased off the log, sitting on the ground and resting against it. My eyelids suddenly felt heavy and I shook my head, fighting off the fatigue of the day.

I heard the lid on the flask of brandy twist off. A minute later, I heard Pete speak. "Diana, you got any boys chasing after you these days?"

Diana responded in her slow measured tone, "No, Pete, I'm still holding on to hope that someday you'll ask me out."

I guess I chuckled a little bit, some people might have called it a giggle, but it was too deep in tone to be a giggle. Even with my eyes closed, I could see Pete giving me a dirty look.

"No need to be shitty with me, Diana, just wondering if you were still seeing Chris Wick. Seems like I heard something last year about the two of you getting together."

I'd heard the rumor but hadn't thought much about it, but now considering Diana's comments about waiting for a rich dude to sweep her off her feet, I opened my eyes to see how she would respond.

"Nothing happened with Chris." Diana gave Pete a shy smile. "He's a nice guy but not interested in a girl that can pin him two out three times."

Pete offered more brandy to Diana.

"What you trying to do, Pete, get me tipsy so you can put the moves on me? Don't you already have a girlfriend like Scabs? I mean, for cryin' out loud, you're going to be the starting quarterback this fall. A stud like you should have a couple of girls."

I didn't say anything wondering how Pete would answer the question. Pete hadn't been out on a date with any girls since sophomore year when his girlfriend Susan didn't show for Homecoming dance because she decided to stay home with her new boyfriend. Although he did give Jessica a ride home from a basketball game one night and her neighbor reported Jessica hadn't arrived home until two in the morning. Pete let us boys in the locker room know they'd run to Lake Como on the way home and went skinny-dippin' in the dark.

"Not that you aren't hot, Diana, but I happen to have a pretty steady thing going for the last couple of weeks, so while I appreciate the offer, I'm not interested in putting the moves on you."

My eyes popped open. I was so sleepy I was having trouble keeping them open. Who was Pete's steady thing? He hadn't said one word to me about a girlfriend. "News to me." I wriggled my back against the log in an attempt to smooth it out as my eyes closed again.

"Nobody knows. She's been real insistent I keep my mouth shut about it, or she's going to turn off the nookie spigot."

"So, you guys are going all the way?" Diana asked. While I hadn't known Pete had a girlfriend, I didn't think he would go all the way with a girl because he had taken the "wait until after high school" oath with Jenny and me. Although, I knew from my recent experience with Jenny it was hard to keep your oath when the other person wanted you to break it.

"So, Diana, how much detail do you want?" Pete said in that almost belligerent tone he had and even with my eyes closed, I knew his upper lip resembled a thin red line.

"Oh, I grew up around dudes with loose tongues and I could use a good bedtime story, so see if you can make me blush," Diane said answering Pete's challenge.

"The first time we just started making out. Just kinda one of those things. Next thing I know, she was on top of me and we were dry humping. Then she suggests we take our pants off and keep rubbing against each other."

Pete paused for a second and I guessed he was taking another drink of brandy.

"She called it sliding."

My eyes shot wide open, but I held my body still. Holy shit. Pete's girlfriend was doing exactly with him what Jenny wanted to do with me and she had the same name for it. That could only mean one thing. Jenny must have got the idea from Pete's girl. That meant Jenny had to be friends with her for them to be talking about something so personal. I wondered if Jenny knew it was Pete her friend was sliding on, and if so, why hadn't she told me? Her friend must really want it kept a secret.

"Whoa." Diana chuckled. "You got to be careful. Pop your top even on the lips and you could end up being Daddy Pete."

Pete didn't miss a beat. "That's why after that first time she made me wear a condom, but she insisted we only slide."

I wondered where Pete got the condoms. I'd heard stories about guys going to Bitterroot Drug and buying condoms. Even in the big town of Hamilton, invariably someone from Darby who knew you and your family spotted you at the checkout counter with your box of goodies. Most guys went the casual route and only purchased the three-pack. That way, when word made it back through the grapevine to their girlfriend's father, the story would be somebody saw Johnny buying condoms, not somebody saw sex-fiend Johnny buying the massive twelve-pack of condoms. HL-100

"We did the sliding thing until everything was nice and slippery. Then I angled my back just right, and whoops, just like that, I was in."

Diana gave a little snort of disgust. "Did she yell at you?"

"More like a squeal of pleasure. From then on, she would suggest I come over to do some sliding, but we both knew that at some point we'd just end up doing it."

I went through a list of Jenny's friends in my head trying to figure out which one was sleeping with Pete. It must have been killing Pete not to brag he was having sex, so what could make him keep his mouth shut? It had to be Jenny's friend Marsha. Marsha was super cool, but she was five foot two and weighed a good hundred and eighty. I'd heard the joke that heavy girls were like Shetland ponies—fun to ride but nobody wanted their friends to see them on one. That had to be it.

Pete turned the tables on Diana. "You got any good bedtime stories, Diana?"

I rose from the ground and rotated to let the warm air from the campfire reach my chilled backside. I thought about bringing my sleeping bag over by the fire to warm it before I crawled into it for the night.

"Oh, I have some real good bedtime stories, Pete," Diana said, her voice lower than usual. "But the difference between good girls and bad girls is that good girls don't kiss and tell." Diana stood. "I'm heading to bed," she announced with a glance at me. "You ready for bed, Scabs?"

I blinked hard, wondering what I'd do if Diana tried to join me in my sleeping bag. I grunted out I was really tired and leaving Pete at the campfire, I stumbled sleepily to my old Coleman bag. I stripped out of my clothes and put them inside the bag with my jacket to use as a pillow. Out of the corner of my eye, just barely from the light of the campfire, I could see Diana slipping out of her shorts. I snuggled inside the Coleman, pulling the bag to my neck, feeling the cool breeze dribbled down the mountain and into the lake.

I heard Diana rustle in her sleeping bag a few feet away. She was pretty cool, not frilly and afraid of the woods like most girls. Someone you could take camping and hunting. Whatever dude she set her sights on was going to be one lucky guy.

The cool breeze paused then returned colder than before. I snuggled deeper into my sleeping bag pulling it over my head. Nestled snug as a bug in a rug, I wondered again what girl Pete had been bragging about. It had to be Marsha. Marsha must have told Jenny about the sliding thing. Had Marsha told Jenny about going all the way with Pete? After Diana left tomorrow, I was going to pester Pete for more details.

Chapter Eleven

I woke up when the birds started to chirp in the predawn twilight. I tried to fall back asleep, but a squirrel let out one of its obnoxiously long trills. Plus, I heard Diana getting out of her sleeping bag and I rolled over and caught a quick glimpse of her pulling on her shorts. Before she could turn her head and catch me peeking, I rolled out of my bag putting my back to Diana. I figured if she wasn't going to be modest, then I shouldn't, or I'd look like a dweeb. I pulled on my socks, hopping around to keep my balance, then pulled my pants on one leg at a time. My shirt smelled of campfire smoke as I pulled it over my head and I figured it would mask my stinking armpits.

When I turned around, Diana stood a few feet away. "Sorry about last night. I hope it wasn't too upsetting."

Even in the predawn light, her green eyes sparkled. I wondered why I had never noticed the color of her eyes before. I didn't understand why she was apologizing for Pete's sex talk. I'd heard worse in the locker room. It made me wonder how fragile Diana thought I was that Pete saying he had sex with a girl would offend me. "It's no big deal. I've heard worse."

Diana arched her eyebrows. "I just thought that, you know, since…" The arched eyebrows disappeared as a sad smile flashed across her face. "Yeah, no big deal." She turned away abruptly.

Pete appeared at the campfire with an armload of dead branches for fuel. I headed into the woods to a blown-over tree to gather more fuel for the morning.

Fog hugged the lake muting the sounds of the birds waking for the day. Somewhere on the lake, a fish rose, the sound of the splash traveling under the fog to my ears. Some of the grass in the low areas around the lake sparkled with frost, but the grass was only wet around our camp. A quick study of the sky revealed no clouds and the promise of another hot day.

Diana mixed powdered eggs, borrowed from her dad's supplies, into the leftover fish and Pete shared his oatmeal. As we ate breakfast, Diana said, "Fishing has been great here. Maybe you boys should just stay here." She loaded her spork up with more eggs. "I could hike the supplies up to Myth Lake then meet you guys back here."

I stopped chewing to come up with a polite way of telling Diana we wanted to check out all the lakes for the kidnapper, without telling her we were looking for the kidnapper.

Pete spoke before me. "I already caught the biggest fish in this lake. Now I want to catch the biggest fish in the other lakes."

Diana didn't object to us coming along and we quietly finished our breakfast. Fish rose on the lake, taking advantage of the morning rush of bugs, as we shoved our gear into our backpacks. The mosquitoes weren't bad, but we sprayed down with Off before tucking it away into a pack.

Diana led us around the lake past the open meadow that ran to the water's edge and past the stump where we laid in the bear grass to dry off. Soon after entering the trees, she switchbacked up the hillside to the ridge separating Trout Lake from Mash Lake. We spooked a mule deer doe and her young fawn. The doe bounced away from us, smashing all four feet into the ground at the same time. It was something I'd only seen mule deer do and I guessed they did it to make noise to scare predators away.

Sweat dampened my shirt under my backpack despite the morning chill. My legs felt strong and even though my shoulders were raw from the backpack straps, they felt good after yesterday's grueling hike. We didn't talk much, mostly about the route through the white pine and lodgepole. We warned Diana not to lose too much elevation and force us to climb again.

As soon as we curved off the ridge, we heard long whistles, like a long drawn-out cow elk call crossed with the chirp of a rock chuck, coming from the hillside below us. Pete said the sound came from owls, Diana said it wasn't owls but another bird, and I suggested it might be Bigfoot. We all laughed at that, maybe a little too loud. We contoured around the hillside, keeping the whistles safely below us, until we spotted the green-tinted water of Mash Lake through the trees. We hurriedly dropped a hundred feet of elevation and stopped on the east shore of the lake. HL-110

Across Mash Lake on the right, rough rocks made their way off a craggy point into the lake, and to the left, steep slopes covered in bear grass ringed a couple of deep bays. I knew from being here with my dad the best fishing was in those coves, but scrambling around the steep hillside behind them with a fishing pole and a stringer of fish could be challenging.

Diana led us around the lake to the right until we came to the outlet stream. A campfire ring and areas cleared of debris indicated this was a favorite place to pitch a tent. Pete and I dropped our packs then unloaded all our stuff, keeping only the items we were carrying for Diana. Pete and I intended to camp here, and didn't want to carry our stuff to Myth Lake and back just for fun. I noticed Pete brought his fishing pole, but I left mine behind. The only thing I brought was Irwin's handgun still hidden at the bottom of my pack wrapped in a bread bag.

With our loads adjusted, we split a candy bar among the three of us. A camp robber flitted tree to tree after us as we crossed the outlet creek, which flowed into Elk Creek, then followed the trail to Myth Lake. It wasn't far through the trees to our destination. Once we reached Myth Lake, Diana turned to the right, following the shore for a quarter of the lake. She slung her pack from her shoulders calling out loudly, "We made it, boys."

Pete dropped his pack and pulled out his tackle box all the while searching the lake for signs of fish rising for bugs. To our left, a rocky point of land stuck out, and similar to Trout Lake, a slope filled with bear grass ran down to the lake with patches of snow stubbornly hanging on to the shadows of the steep hillside. Timbered forest ran the rest of the way around the lake, wrapping all the way around to our right. A dark cloud rose in the sky over the top of the mountain across from us. With it being around noon, I knew the cloud had plenty of time to build into a thunderhead. I just hoped it drifted away from the lake before it started throwing lightning around this evening.

"I'm going to rest for a minute. Then I'll pack everything to my dad's cache. You boys have fun trying to catch a fish in this lake." Looking at Pete, Diana added, "Anything you catch here is going to be big."

Pete snapped a large gold Mepps to the swivel at the end of his fishing line. "You coming?" he asked, looking at me.

"I've never seen Rain Lake. I'm going to hike up there real quick and take a look. See if anything is up there." I didn't want to out and out say I wanted to look for the kidnapper in front of Diana. We'd come on this trip to search for the kidnapper then fish.

Pete gave me a frown. "Suit yourself."

I watched him walk around the shore working his way toward the point of rocks.

Diana glanced up from strapping the supplies to her backpack. "Don't wander around and get lost, Scabs, we can't spend all day searching for you. Maybe you should hang out with Pete and keep him out of trouble."

I laughed, taking her comment for a joke rather than a serious concern. I hoped she didn't really think I could get lost in the short distance between Myth Lake and Rain Lake.

A vague foot trail led around the lake and I followed it, my gaze drawn to the water, watching for any sign of fish. I reached the northwest edge of the lake without seeing any fish rise and left the shore following a scant game trail to Rain Lake. It felt funny to be alone in the grand firs and white pines. The trees seemed to close in a little tighter. The quiet pushed down on me after having the constant company of Pete and Diana.

I studied the trail for any sign of human prints when not scanning the trees for the two B's, bears and Bigfoot. I saw a few deer tracks that must have been made when the trail was wet that were now dried into hard earth. At one spot, I saw a moose track and maybe a hint of a boot heel. I couldn't be sure, as it mixed in with the moose track. The distance between Rain Lake and Myth Lake was shorter than the distance between Mash Lake and Myth Lake, and I hit Rain Lake unexpectedly. The dead-still water of the lake reflected the growing thundercloud in the sky and the mountains rising around the lake. With my head down, I scanned for tracks and worked my way around the lake looking along the shore for any people signs.

I found a single boot print in the wet earth along the edge of the lake a quarter of the way around. The print pointed toward the water like someone had walked to the shore to try fishing. Only with no fish in the lake, nobody would be fishing. It could have been a hiker passing through and stopping to get a drink. I made my way to the water's edge and was surprised by how deep the lake got.

Since it didn't have any fish in it, I had always pictured Rain Lake as a shallow mudhole, but if anything, it resembled a carbon copy of Myth Lake. Freshwater shrimp the size of the end of my pinkie fluttered around in the shallows. If there were fish in Rain Lake, they'd have plenty to eat, but my guess was that so many shrimp in the lake proved it didn't contain any fish. A duck with its lone baby swam out into the lake, putting more water between us, calling to its duckling to stay close.

I heard a cry behind me near where I first reached the lake. My head spun around in time to see a flash of movement in the trees. The cry almost sounded like someone calling out "Scabs." I hurried along the lake toward the sound, wondering if Diana had followed me after dropping off her dad's supplies.

I reached the trail leading to Myth Lake and stood still listening and peering through the trees. "Diana? Pete?" I called in a voice a little louder than normal, my voice carrying across the lake. I didn't get any answer from the woods. I raised my voice a little more. "Diana?"

A camp robber flitted into the branches of a tree near me, looking at me with its black little eyes, no doubt wondering if I had any food. Was that what I had seen? Maybe the cry I had heard had been a bird. I repeated my call for Pete and Diana, surprised at the echo of my voice reverberating on the hillside across the lake.

One human footprint didn't mean the kidnapper was hiding at the lake. Someone hiding out for a week at the lake would have left a lot more sign. Maybe I could convince Pete to fish today and then hike out tomorrow, giving me Sunday to spend with Jenny.

I waited a few minutes and not hearing anything, I trotted down the trail to Myth Lake. I met Diana halfway around Myth Lake as she came out of the trees surprising me enough I put up my fists.

She laughed. "Sorry to spook you, Scabs. Where's the fire?"

I laughed with her, happy to be around other people. Her hair, which had been in a ponytail, hung around her shoulders, framing her face and contrasting with her flushed cheeks. It made her more attractive than her usual tomboy look, enough that I realized I was staring. "Just didn't want you or Pete to worry about me," I said, looking away at the lake.

"What are you off doing in the woods that I should be worried about?"

I started to explain why she might be worried about me but then stopped myself. Diana routinely hiked into the woods by herself, so hiking alone wasn't something a person worried about and she was just pulling my leg.

I laughed and we walked together to the point of rocks to watch Pete fish. He kept at it for over an hour, trying every lure in his tackle box, before throwing in the towel. "There's no damn fish in this lake," he grumped.

"My dad must have caught the last one," Diana said with a smile. "Let's head back to Mash. I've got a freeze-dried meal of chicken and rice I'll split with you guys if you share a candy bar."

We walked quietly down the trail, hopped on rocks across the outlet creek of Mash Lake and stopped at the camp where Pete and I had left our gear. Diana cooked lunch for us, which consisted of her freeze-dried meal, plus a couple pre-baked potatoes Pete and I had packed in, along with a couple of sticks of jerky, topped off with a Snickers bar for each of us.

After lunch, I attached a swivel to my fishing line discussing with Pete how many fish we would need for dinner and who would catch the biggest fish. Diana commented she wanted to take a short rest, wait for the cook fire to die out, and then she would head out to her truck. She thanked us for helping pack in the gear. We thanked her for the food and for cooking. I didn't know if we should shake her hand or give her a hug or maybe a high-five. Pete just said goodbye over his shoulder as he headed for the lake. Diana made the decision for me, she gave me a quick hug saying thanks.

I hustled after Pete, sad to see Diana leave, but it would give me time to talk to Pete about the boot track I'd seen at Rain Lake. When I came up behind him as he stared at the logjam that blocked fishing access to the lake, Pete's attitude indicated he didn't want to talk. He pointed at the east side of the lake. "You fish around that way and I'll go across the creek and fish around the other way. Meet you halfway across and we'll see who catches the most fish."

I wanted to point out that Pete had selected the better half of the lake to fish. He would obviously catch more fish than me. But considering Pete's weird mood on the trip, I decided against it. I didn't want to upset him before asking if he would be willing to leave early so I could spend Sunday with Jenny. I would talk to him about leaving early this evening. He might even be in a better mood since he would have caught the most fish and Diana would be gone.

I headed to my left without a word, leaving the logjam behind. I skipped around a quarter of the lake, determined to fish at least one of the coves where the fishing was excellent before Pete.

I spotted a large rock on the edge of the water and a break in the trees surrounding the lake that would give me room to cast. The trail leading to the rock told me many other anglers considered it a good place to fish. Jumping out onto the rock, I surveyed the water in front of me studying the shallow bottom until it finally faded into the deep right at my maximum casting distance. On the left, a large old spruce tree had fallen into the lake and lay there partially submerged, its trunk and limbs stripped of bark, looking like white spiderwebs in the water. Blue dragonflies danced above the water by the shore in some sort of insect mating ritual. I couldn't see any fish in the lake, but a couple of ripples past where the water level dropped off told me they were rising for bugs ten feet out of my casting range.

I attached the biggest lure I had, a Mepps #2 red and white, to my swivel and whipped my fish pole in the direction of the deep water. The two-year-old mono line whistled off the reel in loops and it took me a half dozen casts before the kinks worked out of the line. I liked to play a game when I fished around mountain lakes. I did ten casts at each new spot. If I saw a fish, I got one more cast, if I got a bite, five more casts, and if I caught a fish, I added ten more casts. It sucked when I caught three fish on my first three casts and then didn't even see a fish for the next thirty-seven casts, so I added a rule that I could only catch two fish in one spot. It kept me leapfrogging around the lake, pausing only where the fishing was good.

With the kinks out of the line, I aimed straight out into the dark-blue water right on the edge of the branches on the fallen tree. I snapped the bail closed and reeled the slack out of the line but let the lure sink for a count of five before I began reeling in fast enough to bring the lure up from the deep and over the rocks at the shallow edge.

A large splash to my left startled me and I turned to see a huge trout dart under the submerged part of the fallen tree trunk. It had probably been hiding in the shadows under the log all along, but now that I had seen the fish, I could determine its shadow from that of the log.

My attention on the fish instead of retrieving my Mepps, the lure clipped a rock on the bottom at the start of the shallow area and snagged. Holding the line tight with my left hand, I opened the bail. Pulling hard straight back with my left hand on the line, I let it go with a snap. A little shockwave rolled out on the line toward the lure. I closed the bail then reeled in, keeping the rod tip high. The snapback worked and had pushed the lure backward off the rock. The snapback trick only worked occasionally, and if it failed, it meant the lure had been hooked bad. It wasn't a trick that should be tried if the lure was hooked on a log because then it would just drive the hook deeper into the wood when the line was pulled tight. Sometimes it worked on rocks and it saved you the time of walking to your left or right along the shore far enough to get a side-angle pull on the stuck lure. If that didn't work, depending on the depth of water, the only option to save the lure was to go wading with a long stick.

I studied the branches by the fish trying to find a place I could cast the Mepps without wrapping it on one of them. I made a tentative cast that fell short of the fish and I let the spinner sink to the bottom before reeling. The fish ignored the flashes of the spinner, holding in its spot under the log. I tried again, holding my breath as the lure hit the side of the log and bounced into the water. The Mepps fluttered in front of the trout's nose as I began reeling as fast as I could to bring the spinner to life, the blade flashing in the sunlight. The trout ignored it and I realized it had reached its gigantic size by knowing the difference between real and fake food.

The lure was only three feet from the tip of my pole when the trout shot out from under the tree streaking toward it. I paused my retrieve in order to keep from pulling the lure out of the water. The great fish rose to the surface and with a slight ripple, snatched a pair of mating dragonflies that had tumbled to the surface of the water in their passionate mating dance. The trout retreated into the jumble of branches under his log as I lifted the Mepps from the water.

I sat on the rock and opened my meager tackle box, reaching for the clear plastic teardrop float and the narrow driftwood stick beside it. The stick had two feet of fishing line wrapped lengthwise around it and an elk caddis dry fly tied to it. I studied the line between the teardrop float and the fly. The last time I used the float was last summer. I used my teeth to bite the fly and the teardrop float free of the line and wadding up the old line, I stuffed it in my pants pocket. I then bit my line a foot above the swivel that held the Mepps and then again, creating a clean piece of fishing line three feet long. Taking my time, I tied the caddis onto the new line, then tied the other end to the teardrop float, then retied on my swivel, and snapped it on the other end of the float. I tested the knots by pulling on the line until I made the drag on the reel protest.

 A teardrop float and leader with a dry fly is a rod and reel way to fly fish. The heavy float made it possible to cast the fly out into the lake without having to bring a fly rod. Leaving the fishing pole on the rock, I removed my camo Sportsman's Saloon hat and hopped to shore. I waited patiently, hat in hand, and swiped at the first dragonfly that whizzed past, trying to catch it in the hat. After a quarter of an hour and numerous swipes, I finally netted one. I carefully reached inside and held the large blue insect by its thorax, careful not to crush it. Hat on my head, I jumped out on the rock, careful not to land on my rod. I ran the hook on the caddis fly carefully through the abdomen of the dragonfly.

 I stood up on the rock, the fly swinging at the end of the line trying to determine the best presentation of the dragonfly to the trout. With a sideways cast, I flipped the teardrop float toward the log in a gentle arc, snapping the bail on the reel closed before the float hit the water in order to bring the float up short and flip the fly past it to keep the line straight. The fly and float hit the water with a gentle splash and I reeled the slack out of the line, careful not to move the float on the water.

The dragonfly struggled on the end of the line trying to escape the water. The trout flashed out from under the log like a torpedo at a loaded merchant ship. I froze while watching the trout cut through the water until it was under the dragonfly. The trout flared its fins and rose straight up nipping the bait off the surface of the water before darting for the bottom of the lake. It happened so fast I almost forgot to set the hook, almost. I whipped the tip of the pole skyward, but it bent over, the tip pointing to the monster on the other end of the line while the drag screeched as the weight of the fish stripped line.

The trout made a dash for the shadows under the log as I frantically tried to turn his head. The drag continued to squeal and I slipped my hand from the reel and turned the drag down two clicks, praying it didn't cause my line to break. The extra drag allowed me to turn his head and the beast of a trout made an arc for the deeper water in the center of the lake but not before it managed to loop the line over an underwater branch sticking out from the fallen tree. I felt the line scrape against the limb as the fish fought to reach the deep water. I didn't know what to do. My line would surely break rubbing against the tree limb as I fought the fish.

"Open your bail."

The command was given with such assurance I

immediately complied even though I worried that as soon as the tension on the line slackened the trout would shake the hook. Line flashed out of the reel for an instant. The trout settled to the bottom of the lake by a large rock barely within my eyesight.

I looked over my shoulder at Diana with a "now what" expression.

"Strip another handful of line," she instructed.

I pulled a length of line from the reel, wiggled the pole gently, and settled the line on the surface of the water.

"Flip the line toward the log."

I didn't understand how this would help me land the fish but did as I was told. I closed the bail, and with a short whipping motion, I lifted the line off the water between me and the limb then flicked the line away from me. It settled into the water away from the limb. I tried to see what the trout was doing, but I couldn't identify the rock he had hidden by on the edge of the deep water. The line on the water in front of my pole wasn't moving, so I decided the trout was either off the hook or sitting still.

"Its mouth is sore from the hook. It'll hold a little bit before taking off," Diana assured me.

That was fine and dandy, but I still didn't see how I was going to get the line unhooked from the limb. Diana eased into the water beside the rock with a six-foot-long stick in her hand. She stepped carefully along the rocky bottom, not creating any splashes, and after a half dozen steps, she reached out with her stick and laid it across my fishing line, sinking it to the bottom. Lifting the stick a foot off the bottom, she said, "Reel in gently until you clear the limb. Then reel as fast as you can."

I dipped my rod tip into the water and slowly reeled, trying to find my line in the clear water. I couldn't see it, but after a dozen turns of the handle, Diana barked, "Now."

I cranked as fast as I could, and when I felt the weight of the fish on the line, I lifted the rod tip. The monster trout fought, but instead of trying to make for his ambush spot under the tree, he kept taking line as he swam out into the dark, blue water. I eased up one click on the drag and let the fish tire itself. The trout made one long run. When the drag quit whining, I turned his head and began working him to shore, keeping the rod tip pointed away from the damn tree and its long fish stealing branches. I had to lift and reel down at first to keep the drag from engaging, but I managed to reel him to within a dozen feet of the rock before he took off again. The drag quit before the fish made it to the edge of the deep water. I cranked the reel, turning the fish to shore.

Diana waded over, and we trapped the fish between the rock and the shore. With deft hands, Diana lifted the trout from the water by its gills. "Holy shit, what a hawg," she exclaimed.

I couldn't believe it. The trout was easily the biggest fish I had ever caught. It had to be over eighteen inches long and it was thick. Its head looked like a nipple compared to the rest of its body.

"You want to keep it? Or should I release it?" Diana looked up at me with a huge smile on her face. I could see her excitement matched my own, but I also saw that if she had caught the fish she would release it.

I couldn't do it. I wanted the fish to show Pete, and I wanted to take it home to show my dad and mom. "I'm gonna keep it."

Diana smiled, her green eyes flashing in the sunlight, as she waded to the shore. "Awesome job, Scabs, you did great fighting that fish."

I proceeded to thank her a hundred times for getting my line untangled from the limb as I fawned over the trout, wishing I had a tape measure and a scale, vowing never to go fishing without one. HL-111

I carefully cleaned the fish using my fake grandpa's method that kept the pectoral fins instead of my dad's method that removed them, and of course, I left the head on so everyone could see its total length. I carried the fish to the outlet creek and found a shady spot in the creek for it to refrigerate while tied to my trusty red stringer.

Diana followed laughing with me and listening politely to me tell the story of how I caught the fish three times. Her eyes didn't sparkle with the same intensity as her smile and I realized I was delaying her from heading home. I started to apologize for keeping her when Pete appeared.

"You guys take another swim? I could hear Scabs whooping it up clear across the lake."

I retrieved the fish from the creek, keeping it on the stringer, to show Pete while telling him the entire story.

At the end, Diana added, "It's even bigger than your fish from yesterday, Pete."

Pete held up a stringer with a half dozen fish, all nice size, but nothing compared to my monster. "We can save my fish for tomorrow and eat yours for dinner."

I hesitated before responding wondering how receptive Pete would be to my suggestion. I had wanted to discuss this with him without Diana around, but in order to save my fish, I spoke now. "I don't want to eat my fish here. I want to take it home and show my family and eat it with them."

Pete snorted. "That fish will go bad before we leave here, even if you keep it in the creek." His upper lip flattened out into his little half sneer as he realized what I really was saying. "So now you want to abandon me and hike out today with your big fish and your"—he glared at Diana—"friend."

"I thought we could spend the night and then leave tomorrow morning early before it gets hot." I didn't want to say in front of Diana, but even with the footprint at Rain Lake, I didn't think the kidnapper was anywhere around.

Diana stepped forward between us. "If you guys are heading out tomorrow, I could stay with you guys tonight then hike out in the morning with you. It'd be nice to have the company."

Pete scowled at her as he said, "Your folks won't worry about where you are?"

"My dad will think I'm with my mom, and Mom will think I'm with Dad in the Big Hole, so I'm good for one more night." Diana ignored Pete's look.

Diana walked away leaving us standing by the creek.

I lowered my trout into the creek, taking in the temperature of the water with my hands. It wasn't ice cold, but it should be cold enough to keep the fish overnight. Pete secured his stringer to a young tree on the edge of the creek and tossed the other end with the fish into the water. He watched the current pull the fish downstream until the stringer line straightened out.

"I didn't see any sign at Rain Lake of anybody around, Pete," I said now that Diana was out of earshot. "We didn't see anything suspicious at Trout or Myth Lake. I don't think we're going to find the kidnapper. He probably asked about the trailhead as a decoy. He's probably over by Salmon, Idaho eating cheese curds right now."

Pete's sneer left his face replaced by a thoughtful look. "So, you don't think the kidnapper is around here?"

"If he was, he's long gone now."

Pete gestured out to the blue-green water of the lake. "I thought we were going to do some fishing if he wasn't around. Build a raft and get out to the deep water."

I shrugged. "We got to fish yesterday and we'll fish the rest of today. Plus, if we leave tomorrow, I can rest Sunday and get back to building fence on Monday. I'm behind schedule, and I guess I was more interested in the reward money than fishing."

Pete looked back along the creek over the logjam on the lake in front of the outlet creek. He stood that way for a minute and I waited letting him think. Finally, he turned to me, a slight grin on his face. "Sure, Scabs, we can head out of here first thing in the morning."

I stepped to him. "Thanks, Pete." I extended my hand.

He gave me a high-five and a bigger grin. "You gonna try to fuck Diana tonight? I got more brandy."

I laughed at him shaking my head. "No, I'm not going to try to sleep with her."

"Okay then," Pete responded. "How about we stop by Sally Parker's on the way home tomorrow and see if she wants to polish your knob?"

I kept shaking my head but stopped laughing. I didn't get Pete's obsession with me cheating on Jenny. "You need to find a girlfriend, Pete," I said as I headed to camp.

Behind me, Pete said softly, "I already have one."

I mulled that over in my head as I opened my backpack and pulled out a candy bar for everybody for lunch. As soon as I got home, I was going to call Jenny and see if she knew who Pete was having sex with.

Chapter Twelve

The rest of the day went better than I expected. Pete's mood improved and the three of us stuck together working our way around the lake fishing. Diana used my pole, and most of the time, only one of us fished while the other two pointed out where a fish had risen to the surface for a bug treat. We didn't keep any more fish except for one Diana caught that swallowed all three hooks on the Mepps so deep we were sure it would die.

On the west side of the lake, we napped in a little opening of bear grass on a plateau twenty feet above the lake. As we worked our way around the steep hillsides above the coves, the thunderhead opened suddenly dropping dime-sized hail into the lake. We retreated into the trees hiding from the hail under the thick branches of a large spruce. The hail thrashed the surface of the lake while thunder rumbled, but I didn't see any lightning strikes. After a few minutes, the hail turned to rain and in few more minutes the rain stopped. The skim of hail covering the ground and floating on the surface of the lake melted by the time we hiked around the rockslide to the outlet creek.

Pete cooked all the fish except for mine in tinfoil in the campfire coals. Diana, like a magician, produced two boxes of macaroni and cheese from her pack, and I boiled water. Diana deboned her fish and mixed it in with her mac and cheese causing Pete and I to question why any sane person would mess with the Kraft family recipe. We scarfed our share sans fish. After dinner, we found spots to roll out our sleeping bags with Pete once again setting his away from Diana and me. Diana disappeared into the woods to visit the lady's room while Pete and I went in the other direction to gather wood for the campfire.

With everything prepped for the night, Pete and I grabbed our poles to do some twilight fishing. At dark thirty, like giant moths, we were drawn to the campfire. Pete pulled out his bottle of blackberry brandy and began to pass it around as we sat on blocks of wood left by other campers who had brought in a chainsaw or maybe an old crosscut saw. After the first pass of the bottle, I pretended to take a drink, but other than letting the brandy touch my lips, I didn't let any of the vile-tasting fluid into my mouth. Diana wasn't even sneaky about it. When Pete passed her the bottle, she just held it for a minute then passed it on to me.

The thunderclouds that dropped the hail in the afternoon had mellowed away with the coolness of the evening then spread out covering the stars and shrouding the moon. Our conversation centered on other lakes and streams we had fished until Pete abruptly changed the subject. "Diana, you got any boyfriends hanging around?"

She shrugged and passed the quarter-full bottle of brandy to me. "Like I said last night, I don't have a boyfriend, let alone boyfriends."

"It seems like an attractive girl like yourself would have someone keeping an eye on you." Pete pulled the bottle from my offering hand and lowered the level of fluid by transferring a large swallow to his gut. I figured Pete was hinting to Diana that I liked her and it annoyed me that he kept pushing me toward Diana.

I needed to tell Pete in front of Diana that nothing was going on between us, but I didn't know how to say that without it sounding mean to Diana. Before I could put my words together, Diana spoke. "There's nothing going on with me and Scabs and if you don't believe me, you can move your sleeping bag in between ours."

"No offense," Pete said, pointing the brandy bottle a Diana, a clear signal that whatever he said next would be offensive. "I've got a girl that's hotter than you, so don't try pulling me into your love triangle."

I didn't have any idea what had made Pete such a pisshead on the trip, but I knew I was getting up early tomorrow and hiking down the trail at sunrise. The sooner I could drop Pete off at his Caddy by Wolverine Creek Campground, the better.

"Good, then you won't be tempted to cuddle with me in the middle of the night," Diana said with a little scorn in her tone. "Why do you need to sleep off by yourself?"

I'd known Pete since before the first grade and had spent many a weekend sleepover at the ranch with him. I knew the one thing he would hate for any girl to know about him. I'm not sure why I said it, maybe because Pete had been so heinous during the trip. Anyway, the worst thing I could say came out of my mouth before I could stop it. "Pete's a member of the rubber sheet brigade. He probably wants to sleep off by himself so that if he wets his sleeping bag he can hide it from us." If I had reached across the fire and sucker punched Pete it wouldn't have made a bigger shock.

Pete glared at me over the fire. "I am so fucking sick of you, Scabs, and your bogus attitude that you are better than everyone else."

"I don't think that," I protested.

"The fuck you don't."

The anger in Pete's voice hit me like a physical blow. I shouldn't have pushed his button by bringing up his bedwetting.

"You walk around like your shit doesn't stink when your family is nothing but poor white trash."

I struggled for a comeback, something to calm Pete down. "Being poor doesn't make you trash, Pete."

"How about prostitution and draft dodging? Do those make you trash, Scabs?"

"Pete, shut up," Diana said, faster than her normal cadence.

"There it is. Everybody walks on eggshells around poor little Scabs, don't want to hurt his feelings, don't ever talk about his parents."

No one said anything after that, and in the silence, I tried to make sense of Pete's words, but I didn't have any answers other than he must be losing his mind from the brandy.

Pete didn't let the silence last. "Your dad didn't go to Canada during Vietnam to find draft dodgers, Scabs. He went to Canada because he dodged the draft. Why do you think he only works for cash and can't get a decent full-time job? Your daddy is a coward draft dodger but flies the flag out in his yard every Fourth of July and every November tenth. He's a fucking hypocrite."

I thought through Pete's words, struggling with the anger in his voice and with the ring of truth in his words.

"C'mon, Scabs. You're supposed to be wicked smart. Have you ever heard about the military sending soldiers to Canada to look for draft dodgers? You haven't because it's just a bullshit story from your dad to explain why he was living in Canada while my dad took two rounds in his leg and has nightmares about it the rest of his life."

The anger scared me. Pete and I were buddies and it shook my world to think he hated my dad. Did he hate me too? "Whatever, Pete, I'm not going to argue with you."

"No, not whatever," Pete rasped then took another drink of brandy. "Either you know the truth and you're in on the lies or its time you learned about your parents' lies. Like why do all the men in town smile and wave at your mom."

Diana rose from her log. "Shut up, Pete," she demanded.

Pete ignored her pointing at me across the fire with the bottle of brandy in his hand. "Her massages have a happy ending, Scabs. For a little extra cash, your mom gives her customers a handjob or maybe more."

I slumped on the stump, unable to meet Pete's stare. My mom was a licensed massage therapist not a hooker. I held my rising anger in my throat and choked on it. Nothing I could say to Pete would calm him down. I could only sit here and wait out his tirade.

"Yeah, got nothing to say about that because all you have to do is think about it for ten seconds to know I'm right. Every Sunday after church, you and your dad are off sighting in your rifles and your mom is whackin' off a logger every thirty minutes."

Diana stepped toward Pete who ignored her as he gulped brandy. I stood. I didn't have to sit and take Pete's abuse and I didn't want Diana to get any closer to Pete for fear he might start yelling at her. I didn't trust Pete not to strike out in his drunken state. "My mom's not a whore," I said as I turned to walk away.

"How would you know," Pete snarled at my back, triumph in his voice. "You don't know anything. You don't even know I'm fucking Jenny."

I turned to the fire and watched Pete drain the last of the brandy from the bottle. "What?"

Diana stepped back then sat on her log and by the look on her face, I knew she thought everything Pete said was true.

"Jenny's a hot young woman with a great bod. She knows that bod ain't gonna last after she pops out a couple of calves. She wants to use it while she can and you dumbass, are too fucking stupid to take advantage of that." Pete tossed the empty bottle into the coals of the fire, sending a shower of spark floating into the dark.

"She took the oath" was all I could manage to say.

Pete laughed. "She took the oath to keep her dad from worrying about her going out on dates. Same reason I took the oath—so our parents could convince themselves that their little angels weren't out screwing all night instead of going to the movies."

Pete reached out and nudged the end of a burnt log deeper into the coals with the heel of his foot. "Everybody but you, Scabs. You had to stick to your oath, so when I ended up lying on my back with Jenny sliding up and down my dick, I just grabbed her by the hips, slammed it home, and listened to her squeal."

I jumped across the fire at Pete, not caring if he kicked my ass or not. I just wanted to feel my fist smash his nose flat. Pete must have been ready for my jump or just quick as a cat. His foot rose and caught me in the groin, stopping me mid-jump. I twisted in the air as gravity pulled me toward the hot coals. Diana grabbed on to me, one hand in my hair and the other by my shirt. She pulled me toward her. My ass hit the edge of the rock ring and I rolled toward Diana. I landed on top of her trying to figure out if I had burned myself or if my clothes were on fire while Diana scrambled out from under me.

I pushed off the log Diana had been sitting on balling my fists to hit Pete. I turned toward him and he sprang off his stump toward me. His right hand cocked back like he was ready to throw a long bomb touchdown pass until it shot forward into my right eye.

The world went dark except for the stars exploding in my head. My feet felt rubbery and I went down with barely enough sense left in my noggin to fall away from the fire. I struggled to my feet, aware of Pete hovering over me, waiting for me to get up. Diana pulled me farther away from the Pete and the fire.

They call it a fight-or-flight response, and Pete's fist had eliminated one half of that equation, I focused on my other option and ran away. The talk about my parents, Pete saying he was sleeping with Jenny, and his fist overwhelmed me.

~ ~ ~ ~ ~

I guess that brings us around to where I started telling the story. The point where I ran away from Pete and Diana into the dark and smack dab into the kidnapper. The kidnapper we had been looking for but hadn't seen even though he had been spying on us. Now hopefully you'll understand why my life became a story that graduation day when Pete drove Jenny home from the party. The night before I helped a kidnapper on my way to a job interview. HL-120

Chapter Thirteen

I squeaked, "No, we don't have any guns," hoping he would believe me. I thought he might question me more, but instead, he cussed then said the word shit over and over. I followed along with him in my head. He started mumbling to himself and I caught enough of what he said to know he wanted to let me go but was worried we'd go fetch the police. As his self-debate continued, I could tell he had settled in on three potential courses of action. One, he could keep us with him, which I gathered he thought would be a pain in the ass for him. Two, he could let us go and while we hiked out to tell on him, he could hike to somewhere else. Three, he could just kill all of us. That would make sure we wouldn't tell anyone about him. In between these thoughts, he did a lot of cussing at himself for letting me run into him in the woods.

I thought about that. If Pete hadn't been such an ass, I wouldn't have run away from the fire and into the kidnapper. Then we would never have known he lurked outside the campfire light spying on us. We would have left the next morning safe and sound. I decided this was all Pete's fault. What a dick, fucking Jenny behind my back and telling me my mom was a whore and my dad a draft dodger. I should tell the kidnapper that if he shot Pete I wouldn't tell anyone anything.

"You let me go and I won't tell anyone anything. We'll all go home and I'll pretend like I never saw you, ever," I pleaded.

"Scabs?" Diana's voice came from the dark maybe ten yards away. The brush rustled as she walked closer, honing in on the sound of my voice.

"Go back to the fire. Leave me alone," I cried out, trying to keep her from seeing the man with the gun pressed into my temple. I could tell how the kidnapper's eyes glinted Diana had already seen him.

"I didn't mean for this to happen," he said, his voice oddly calm. "He ran into me. I don't want to hurt him."

The gun muzzle swung away from my temple until it pointed at the ground. I twisted my head to see Diana in the cloud-screened moonlight standing with her hands out away from her body staring at the kidnapper. She probably had no clue who the guy was or why he would have a gun to my head. Probably scared — well, at least as scared as Diana got.

The kidnapper pivoted above me growling, "C'mon," as he pulled me to my feet. "To the fire," he commanded.

Diana waited until we reached her, and without a word, she led us to the fire. Maybe Pete had searched through my pack, looking for more booze but instead found Irwin's revolver and when we reached the fire, he would get the drop on the bad guy. Then we would tie him up, march him to Darby, and turn him over to Marshal Rose to collect the reward. Pete would share it with me because we were still best friends. Then he'd tell me he'd lied about screwing Jenny, my mom being a whore, and my dad being a draft dodger. He'd buy a new Ford F150 with his share of the reward and I'd pay for college. Ten years from now, we'd drink a couple of real fancy beers, like Heinekens, and laugh about this trip. Or maybe Pete would be standing at the edge of the fire pit pissing a stream into the coals putting a foul burnt ammonia smell into the air. I should have guessed that because then I would have been right.

The firelight revealed the kidnapper wasn't any taller than me and probably weighed the same. The vee shape of his back and the size of his forearms indicated he exercised more than me, probably more than most people. He had black hair, short in the front and on top, but in the back, it reached to his shoulders. He had a large nose shaped like a ski jump that stuck out on his face, making him look like a vulture. The kidnapper had Diana tie Pete with some cord from her pack. She tied his hands behind his back and his feet together. Halfway through being tied, Pete started to yell. I guess to alert help even though no one else was around for miles. That annoyed the kidnapper who then searched through Pete's pack, found a pair of his underwear, and stuffed them in Pete's mouth. He had Diana run a loop of cord around his head to hold it in his mouth. They left Pete in the dirt beside the fire struggling to breathe through his nose. I decided I wasn't going to yell for help.

Diana tied me next, the same as Pete, but thankfully, I didn't get any underwear shoved in my mouth. I ended up on the dirt with my feet near Pete's head. The kidnapper checked how well Diana had tied us. I hoped the kidnapper didn't feel threatened by Diana because she was a girl. Maybe when he dropped his guard she would disarm him. Then I started to worry maybe he would shoot her if she tried anything, so I alternated between hoping she would do something and then hoping she wouldn't try anything.

After he checked the knots on the cord holding my legs together at the ankles, the kidnapper announced, "I'm going to take the girl off in the woods to have a private chat. You make any noise and I'll come kick you as hard as I can in the guts." To demonstrate his sincerity, he kicked me in the left butt cheek.

I went cold inside ignoring the pain in my ass. What did he mean by private chat? Up till now, I hadn't even thought about the kidnapper also being a rapist. What if he raped Diana? Coldness settled into my stomach. "Why do you need to talk in private?" I asked, my voice cracking a tiny bit.

The kidnapper gave me another kick in the left cheek. "I'm going to talk to all of you in private. That way, I'll get the truth out of you because you won't know what the others said."

He waved the pistol and pointed at the trail to the outlet creek with the other hand.

Before she meekly walked away into the dark, Diana said, "Don't do anything stupid, Scabs, I'll be okay."

With a foot jab to my thigh, the kidnapper followed Diana into the dark. Bile rose in the back of my throat, forcing me to cough. I wanted to yell, to scream at him not to hurt Diana. That I'd already told him the truth. But

I knew if I did he would kick me in the gut. Pete grunted and I rolled around on my side to see him. He grunted again, sliding his head across the ground toward my feet.

In the dim firelight, I could see some of the waistband to the underwear sticking out past the cord holding it in his mouth. Sliding my feet by his head, I forced my toes apart then pinched the fabric between my toes. Pete shifted his head, pulling the underwear out of his mouth. I lost the grip with my toes with it half out, but with a couple of more tries, I snagged the cloth completely out of his mouth. I spun around like a top, rotated my head away from the fire, and put it where my feet had been.

The cord pressed tight into Pete's mouth, but with the underwear removed, he could talk. I kept my voice low. "Pete, crawl around and put your hands by my mouth. I will try to chew the cord loose."

Pete whispered, his tone flat, "He comes back before we're free he might kill us."

I almost spit at him in my disgust. "He's probably raping Diana. We have to save her." My voice got too loud and I brought it back to a whisper. "I've got a gun in my pack. If we get that, we can stop him."

Pete made an odd choking chuckle. "You really are naive, aren't you, Scabs." Pete rolled his jaw, positioning the cord in his mouth so he could talk better. "They might be screwing right now, but he's not raping her."

If Pete had said don't worry the moon is going to fall out of the sky, turn into a rock the size of a fist, and fall on the kidnapper's head saving us, I would have been less skeptical.

Pete whispered, "Have you ever heard of Diana's dad having a hunting camp at these lakes?"

I opened my mouth to say of course, then closed it. Diana's dad had a hunting camp by Quartz Mountain in the Big Hole, and he had another one up Nez Perce Pass in the Selway Wilderness, but I'd never heard anyone mention him having a camp in the East Fork.

"So why do you think Diana brought all that food in here?" Pete asked.

A hundred thoughts swarmed through my head trying to piece together this new reality. Nothing in my life resembled what I had thought it was an hour ago. I had thought my dad served honorably in the military, but now I knew everybody thought he'd dodged the draft by hiding in Canada. I thought my mother was a nice lady that everybody liked and women were jealous of because of her good looks. Now she was just a woman who gave handjobs to horny men in order to put food on her family's table because her husband couldn't get a real job since he was a draft dodger. Diana wasn't a lifelong friend flirting with me because she thought I was fun to be around. She was just distracting me from figuring out she was helping a kidnapper. My sweet innocent girlfriend was really a horndog screwing my best friend. And my best friend—.

I slammed my forehead into Pete's mouth, feeling satisfaction at the pain of his teeth cutting into it since I knew I must have busted his lips. Pete squirmed away from me, but I pivoted on my side, using my stomach muscles to lift myself off the ground and I drove my head into his face. Only I missed, smacking my head into his shoulder. Then as quickly as the rage in me had blossomed, it faded away leaving me feeling hollow.

"When did you know about Diana?"

Pete wormed across the ground as he responded, "Saw her truck parked off the road by the creek near the Guard Station when I drove to the campground." Pete rolled over on his back putting his hands near my mouth. "Then you think you see the kidnapper's car drive down the road while we're at the campground. Then later, we see Diana's pickup drive to the trailhead, and when we saw her at the trailhead, she said she had come over late from the Big Hole."

I gripped the knotted cord with my front teeth and tried to pull.

"I thought that was odd and then when she said she was hauling in supplies for her dad's camp, I knew something was up. I figure she parked her truck along the road, hiked to the kidnapper's car parked at the trailhead, drove it to her truck, then drove her truck to the trailhead. That way if the cops found his car it would point them away from the lakes."

I turned that over in my brain then decided it would have been hard for me to figure out since I hadn't recognized Diana's pickup at the Guard Station. Pete could have been more forthcoming with his insights. Instead, he'd acted like a gnarly dick the whole trip waiting for the best time to tell me he was screwing Jenny.

Right then, I didn't want to free Pete. I wanted to free

myself and run away. Run all the way to the old road by the spring then jog all the way out to my truck. I lifted my head to look at the coals in the campfire. I could swing my feet into the coals and burn the cord around my ankles. My ankles would probably get scorched but maybe not too bad. With my feet free I could run away into the dark.

I didn't get a chance to try it because the kidnapper and Diana appeared on the edge of the firelight. The kidnapper wordlessly dragged me away from Pete. Diana added more wood to the campfire then sat on a log. The kidnapper dragged Pete to a tree, untied his hands, and tied them back together around the tree. It didn't look comfortable to have your shoulders pulled so far behind you. A few minutes later, tied to my own tree, six feet from Pete, I wished I was double jointed.

Diana didn't look at Pete or me and didn't say anything. I couldn't tell if her face was flushed in the red firelight. Her hair looked more messy than usual, but I couldn't really tell with it being in a ponytail. Diana sat quietly first looking at the fire then staring off into the dark in the direction the kidnapper had taken her. From time to time, she added another stick to the fire.

The kidnapper disappeared into the darkness where he had taken Diana. Diana didn't make any move to set us free or even acknowledge my whispered pleas for help. At that point I realized Pete must be right about her helping the kidnapper. My heart broke. It seemed like Pete was right about everything.

The kidnapper returned leading the kid he had

napped by the hand. The boy had blond almost white hair with the same big eyes I remembered from when I had jumped their car. I guessed he was eight years old, but he was skinny, so he might have been older and just small for his age. The boy sat on the log by Diana, snuggling against her, as she put her arm around him. The last remaining doubts I had about Pete's ability to judge people left my mind.

The kidnapper tucked his gun away into a holster on the back of his belt. It seemed an odd place to have your holster, but I guessed it kept the gun out of his way. He stood near the fire by Diana holding his hands out to warm them.

"You boys have put me in a pickle. But the first thing I want you to know is that I'm not a bad guy." He squatted on one knee and leaned forward, putting his hands closer to the flames. I guess tying us up made his hands cold. "My ex-wife is a real bitch." His eyes flicked to the kid briefly then went back to looking over the fire at Pete and me. "We got divorced a year ago and I only got weekend custody of my son. Now she's met this rich asshole that works for a car rental business and she wants to move to France with him for his work and take my boy away from me." He walked around behind Diana. "I can't see my boy if she moves to France, so when I picked my son up for the weekend, I left with him."

He tousled the boy's hair who smiled. "She called the police when I didn't bring him back on Sunday night saying I kidnapped him. You can't kidnap your own son. I've got an attorney right now working on things with her new husband's attorney. This mess will all be straightened out, but I need to keep out of sight until they can reach an agreement. If you boys turn me in, then they'll send my boy to his mother, she'll leave the country with him, and I won't ever see him again."

Diana walked to her pack and came back with her jacket that she wrapped around the boy who snuggled to her when she sat on the log next to him. I tried to think like Pete and evaluate what the kidnapper was telling us. I figured Pete wouldn't believe any of it. I couldn't find any reason to think the kidnapper was lying, but he probably wasn't telling us the whole truth.

Diana spoke. "Seth doesn't want to hurt anyone. He just needs to stay hidden for another week and then his attorney will convince the judge to have a custody hearing. His ex-wife won't be able to leave the country until after the hearing."

I wondered what would happen if Seth lost the custody hearing. Seth walked around the fire and stared first Pete then me in the eyes. "I can't free you because I can't trust you to keep your mouths shut." He smiled at both of us. "I can't kill you because I don't want to upset Di." He laughed. "I'm just joshing you. I'm not going to hurt anybody. I just can't have you telling anybody about me, so you're going to have to hang out with me for a few days." He glanced over his shoulder at Diana with his son nuzzled against her. "If we all cooperate, we can make this work without it being too uncomfortable."

He leaned in close to me and whispered, "And if you try to escape, I will let you run away, then I'll find you, gut you, go back to Di, and tell her you got away." His voice rose in volume. "Right. No reason for anybody to be scared. I don't plan on hurting anyone."

Seth took my sleeping bag for his son and Pete's sleeping bag for himself. Diana used her own sleeping bag and they stretched out on the ground near the fire. Seth slept a little farther from the fire in the shadows, where I couldn't make out if he was asleep or watching me. Diana draped my jacket over my shoulders. Seth told me that if I didn't move around too much it would stay in place. They did the same for Pete and I wished I had brought a heavier jacket like Pete did.

The night lasted a long time since I didn't sleep much. I tried to pull my legs close to me to hold in my body heat. I'd sleep for ten minutes then wake up running everything that had happened since graduation day through my mind.

Pete gave Jenny a ride home from the graduation party and somewhere along the way, they had sex. I wasn't sure if they had done it before then, but something happened that night. After that was when Jenny and Pete both started acting weird. Why didn't Jenny just break up with me if she loved Pete? Maybe Jenny didn't love Pete. Pete had been pushing me to dump Jenny and chase after Sally Parker. He had even pushed me to chase after Diana, but a second review of that made me think that had been more to test Diana than me.

Pete sputtered. I had enough light to see his chin hanging on his chest, snoring as his breath forced its way out. Jenny might have had sex with Pete, but she stayed with me. That could only mean Jenny wanted to be with me, not Pete. She had slept with Pete because I wasn't sleeping with her. All I had to do to keep Jenny was start having sex with her. That seemed like a great idea, except for two things. I'd made a vow not to have sex until after high school and I wasn't sure if I still wanted to be with Jenny. HL-130

I ran that around my head every time I woke, along with horrible thoughts of my mom giving handjobs to her customers. The faces of all the men I knew had been her regulars would flash through my head like an endless View-Master. My math teacher constantly asked about my mom, never my dad. I began to picture me smashing in the noses on the men. Somewhere in the middle of the night, I remembered that last February Pete's dad had hurt his back throwing hay bales out of his truck while feeding their cows. He'd been getting a massage from my mom every week since then to help with it. That might be why Pete's folks weren't getting along. Nope. I couldn't believe it. My mom was not jerking off people at the end of her massages.

She was a certified massage therapist specializing in clinical massage who saw both male and female clients. I then started thinking about the few women who saw Mom. I stopped thinking about them because they were all single ladies with short hair and I didn't like where that train of thought was chugging. I fell asleep for a few minutes and when I woke, I remembered Jenny's dad had seen my mother for massages before Jenny and I started dating. I ran everything through my head again—first

Jenny and Pete, then my mom.

I wanted to jump for joy when the birds tittered from a tree by the creek since I knew that signaled the end of the night. Dawn arrived with light to see by, but I knew it'd still be a while before the sun climbed over the mountains.

Seth and Diana huddled together whispering quietly to each other. Diana woke Seth's boy then packed all the sleeping bags. I saw her sneak a candy bar out of my pack to give him for breakfast. Seth adjusted the cord around my feet so that instead of holding my legs tight together I had two feet of cord between them. I could hobble along but not run away. He untied my arms from around the tree and my shoulders screamed in pain as they returned to their normal position. To keep me from running away while he did the same with Pete, he put a small loop in the end of a four-foot piece of cord then ran the other end of the cord through it, looped it around my neck and tied it to my sleeping tree. If I tried to run away now, the cord would choke me. I had to piss like a racehorse, so I turned my back to Diana and got my pants down enough to piss all over the tree I'd hunkered against during the long night.

Nobody said anything except for Seth's little boy who announced he had to pee. Diana led him out in the woods to do his business. As soon as Pete could, he began to piss, not bothering to turn away from anyone. I couldn't help myself. I peeked at his dick thinking about how it had been inside Jenny. I didn't hate Pete for screwing Jenny, but I hated him for doing it behind my back. I hated him for throwing it in my face the way he did, and I hated him for telling me my mom was nothing but a whore.

I decided right then, if I lived through this ordeal with Seth, I was going to kick Pete's ass. And not one of those fights where we meet down by the Silver Bridge after school and shove each other around a bit before someone makes us shake hands. No, I was going to punch that two-faced son of a bitch until my hands hurt so bad I couldn't punch anymore.

The anger must have been written on my face because Seth leaned in close and said in a low voice that only Pete and I could hear, "Di told me about your bud here, slippin' your girl the Polish frank. If you want—" The knife Seth used to cut the cord appeared in his hand flicking open. "I can cut on him a little for you. Maybe put a nice 'X' right on the head of his dick."

I'm not sure anyone has ever been more tempted than me at that moment. "No," I said. "When you let us go, I'll deal with him."

Seth smiled. "Sure thing. If you change your mind, let me know. If I had the prick that's bumping uglies with my ex-wife here, I'd cut him in a second." His smile changed to a grin. "I'd slit that bitch's throat too. But that's just me. I don't like people messing with me."

Chapter Fourteen

Diana and the little boy reappeared as Seth's knife blade folded into the handle. Pete buttoned his 501s as we hobbled to the campfire. Seth instructed us to shoulder our packs then he tied our hands together in front of us. Not that I wanted my large trout to be eaten but I didn't want it to go to waste in the creek. I asked Diana if she would grab it so we could have it for lunch.

When Diana returned from the creek, Seth, with a wave of his hand, told us to lead, and we headed to Myth Lake. Pete and I shuffled in our makeshift hobbles, while everybody else walked.

I wished someone would come along and see us trudging with our legs hobbled and set us free. That would mean they would have to confront a pistol-packing Seth. I didn't want Seth to hurt someone because they were trying to save me. Seth intended to let us go in a day or two, so I resigned myself to being a captive for a few days and some sleepless nights.

We made it to Myth Lake then followed the trail around the lake to the east. I tripped on an exposed tree root and tumbled to the ground. I rolled down the steep bank of the lake, flailing my tied arms around, trying to grab something to stop from rolling into the lake. The water wasn't deep, but if I came to a stop facedown in it with my pack on my back, I could drown. Diana jumped between the lake and me then grabbed my shoulders. She helped me to my feet by lifting my backpack asking if I was all right. I nodded my head while I hobbled to join Pete on the trail.

I hadn't meant to grab the rock. I was grabbing for anything and had managed to pick up a small flat rock. I turned it around in my hand the best I could, feeling it with my fingers, noting a jagged edge. I stuffed it in my pants pocket hoping no one noticed. Seth told Pete to turn off the trail into the trees following the route Diana had taken to hide supplies for her dad's hunting cache. I realized that while I was searching Rain Lake for the kidnapper, Diana had been delivering groceries to him. I also noticed that the point of rocks Pete had been fishing from gave him a view of the entire lakeshore. He probably hadn't been fishing but watching Diana. Seth stopped us then wandered off into the trees and returned a minute later with a half dozen Indian paintbrush flowers in his hand. He handed them to Diana who accepted them with a smile.

Diana puzzled me. If she was hooked up with Seth then why had she made the comment to me about missing my chance if I had tried to kiss her? It seemed odd that while on a trip to bring supplies to your lover you would be open to kissing another guy, especially a younger, dumber, not as rich guy. That didn't fit quite right, so maybe Pete didn't have it all figured out. Maybe Seth was just a good family friend Diana was trying to help. Or maybe Diana was the reason Seth divorced his wife, Bonnie to his Clyde.

Those thoughts flitted around my brain for the next two days as we hunkered at Seth's camp. The mornings were damp, the afternoons hot, and the nights cold. At night, Seth's little boy, Adam, slept in a tent by himself while Pete and I slept tied to trees with our sleeping bags draped over us. If we wiggled around during the night, the sleeping bags fell off and since our hands were tied, it was impossible to pull the bags back into place. Once the bags fell off, the mosquitoes feasted on our cold flesh. I tried to hold motionless through the nights thinking about beating the shit out of Seth then Pete and trying to figure out what to do about Jenny.

Seth and Diana slept off in the trees and on the first night I heard a lot of rustling in that direction. Pete kept his mouth shut the whole time. Maybe he had used up all his words telling me about my shitty family. Or maybe he didn't want his skid mark underwear shoved in his mouth again.

I didn't say much either except to ask to visit the trees to relieve myself and say thanks for any food Diana brought to me. I spent a lot of time wondering what to do if Seth decided not to turn us loose. I didn't think Diana would let him hurt us, so I wasn't that concerned. The rock in my left front pocket might be sharp enough to cut the cord binding my hands if things went bad. I definitely didn't say anything about the revolver in my backpack. It remained undiscovered even though Seth had fished a hand around inside it and had stolen the last of my candy bars. He gave them all to Adam, so I wasn't mad about it, just happy he didn't find Irwin's handgun.

On the afternoon of our second day at the little camp near Myth Lake, Pete finally spoke. Diana had made another meal of freeze-dried food for everyone. We were only eating two meals a day to save on the food supplies, so it was our late lunch, early supper meal.

After everyone had eaten, Pete said, "Seth," in a commanding tone. Well, since he hadn't talked in two days, it got everyone's attention. "Let me and Scabs go tomorrow morning, or you're screwed."

Seth grinned while walking over to Pete then stood in front of him with his hands on his hips. Pete was physically bigger, but Seth's body language stated he didn't think, tied up or tied down, Pete was a match for him.

"Scabs and I are supposed to be home tomorrow." Pete grinned at Seth. "If we don't make it home, my folks will have Search and Rescue in here the next morning turning over every rock looking for me." Seth didn't appear to be impressed with Pete's statement since he turned away. Pete called after him, "Turn us loose, we hustle out of here, get home on time, and we don't say anything about you. I mean, I get it. Your ex-wife's new boyfriend is a dick. We keep our mouths shut. You guys have more food to eat. Everybody wins."

Seth sat down on a rock then pulled his pistol from the holster at the back of his belt. He ejected the magazine with the push of a button, made a show of looking at the bullets in the magazine, then loaded the magazine into the pistol, and worked the slide.

"Yeah," he said, "Diana already told me when you

boys were supposed to be home. I don't think Search and Rescue is going to make it this far."

I couldn't help myself and asked, "Why not?"

Seth gave me a sly grin. "Once they find your bodies floating in Mash Lake hooked together in a homosexual suicide pact, I don't think they'll hike on up here looking for you." He laughed and I couldn't tell if he was really going to kill us or if he was just messing with our heads.

Seth continued, "I haven't decided if they will find you floating in the lake with your cocks in each other's mouth and your thumbs up your own asses"—Seth paused a second before informing us of the other option—"or hanging from a tree in a mutual autoerotic asphyxiation circle jerk."

He laughed at his joke. Even though I didn't know what autoerotic asphyxiation meant, I decided I didn't like either of the options. Seth continued to chuckle as he holstered his pistol. Diana gave Seth a dirty look saying to me, "He's not going to do that, he's joking." HL-140

Seth quickly stood and for a quick second, I thought he might yell at Diana, but instead he gave his creepy little smile. "She's right. I'm not going to hurt you. We're going to wait until it's almost dark. Then I'll truss you up like I did that first night and leave you on the ground. You should be able to untie each other with a little effort. Hopefully, for me, it will be after dark and since I'm going to take all the flashlights, you won't be able to see where I've hidden your boots along the lake."

Well, that didn't make much sense to me. Pete and I could get untied, find our shoes at first light, hike to the trailhead, and go home to call the cops on Seth.

Seth walked over and tousled the hair on my head similar to how I'd seen him do it to Adam. "I'm going to walk out of here tonight in the dark. By the time you boys make it out of here tomorrow, I'll have a good twelve-hour head start on you." He shoved my head hard at the end of the tousling. "I could be anywhere within eight hundred miles of the trailhead. Now if you boys choose to make a complaint to the cops, then I'll have kidnapping charges against me, so I'd appreciate it if you pretend this didn't happen and when I get this issue with the ex squared away, I'll send you a gift. Say five grand each."

Seth walked over to Pete but didn't try to touch him. He just stared at him for a minute. "If you do tell the cops, maybe someday I pay someone five grand to come beat you senseless then smash your nuts with a ball-peen hammer." He chuckled. "Get it, smash your balls with a ball-peen hammer."

When neither Pete or I laughed, he turned away shaking his head. Why was Diana helping this jerk? She must really be in love with him, or maybe like she said, she liked the idea of his money and getting away from barely scraping by for a living. Maybe once Seth resolved the custody issue, he planned to take her to his mansion where she wouldn't ever have to work again.

Not for the last time I wished I hadn't run away from the campfire. I shouldn't have run from the fight with Pete. I should have stayed and beat his ass or taken a beating. That's what I should have done. I made a vow that if I got out of this I would fight Pete, beating be damned.

I watched Diana and Seth load their backpacks worrying they might go through my pack one last time and discover the revolver. Not that I thought Seth would shoot me with it, but he would take it and since it belonged to Irwin, I didn't want to lose it. They loaded all the food and flashlights into their backpacks. An hour before dark, Seth stripped our hiking boots off our feet. He untied us from the tree, walked us over by the campfire then tied our feet together. He tied our hands behind our back as we lay on the ground.

Diana and Adam carried canteens of water from the lake to douse the campfire. Damp ash, carried by the steam, settled out of the air onto my face as I lay on my side. I twisted my hands around to see if I could reach my pocket where I had stashed the rock. I couldn't reach the rock, not without contorting my body around noticeably. I decided to wait until after Seth, Adam, and Diana left.

Seth knelt by Adam. "Son, do you remember the big rock by the lake? The one you and Diana sit on?" I couldn't see Adam, but after a pause, Seth said, "Okay, good. Walk out to the lake and wait for me at the rock. I'll be along in a few minutes."

Adam noisily walked off through the woods toward the lake. My stomach twisted into a burning knot. Maybe Seth was going to kill us before he left. Why else would he send his kid away, unless he planned to do something terrible to Pete and me? I rolled over so I could see Seth and watched him quietly slip his pistol out of its holster.

Seth's face wore a sad grin as he pointed the pistol at

my face, his thumb resting on the hammer. "Diana, honey, I'm sorry, but you need to come over here."

I heard Diana move closer then stop, probably when she saw the gun.

"Sorry, Di. I can't take you with me. If it's just Adam and I, then Scabs here won't care. But if you go with me, then that pea brain will be worried about you and will tell the cops for sure."

The muzzle of the pistol wiggled when he said pea brain. Even though I didn't want to draw any more attention to myself, I rolled around to see Diana. She stood with her hands at her side a few feet from me, maybe five yards from Seth. Her face didn't show any emotion as she stared at Seth.

Behind me, Seth spoke. "It's not that I don't like you. I mean, you helped a shit ton by telling me about this place and bringing in the extra food." Diana's face remained blank. Seth might like Diana, but he didn't say love and he felt the need to have a gun in his hand when he broke up with her. "You're a great girl. I mean, you tried your best with the blowjobs and your sweet little coochie is an E-ticket ride all day long. But it's better for both of us if you stay here."

If anything, Diana's eyes flashed at the sex talk, whether from anger or embarrassment, I couldn't tell. Pete laughed, a shortened chuckle, like he found the word coochie funny, or maybe he thought it was funny Diana had been used. Diana didn't cry or say anything about loving him or being hurt. She just stood there with a blank look on her face. Right then, I wished I could get my hands on Irwin's revolver.

Diana said in her slow way of speaking. "Okay. I get it. I won't say anything to anyone."

I didn't want her to say that. I wanted her to be pissed at Seth for using her, leap at him, wrestle him to the ground, and beat the crap out of him. I guess if Seth hadn't had the pistol in his hand that's what would have happened, but maybe not. I'm not the best at predicting what people will do.

Seth tossed her a loop of cord, pre-tied with tightening loops and made her slip it over her legs to the knees then pull the loop tight. Then he had her sit on the ground facing away from him. He came into view over my shoulder as he tied her hands behind her back. He removed her boots, tested the knots on all of us, and walked away into the trees toward the lake with his backpack and our boots.

Chapter Fifteen

After the sound of Seth leaving died away, I waited a few minutes, expecting Diana or Pete to start talking, but nobody said anything. I rolled toward Diana until my head lay on her legs. I forgot about the rock in my pocket and bit at the knot binding Diana's legs together. Brush broke in the direction of Pete. I hoped he would be smart enough not to make too damn much noise and bring Seth back. The cord was pinched tight around Diana's legs with the knot at the back of her knees. I couldn't get my teeth against the knots without burying my face into her legs.

"Push your legs together to loosen the cord so I can pull at the knot," I whispered.

Pete giggled from across the fire ring. "I hear she has trouble doing that."

"Dick," I hissed toward Pete. Once I freed Diana and she untied me, I was going to suggest we leave Pete tied for the rest of the night. But then Pete materialized in front of me ruining my plan. He shoved my head away from Diana's legs. He looked down at me holding out a piece of glass.

"Pocketed it that first night by the campfire. I didn't want anyone to step on it, but I guess picking up litter is rewarding." Pete knelt on one knee and held the glass near my face. "I cut you loose, I don't want any bullshit out of you. No whining about me and Jenny. You shut your trap and do what I tell you."

I thought maybe Diana might say something to Pete but she didn't, so I said, "Sure, no problem from me."

Pete smiled, his upper lip thinning into its hard sneer. He walked to my backpack and returned holding Irwin's .357. He waved the gun in my face then stuffed the barrel awkwardly into his pants, the butt sticking out of the waistline. "Just making sure you don't get any crazy ideas."

He pushed me over to my belly then cut me free. I remembered my vow telling myself if we got back to civilization one day I was going to smash that thin upper lip of his until it swelled to normal size.

Pete cut Diana's bonds as efficiently as he had mine then pocketed the little piece of glass. He held his hands out to Diana. "I have a couple matches, had them in my coin pocket, see if you can get a fire going. I'm going to look for our boots."

I stood rubbing my wrists watching Pete step gingerly through the trees into the twilight toward the lake. Diana walked to the campfire ring with Pete's matches in her hand. I hustled up some green moss from the side of a tree along with a few dead dry branches for starter fuel. The sizzle of the match flaring sounded great to my ears. The flames licking at the moss calmed me. We added more branches and the contrast of the flames with the deep shadows around us emphasized the sun had set.

I felt a great easing of tension in my body. The ordeal was over. In the morning, we could hike out to the trailhead. By suppertime, I'd be home with my parents. By the next day, I'd be back to work on Cherylann's fence and everything would be normal. I gathered more branches for the fire and nestled them onto the handful of flames Diana had created. The flames disappeared, taking their red light. I knelt beside the rocks and blew a stream of air at the base of the sticks. The smoke burned my nostrils, but the flames popped into life, spraying light around our quiet little campsite, as I held my hands out to the mini inferno.

A drop of rain hit the brim of my hat followed by the pitter-patter of raindrops hitting the ground. It wasn't a heavy rain, but Diana and I huddled under the branches of the fir tree closest to the fire. We sat down so we didn't have to stand on our tender feet. Diana still hadn't said anything when any other girl would be crying their eyes out.

"Sorry," I said, not knowing what else to say.

She put her hand on my arm and, with a sigh, squeezed it. "Better this way, probably. Seth was using me. Better to find out sooner rather than later that he's a prick."

I didn't know how to respond. I thought about my own situation. Was it better to find out about Pete and Jenny and about my mom and dad now or find out later? I was glad I knew about Pete and Jenny, but I would have preferred to never know about my mom and dad.

I faced Diana. "My mom and dad. Is what Pete said about them true? Is that what everybody thinks?"

Diana didn't look me in the eye. "That's what some

people say, Scabs, but that doesn't make it the truth."

It didn't matter what the truth was in a small town. If town gossip said it, then that was what it was, regardless of the truth. It hurt to think everyone in town had been nice to me because they felt sorry for me. I decided not to tell anyone about Diana and Seth. If the town didn't know, then it would be like it never happened. Somehow, I'd have to find a way to keep Pete from talking.

I must have thought of him one too many times because Pete tromped to the campfire, his head swinging back and forth, his boots made a squishing sound with each step. As soon as he spotted us, he tossed us our boots. "Pretty smart. He tied them to the fish stringer and tossed them into the lake. I saw it and thought maybe there was a fish on it for us to eat and pulled in our boots."

I picked up my boots, the leather soaking wet to the touch. Even if I had dry socks, as soon as I stuck my feet in these boots, they'd be soaked. I decided it'd be better to go barefoot for the night while I dried the boots by the fire.

Pete had other ideas. "Get your boots on and gather your shit. We got to get a move on if we're going to catch him."

I couldn't believe it. Pete wanted to chase after Seth. Even in the dark, my hesitation must have been apparent.

"C'mon. He's got a little kid with him. How fast can he go? We can catch him." Pete patted the butt of the .357. "Then we make him our prisoner and we take him in for the reward." He chuckled. "Scabs get his reward money and Diana gets to screw the guy that fucked her."

Pete gave another goofy chuckle. "Everybody gets what they want."

Diana said slowly, "What do you want Pete?"

For a second, I thought Pete was going to pull the revolver out and wave it around. Instead, he waved his hands. "I want Scabs to get his money and get the fuck out of town." He sniggered. "And I want to protect your honor."

Pete's snigger died out, leaving only the sound of the rain pitter-pattering on the trees around us with the occasional hiss of steam when a raindrop struck our wilting fire. I didn't want to do it, not even for the reward. All I wanted was to build a stack of logs three feet high on the fire then sleep on the ground inside a sleeping bag. After that, I'd be happy to chase after Seth.

"Have fun, Pete, I'm not going," I said to the darkness.

Diana sat on one of our chair logs and pulled on a wet boot. "You can stay if you want, Scabs," she said as she reached for her left boot. "I'm going with Pete."

Well, I certainly wasn't letting Diana hang out in the dark with an armed Pete. I grabbed my boots and sat on the log next to Diana. Fir cone pieces coated my wet socks and I brushed them off. My feet slid into the cold boots and I went to tie my laces. Seth had taken it upon himself to run a knife blade through the middle of the laces that ran through the eyelets below the hooks. I tied two figure-eight stopper knots then tightened the uppers of the boots the best I could. I guess Seth wanted to give me a special present since nobody else had cut laces. Or maybe, I thought, looking at the ragged edges of the cuts, they had been cut with a piece of glass. By the time I got my boots on, Pete and Diana were waiting for me.

"What about our packs?" I asked.

"Shit, Scabs, do you want him to get away? I'll come back for mine later," Pete responded.

I hurried to my pack, feet squishing in the waterlogged boots, grabbed my sleeping bag, and stuffed it inside the main compartment. I grabbed Pete's pack and for a second thought about carrying it but then hung it from a branch on the large fir tree near the campfire. I couldn't see anything else in the dark, so I squished my way to Pete and Diana.

As soon as I started toward them, they turned, and with Pete leading, we walked to the lake. The break in the trees along the lake allowed for more light from the sliver of moon hidden by the rain clouds. Pete lengthened his stride, following the trail around the lake, but slowed once we left the lake entering the darkness under the trees. I slipped every third step going downhill to Mash Lake, the downgrade ramming my toes into the tips of my boots with each step. My waterlogged feet pruned and I could feel the skin on the pads of my feet blistering with each step. Pete jogged around Mash Lake as the trail became flat. The increased pace made my back sweat and I thought about leaving my pack along the trail. My family couldn't afford for me to lose my camping gear. I tightened the belt and loosened the shoulder straps, trying to shift the weight to a new spot on my back.

We climbed the ridge heading to the saddle with the

spring leaving the lake where a little stream tumbled noisily into it. The incline and the added darkness under the trees slowed Pete, but it didn't help the pads of my feet. I thought about tackling Pete from behind and wrestling the gun away from him. Once I tackled him, I thought Diana would help me subdue Pete. I'd feel a whole bunch safer with Irwin's revolver in my possession. Pete kept stepping up the trail, sometimes slowing to a crawl but never slow enough for me to gain any ground on him. Several times, I almost stopped to suck in air, but worried I might lose them in the dark, I kept my feet moving.

The terrain flattened as we curved into the saddle. I waited for Pete to turn from the trail and head to the spring for a drink of water, but he made his way straight to the old Jeep road. I lowered my head as we climbed the bump on the ridge. When I crested it, my face twisted into a grim smile knowing it was mostly downhill to the trailhead.

I couldn't believe we hadn't caught Seth and Adam. They didn't have that big of a head start. I didn't think Adam could hike very fast, even in the daylight. I expected to blunder into them around every turn in the trail. I pressed as close to Pete as I could to be ready to stop him from doing anything foolish. Pete doubled his walking pace, and on the steeper downhill sections, he jogged. Diana fell in front of me and I tripped over her and fell hard, popping my chin on a rock. Pete didn't wait for us and we scrambled to our feet and raced after him.

The blisters spread across the balls of my feet until

they joined into one massive hot sore sending jolts of pain across my soles each time my cut laces let my feet slide across the damp leather. The pain gave me something to focus on. Each step meant one less step in front of me and another lurch of pain behind me.

My ball cap couldn't shed or absorb any more of the persistent drizzle. The water ran down my neck into my sweat-soaked shirt. Unlike sweat, the cold rain chilled my torso. After another mile the water flowed from my shirt into my pants.

Two lines of a song about catfish cycled through my head like a skipping record needing a couple of pennies taped to the head of the tone arm. I tried to remember more of the lyrics and the name of the band as I plodded after Pete—anything to take my mind off the pain in my feet. Was it Seals and Crofts or Steely Dan? Did catfish really jump out of the water? I'd never seen a catfish other than deep-fried chunks of it I ate at a restaurant in Missoula one time. I thought catfish were bottom-feeders, so I doubted they ever jumped out of the water like a trout did going after flies. Did the songwriter know that and didn't care because it sounded good in the song. On the other hand, maybe catfish did jump. They kept jumping in my head, keeping me from thinking about anything other than putting one foot in front of the other.

We hit the last stretch of the trail with its ups and downs. I forgot about catfish as I struggled to keep pace with Pete. Head down, I ran into Diana when she stopped on the trail and called ahead to Pete. I didn't see Pete stop, but I heard his footsteps stop. Silence filled the woods around us.

"The old road is off this little draw just across the ridge. It's a little farther, but we can go faster on the old road." Diana spoke as if she hadn't just walked six miles nonstop in the middle of the night in the rain with wet boots. When Pete didn't answer, she added, "It's the gated road past the trailhead."

Diana didn't wait for an answer. She turned off the trail through the trees, and I followed, happy for the chance to leave Pete. After a hundred yards, even in the dark, I saw the remnants of the old road. Diana led us down a little draw on the other side of the ridge the road appearing to our left. Pete pushed past me in a jog.

I marveled at how damn fast that kid Adam could hike. Diana broke into a jog in front of me and holding the bottom of my backpack against me, I ran the best I could in my loose boots without tripping. The blisters spread to my heels and I was pretty sure the moisture in my boots wasn't water but blood.

Pete grunted and Diana came into view in front of me. I slowed from my limping jog to a walk then came to a stop. Pete had run into the white bar of the gate the Forest Service used to close off the road. That meant we were on the edge of the trailhead parking lot. Close enough to the trucks that Pete's grunt might have alerted Seth to our presence, if our footsteps on the dirt road hadn't. We bunched up at the gate then went around on the uphill side, staying within arm's reach of each other, as we tiptoed down the middle of the road into the parking lot expecting to see Seth any second.

Chapter Sixteen

The Courier looked like a long-lost friend sitting exactly where I had left it right next to Diana's brown Ford. I shrugged out of my backpack, letting it fall to the ground behind the Courier. Pete and Diana knelt between the two trucks as I joined them.

Diana whispered in her same slow cadence as she talked. "We must have passed them in the last section. They should show up any minute."

Pete grunted his agreement. "Okay, we wait, quietly, until they come to the truck. Then I get the drop on Seth."

I sat on my butt in the dirt letting my aching feet rest. As the minutes dragged by, I began to doubt Seth would show. He had probably decided to take the trail from the ridge to the northwest to come out of the woods by Philipsburg. I reconsidered as that was a long hike for Adam. It was more likely Seth had hidden off in the trees letting us go by in the dark when he heard us coming down the trail. That didn't make much sense either. If we beat them to the vehicles, then he'd have to walk the road out to Springer before he could find a ride.

The whisper of raindrops stopped as a gentle breeze swept across the hillside. Lacking the heat generated from hiking, I started to shiver.

A half hour later, I spoke through chattering teeth. "Screw this, I am getting in the truck out of the wind."

Pete grumbled, but he didn't try to stop me. I kicked the rock away from the back tire of the Courier then picked up my keys.

Diana wanted to get in her truck, but Pete waved the gun toward the Courier. "I don't want you driving off."

Pete got behind the steering wheel, I guess to make sure I didn't drive off. Diana slid into the middle of the seat and I sat on the passenger side. I tried to talk Pete into starting the engine so we could run the heater, but he didn't want to for fear of Seth hearing the engine. Pete held the revolver in his left hand against the door. I rested my head against the rear window and crossed my arms against my chest, making it clear Pete didn't have to worry about me trying to take the gun from him.

The next time I went on a camping trip, I was going to make sure I left a full set of dry clothes inside the truck. That way, I'd always have dry clothes for the drive home.

Being out of the wind helped with the chill and it didn't hurt that Diana pressed against me, sharing her warmth. I couldn't see anything in the dark anyway, so I shut my eyes and listened intently for Seth's footsteps.

I tried to fall asleep, but the cold wouldn't let me. After an eternity, the sky lightened, indicating sunrise was only a half hour away.

Pete murmured, "Where did he go?"

Diana shifted sideways putting an arm across my chest as she rested her head on my shoulder. I decided Seth must have had another vehicle hidden somewhere or he had decided to come out of the woods in a different spot. Finally feeling warm, I let out a long breath, snuggled closer to Diana and fell asleep.

I woke with a single ray of sunlight glancing off the rear window. The little bit of sun provided more heat in the crowded truck cab fogging the windows by mixing with our wet clothes. Diana's head rested on my arms with her legs curled under her. Pete's head rested against the corner of the cab with his legs stretched over the transmission hump. I wasn't sure what time it was and didn't care. I liked the feel of Diana's body close to mine. When she woke, we'd go home. I wasn't in any hurry to see my folks or Jenny, not after what Pete had told me. Content for the moment, I fell down the well of slumber.

I woke to a tapping sound on the front windshield. Diana pushed off my chest. Pete leaned forward and wiped the fog off the inside of the windshield, revealing Seth standing beside the Courier tapping the windshield with his pistol.

When he saw the movement inside the cab, he waved with his free hand. "Get out here," he commanded. "Keep your hands where I can see them."

I cracked my door then looked over at Pete to see what he was planning and saw him pushing the revolver down the back of his pants like he was Magnum P.I. My hands in the air, I crawled out of the Courier followed by Diana. Seth kept motioning with his gun to come forward. Diana and I walked past the hood of the Courier before Seth stopped waving the gun. Adam stood across the pullout by the "Pack it in, Pack it out" sign at the start of the trail wearing his same sad face and, despite all the rain last night, dry clothes.

Pete came out the driver side of the Courier with his hands up. Leaving the door open, he walked until he was slightly behind Diana then stopped. I hoped he didn't try anything stupid. It seemed pretty simple to me. We let Seth take one of the trucks and we would promise not to tell anyone about him.

"The keys to the Courier are in my pocket. I'll give them to you. We'll wait here until dark before we head home. We won't tell anybody about you. I'll just report my truck as stolen, that's it," I offered.

Nobody but me seemed to think that was a good idea. Diana inched toward Seth, "Sure, right after he explai—"

"Stop." Seth pointed his pistol at Diana taking a step back to keep his distance. Behind Seth, Adam started to sniffle.

I stepped to Diana's side. "Hey, point the gun somewhere else, Seth. Nobody needs to get hurt. I'm sure we can work something out."

Diana took a half stride toward Seth.

"Diana, stop," I pleaded. "Seth's a dick but he's a dick with a gun, don't do this."

Diana brought her lagging foot up even with the other then held still, resembling a bobcat waiting to pounce on a rabbit.

Pete asked from behind us, his hands over his head just like mine were, "What took you so long getting here?"

Seth didn't take his eyes off Diana, but he lowered the muzzle of the pistol so it pointed at her feet. "We camped on the ridge by that little spring. I didn't want to hike out in the dark with Adam." He smiled. "I saw your tracks in the mud on the way out this morning. Gave me quite the shock you'd gotten free so quick. I expected to see the police waiting at the trailhead." His eyes shifted from Diana to Pete. "But it looks like you dumbasses sat around waiting for me."

Pete lowered his hands a little. "Scabs has the right idea. Let him toss you the keys to the Courier. You can take it and flatten the tires on Diana's rig. You'll have a head start before we get to the police." Pete kept slowly dropping his hands as he talked until they rested on his hips. "We got a deal?"

Diana started to cry and her stumbling way of talking became more pronounced. "I hate you," she said to Seth.

Seth kept his pistol pointed at Diana's feet but talked to me. "Toss the keys over nice and slow. Then everyone needs to walk over to the gated road while I leave."

I brought my right hand down, wiggled it into the wet pocket, and pulled out my keyring. Diana was slightly between Seth and me, so I sidestepped to my left in front of Pete. With an underhand toss, I threw the keys to Seth.

A lot of stuff started to happen when the keyring left my hand and time slowed for me. Seth's eyes widened as he jerked his pistol up to my left. My mind, in the form of a news flash, informed me: this just in, Pete did something stupid. My left leg disappeared out from under me, and I started to fall.

Seth's fingers flexed open and the pistol left his hand, floating sideways in the air. The dirt road rose slowly toward my face, but before it covered my view, I saw

Diana jerk to her left, a red dot appearing on her shoulder. I twisted my hands in front of me to cushion my fall. Pain flared briefly as my right wrist bent as I rolled to my side. The pain in my wrist faded but was replaced by the feeling that a red-hot fireplace poker had been shoved into my leg. I curled my head around and saw Pete with Irwin's revolver in his right hand. Blood dribbled out of my jeans below my crotch into the brown dirt road.

Like a blow to my entire body, time ramped back to normal speed along with the sense of sound.

"Oh shit," Pete said in a hollow tone.

Seth dropped to his knees beside Diana who lay on her side, blood everywhere on her upper body. I tried to stand but couldn't make my left leg work, so I crawled to Diana. There was a lot of hollering going on. Pete screamed at Seth to hold still, Seth shouted at Pete to help with Diana, little Adam cried hysterically, and I yelled for everyone to shut up. The only person not making a sound was Diana.

Seth clamped one of my hands on the front of Diana's shoulder and one on the back. "Push hard." He frantically searched the ground for the keyring I had tossed to him.

He snapped it out of a rain puddle then brushed past Pete to the Courier. Pete stood there with the revolver hanging at his side staring at Diana, not saying anything now, just looking at me like it was my fault he'd shot Diana. The Courier's engine came to life then it rolled beside Diana. Seth ran around the side of the truck yelling at Pete to help then he knelt beside me.

"Help me put her in the bed of the truck. Then you'll need to keep holding her shoulder to stop the bleeding."

I kept my hands on Diana's shoulder and nodded at the blood on my leg. "Not sure I can stand."

Seth eyed the blood on my jeans then his focus flickered back and forth between Diana and me. Without a word, he grabbed Diana around the shoulders and half dragged her to the Courier. Pete helped by lowering the tailgate and Seth hopped up and pulled Diana into the truck bed. He jumped out of the bed and landed on the ground next to me. Using the same hold on me, he dragged me to the truck, laid me beside Diana, and instructed me to push on her shoulder.

There was more yelling. Seth trying to get Adam in the Courier. Pete yelling at Seth not to try to escape. Diana continued being quiet. I wondered why nobody needed to put pressure on my wound. I decided it must not be that bad. Looking at my leg, I was shocked at how much blood had pooled on the bed of the truck. Diana's face, even her lips, looked deathly white. Pete climbed over the side of the bed of the truck and sat next to me. Seth popped the clutch lurching the little truck out of the turnaround.

"What do you think, Scabs? Nearest phone at the Guard Station?" Pete asked.

I nodded my head, trying to focus on pushing against Diana's wounds. Her head lay against the bed of the truck bouncing against it as the Courier sped down the road and I wished I had a pillow for her. It got harder to keep the pressure. I had to concentrate to make sure I was pushing on her wounds. I felt exhausted, like I could just roll over onto my back and go to sleep. I didn't dare though. I had to keep the pressure on Diana's shoulder. I whispered in her ear telling her everything was going to be okay. I didn't believe it. I was sure Diana was dying.

We bounced along, my world existing only of Diana's face, forcing my hands against her shoulder, and trying to brace my body so Diana didn't slide around the bed of the truck.

The Courier came to a short stop and we slid forward, Diana's head bumping into the front of the truck. I mustered the energy to raise my head to look over the side of the truck bed. An old guy with a long beard driving a Ford a shade of brown that could only be described as turd sat alongside the road. My eyes closed for no reason, and I forced them open, but the world blurred into shades of gray. I laid my head against Diana, listening to Pete and Seth try to explain we needed an ambulance. With effort, I raised my head and saw a straw cowboy hat wearing eyes. The eyes didn't seem excited. They swept the scene, taking in the gun in Pete's hand, the young boy in the front seat crying, and he jumped into his turd brown truck. My head floated to Diana as I felt Seth beside me pushing my legs around. I managed to flutter my eyes open enough to see he was wrapping his shirt around my leg and tying a knot in it. I heard him say something to Pete and then Pete rolled me off Diana's shoulder.

The driver of the turd truck was talking crazy. "Breaker one nine, this is Twenty-two Charlie. Country

Girl, you got your ears on." I drifted off hearing him say, "Copy that, rally at Fred Wetzsteon International Airport."

A spike of pain ran through my body. I heard a groan and realized it came from my mouth. I opened my eyes to a stranger hovering over me talking into a radio. I couldn't hear anything other than a droning roar. Then I saw the tail rotor of a helicopter and realized they were loading me onto it using a gurney. I tried to tell them to take Diana first, but I couldn't make my mouth work, or they couldn't hear me over roar of the helicopter. I tried to stay awake. I'd never ridden in a plane or a helicopter before and didn't want to miss out on the experience. The stranger beside me shifted out of sight except for his bloody hands. I wondered just how much blood a person had inside them. With a long exhale, I fell asleep.

Chapter Seventeen

At the hospital, they pumped me full of fresh blood and cleaned out my gunshot wound. The doctor explained people have about a gallon and a half of blood in their body and I'd lost half of mine. The doctor said if the EMT on the helicopter hadn't done a transfusion directly from his arm to my arm, I would have died from blood loss. I thought about Seth tying his shirt around my leg. If he hadn't done that, I wouldn't have made it to the helicopter.

Diana's wound was worse than mine. She hadn't bled as much, but the bullet had broken her shoulder blade and after spending one night at the hospital in the room across the hall from me, they loaded her in an ambulance and sent her to Missoula to have surgery.

The doctor also explained I didn't have a special gift to make time slow. The phenomena happened to everybody when they got excited and their amygdala started writing more memories. It had something to do with the brain using memories to tell how much time had passed and more memories tricked the brain into thinking one second was like fifteen. Noting my disappointment that I didn't have a special ability, he did say that maybe my amygdala was bigger than most causing it to happen to me more than other folks.

They arrested Seth at the little airstrip alongside the

road before Springer Memorial where the helicopter landed to pick up Diana and me. They tried to question Pete at the airstrip, but he refused to talk until his dad was present. Pete's dad refused to let Pete talk until his attorney was present. Pete claimed Seth had pointed his pistol at him and he had shot in self-defense. The sheriff confiscated Irwin's revolver and I worried Irwin was going to be pissed at me for involving his revolver in this mess. The sheriff questioned first Diana and then me at the hospital before they took Diana to Missoula. I told the sheriff Seth didn't have his pistol pointed at anybody when Pete started shooting.

The doctor let me go home after two nights at Marcus Daly Memorial and I was happy to get out alive since the locals called it Carcass Daly. On the ride to the East Fork, I realized someone would have to pay my hospital bill. While I didn't know how much two nights in a hospital cost, I had an idea it would be more than what I made building Cherylann's fence. HL-170

~ ~ ~ ~ ~

My folks made me stay in bed for a week, per the doctor's order, moving as little as possible to let the wound heal. I had to suffer through some awkward sponge baths since they wouldn't even let me shower. The sheriff came by the house to return Irwin's revolver. He said Seth had hired a fancy lawyer and was out on bail. He thought Seth would probably plea bargain down to a lesser charge. No one got a reward for Seth's capture as Seth's ex-wife refused to pay saying the paper had misrepresented her statement about wanting to post a reward, not that she had posted a reward. No charges were filed against Pete as the sheriff said it had all been an accident. I wondered if the sheriff getting to hunt on Pete's ranch every fall had anything to do with the outcome. I guess I didn't care. I was happy to get Irwin's revolver back. Dad told me to clean it before I returned it to Irwin.

My folks made me stay in the house doing the stretches the doctor told me to do for my leg for another two weeks after the week in my room. The week after they let me out of the house but wouldn't let me leave our property. I walked a path around our property trying to build the muscle in my leg even though it itched liked crazy.

Jenny never came to see me. She called the day after I got home from the hospital. All she said was that she hoped I got better quickly, but she hung up before I got the nerve up to ask if she still wanted to go out with me. I didn't call her back because I was trying to figure out if I still wanted to go out with her. Besides, I had plenty of things to worry about other than Jenny—healing my leg, getting the fence done on time, the hospital bill, what I was going to do after high school, and punching Pete in the nose. Not necessarily in that order. Another week passed before my folks let me start working on the fence.

Chapter Eighteen

Irwin sat on the tailgate of the Courier drinking a Milwaukee's Best, wearing a Camels' ball cap, and his gray shirt read "mother trucker" on it in black letters across the chest. I rolled the three-wheeler to a stop beside him and he tossed me a beer. The can of Pabst felt warm, but more importantly, it was free. Irwin had taught me there were only two kinds of beer, cold and free.

"Thanks," I said after my first drink.

"All done?" Irwin asked, sliding off the tailgate and walking to the wheeler, his round beer belly looking like he might give birth to three-quarters of a basketball any day.

I shook my head. "Nope. I still got one more strand of wire to run on the far side and I need to pull and roll the wire from the old fence."

"Well, shit, boy," Irwin drawled. "I was rooting for you to finish on time. You should have let me help you."

I smiled at Irwin. "I appreciated the offer, Irwin, but the agreement with Cherylann was that only I work on the fence. Not your fault or Cherylann's I didn't get the fence done on time."

I took another drink of PBR thinking that it probably tasted better slightly warm than cold. On my first day back to work on the fence, Irwin had stopped by offering to help. I had refused, wanting to honor my agreement with Cherylann. At the time, I still hoped I could finish the project before the deadline. After that, Irwin began appearing at the Courier at the end of each workday, always with an extra beer.

I hated losing the bonus money, but I'd shaken hands with Cherylann and it wasn't her fault I couldn't hold up my end.

After I finished the fence, I hoped to work a few jobs with my dad, but he didn't have any work lined up for the fall himself. My hospital bill for the gunshot wound had come in the mail, and even though my folks didn't ask me to help pay for it, I planned to give them the money I earned doing the fence. Summer would end and I wouldn't have anything to show for it. Zero progress on my goal of going to college after high school. I had a plan B for after high school, so I focused on another goal I wanted to complete before school started.

I studied Irwin's skinny frame with his beer pooch belly and decided to ask anyway. "Irwin, do you know anything about fighting? Like if a smaller guy wanted to smash the nose of a guy bigger than him, would you have any advice?"

Irwin drained his beer in a long gulp and slid off the tailgate. Setting his beer can on the ground, he stomped it into a biscuit before tossing it into the bed of the Courier. "This smaller guy might be you?" he asked with an eyebrow halfcocked.

I shrugged and took a drink of beer.

Irwin nodded. "The bigger guy that asshole buddy of yours, Pete?"

"Yeah. I don't need to win the fight. I just want to smash his nose."

I hadn't told anyone everything that happened at the lakes. It wasn't like I could tell my mom and dad. I hadn't even told the police the things Pete had said about my family. I hadn't told Irwin about it. Even though, unlike everyone else, Irwin had never asked.

It spilled out of me there standing by the Courier. Not the whole trip but the mean things Pete said to me around the campfire about Jenny and my parents.

"Well, that is certainly reason to fight someone," he said quietly when I finished.

I couldn't help but ask, "Is it true Irwin?"

Another beer, this one a Buckhorn, had appeared in his hand. He took a drink of beer before answering me. "Well, it's been a long time, but I seem to remember that teenage girls can be just as horny as teenage boys, so I expect it's true that your girl screwed around on you."

That hadn't been the part of Pete's story I wanted his opinion on. I was sure Jenny had fooled around with Pete. "What about my folks?"

"Well," Irwin said slowly in his two-syllable way. "I don't have any idea about your dad skipping off to Canada to avoid Vietnam, but he doesn't come across as the type of guy that would do something like that." He didn't say anything else. He just stood there taking another drink.

"And my mother?"

Irwin stared straight into my eyes. "I don't like to say it, but I've heard those things about your mom myself."

He took another drink. "But when I first came to the valley, I twisted my back moving around some of Cherylann's knickknack paddy crap. I went to see your mom to work out the kinks. She never did anything that wasn't completely professional. Never suggested anything like a happy ending."

Irwin rubbed his chin for a second as if trying to rub color into his gray stubble. "I guess I'm not going to be able to talk you out of fighting, so I should probably try to keep you from getting your ass completely kicked. This Pete fella, he been in any other fights? Did he win?"

"Yeah, freshman year. After football practice in the locker room, the upper classmen would pee on the freshman in the shower. Usually when you had your eyes closed rinsing out your hair. Anyway, this sophomore Brian pissed on Pete and Pete didn't like that a guy only one year older than him and worse at football did it."

Irwin nodded, encouraging me to go on with my story, then took another swig of beer.

"They met out in the parking lot and Pete knocked him down."

"How'd the fight go? Did it last a while? Did this Brian get in any good hits?" Irwin asked.

"Not really. Pete charged at him, swinging with both hands. When they got close, Pete hit Brian on the side of the head and Brian went down. Didn't knock him out, just hurt him real bad."

Irwin finished his beer. "Pete been in any other fights?"

"No. That pretty much gave Pete the tough guy

reputation. Nobody has had the nerve to challenge him since then."

Irwin crushed his beer can, tossed it into the bed of the Courier then faced me. "He might not even fight you." The puzzled look on my face must have revealed my disbelief. I knew Pete thought he could kick my ass anytime he wanted to, so I didn't understand why he wouldn't fight me.

"Pete's the big jock at school. The quarterback of the football team. He's bigger than you and already has a reputation of a badass fighter. If he fights you and wins, none of that changes, except maybe people think he's a jerk for picking on a wounded kid."

Irwin continued, "If he loses the fight to a smaller guy, well then, he's not such a badass anymore, and he isn't top dog anymore. Maybe some of those other kids that have let him push them around because he's such a badass will take a crack at him. He's got a lot to lose and not a thing to gain by fighting you."

I agreed with Irwin, but I thought Pete would win the fight, so I didn't see him worrying about losing.

Irwin stepped away from the Courier, moving out into the field, and I pivoted to face him. "Pete will probably try the same thing with you. He's not going to change a tactic that worked in the past. He's going to rely on that fast and furious attack to intimidate you."

Irwin rolled his shoulders in an exaggerated shrug and after a deep breath brought his fists up. "Okay, come at me just like Pete did to Brian, only keep it about one-third speed. Don't go full throttle."

It took a second to process what Irwin wanted me to do. I hesitated even more because I didn't want to accidently hurt Irwin throwing punches at him. I came at him slowly throwing exaggerated, wide haymakers with both hands. Irwin stood still, a hint of a grin on the corner of his mouth. I smiled back because I realized how ridiculous I looked.

When I got close enough to actually hit Irwin, I expected him to duck. Instead, he stepped to the side in slow motion. His right hand pushed my right arm down alongside my body and sliding behind me, his left arm grabbed it, pinning my arm to my gut. I twisted to get away and Irwin tripped me face-first into the dirt.

The side of my face slammed into the ground. I tried to get up and realized Irwin still had ahold of my arm, pinning it under my body. He was on his knees, leaning over me pushing on me with his chest.

"Hold still for a second," Irwin commanded and I stopped struggling. He said, "Look at where my knee is at. I can use it to bash you in the face from this position." I rotated my face away from Irwin's knee and he brought his elbow down into my forehead. "If he turns away, you can either knee him in the back of the head or smash his nose with your elbow."

He dropped his full weight onto my back and I felt something digging into the base of my neck. The pressure eased. "The weight of my body helps keep that arm pinned, and I can dig my chin into your back to hurt you."

Irwin shoved off my back pushing the air out of my

lungs as he stood up quickly. "You can also use your feet." He kicked at my face, stopping his foot right in front of my nose. Irwin smiled as he helped me to my feet. "You want to bloody Pete's nose, you get him down and you smash your knee into his face a few times. It will be bloody."

I dusted my pants off wondering if any of this would work on Pete. Irwin stepped back a few feet. "Okay, let's do it again really slow this time and I will talk you through what I'm doing."

We repeated everything, this time in super slow motion, with Irwin explaining each step. Then he played the part of Pete working with me on how to get behind and pin the arm against the body. After a few tries, Irwin said, "Okay. I'm going to rush you about quarter throttle and you take me down."

I messed up the arm grab the first go, so we started again. I got the arm but hesitated on the trip to the ground.

"Dump my ass. You ain't going to hurt this old man." Irwin's hand shot out and cuffed me upside the head.

The blow wasn't hard enough to hurt, but it did piss me off. I did exactly what Irwin asked. I dumped him on the ground. After that, things began to speed up, and each time I hesitated, Irwin cuffed the side of my face. I didn't know how much throttle Irwin was using, but I had mine mashed to the floor after three cuffings. After each pileup, Irwin would talk though what I did right and what I could do better.

On our last practice run, we went full speed. I'd

already thought Irwin was going all out, but he surprised me by being stronger than his skinny frame indicated and fast. He connected with a blow to the side of my temple, making a bell ring inside my head. I caught his arm, twisting it in front of him and then Irwin leaned forward trying to pull out of my grasp. I stumbled after him and tried to trip him when his head shot back into my chin. The blow didn't loosen my teeth, but it sure felt like my two front teeth were rattling around in my mouth.

I swung my leg around his and lunged, tackling him to the ground in a pile of dust. I landed in the right position and shifting my legs slightly, rammed a knee into Irwin's guts. Irwin grunted then laughed as he called out, "Uncle."

We got to our feet, Irwin laughing for some reason I didn't quite understand. Maybe the old guy just liked to fight. I wiggled my shoulder around to work out the kinks. I couldn't help but smile at Irwin. "If none of this shit works, Irwin, then what?"

Irwin's laugh morphed into a wide grin. "You bite him. No matter what happens, or how bad somebody has you wrapped up, you can always bite. Nothing hurts worse. Bite somebody hard enough, their only thought will be getting the hell away from you."

Irwin dusted off his clothes, and I noticed his lower lip had blood on it. "Good workout, kid. Haven't had this much fun since that big old boy Jim beat the shit out of me at Dotson's Bar for refusing to pay a quarter to use the bathroom."

We shook hands and Irwin jogged down the road to

the ranch house saying something about needing to be home before dark. I gathered the beer-can biscuits out of the bed of the Courier and put them into a brown grocery bag behind the seat. I didn't need my dad seeing beer cans in the bed of my truck, even if most of them were from Irwin.

Chapter Nineteen

I turned left off Water Street down the road leading to the Darby Silver Bridge my stomach full of bees. On the left, I went past a modern log cabin where a guy had been murdered a few years back, a nice man caught in a bad situation. Somehow, my dad had ended up with his cowboy hat. I drove across the bridge keeping the Courier between the metal girders that formed triangles on either side.

Often, kids from town walked to the bridge to swim in the deep pools under it. They jumped off the bridge into the river. A few adventurous or maybe crazy ones climbed the girders and jumped from the top of the bridge. I didn't live in town, and I didn't swim that well, so I'd never jumped from the bridge at any height. I drove past the cottonwoods on the edge of the river, straight for the open hillside of arrowleaf balsamroot, and parked with the front of the truck nudging the hillside. The heat of the sun reflected off the hillside, contrasting with the cool air from the river. I dropped the tailgate, took a seat facing the bridge, and waited for Pete.

The football team was still practicing twice a day, once in the morning then again in the afternoon. Pete had agreed to meet me here after the second practice. I hadn't told him I wanted to kick his ass, but I figured since I wanted to meet at the bridge he'd get the idea. While I waited, I walked through everything Irwin had been teaching me over the last week. After that first night of training, Irwin had met me at the Courier after work each night, and before drinking our beer, we had practiced fighting.

Pete's giant Caddy came hurtling down the road less than ten minutes later. It bounced over the bridge and as soon as he cleared it, he gave the Caddy even more gas, doing a cookie right in front of me, throwing dust in my face. Rock music blasted out the windows, the bass line thumping hard, and the lyrics shouting about drinking liquor at bedtime contrasted with the peaceful gurgle of river. The Cadillac came to a wobbly, bad shocks, stop on the north side of the bridge and the music died. Pete and four of his football buddies poured out of the car laughing at all the dust in the air. I recognized Bob, Brian, Billy and a goofball called Bing. They all had ball caps on except for Bob who had on his black cowboy hat.

Pete separated from his pack and walked over to me. I got to my feet and met him halfway. I hadn't seen him since the trip to the lakes. I'd forgotten how damn big he was.

I started to say hi, but Pete spoke first. "So, what does your lame ass want, Scabs? Here to beg me to stop dating Jenny so she will go out with you?" He laughed and a few of his teammates behind him chuckled.

I grimaced inside but tried to keep my face calm. That told me Pete had made sure the locker room knew he had slept with Jenny. Great, he was willing to make the girl he wanted to date look like a cheating slut in order to hurt me. Right then I wondered if Pete had always been a dick, and I just hadn't noticed it, or had he become a dick recently. Before I could change my mind, I spoke the words I'd rehearsed in my head a hundred times. "I'm here to beat the shit out of you."

A few of the guys behind Pete laughed. Billy turned his hat around backward like a character in one of the Clint Eastwood orangutan movies. Pete didn't laugh and by the look in his eyes, Irwin had been absolutely right. Pete didn't want to fight.

"What's a matter, Pete? Scared to face me after shooting me in the back?" That shut everyone up behind Pete.

"I'm not going to fight you, Scabs, not fair with you being so injured you can't play ball." Pete smirked.

That was a smart remark from Pete. If I fought him, it would be admitting I hadn't played football because I just didn't want to, not because of my wound. In Darby, not playing football if you could was a sin, worse than peeping in on the girls' locker room shower. He had put me in a bad spot, but as Pete had already explained to me, my family didn't have a good reputation in town, so I didn't have much to lose.

I knew what to do to make Pete fight me. "Fuck you. You bedwetting pussy." I said and spit on him. I tried to hit his face, but the distance, breeze, and my aim caused the wad of phlegm I'd horked up from the back of my throat to hit his shoulder. He'd either have to fight me or walk away with my spit on his shirt. I took a step back, giving Pete more room to charge me, bringing my fists up.

The guys behind him gave an audible intake of breath and one of them said, "Ten bucks Pete knocks him out with one punch."

Pete charged, just like he had done in his first fight and just like Irwin and I had practiced. I ducked his wide swing, stepping to the side my hands grabbed at his forearm and pinned it to his side. Instantly I realized that as strong as old Irwin was, Pete was stronger. I struggled to hold him but managed to position my foot then swung my upper body, tripping Pete into the dirt road.

The side of his face scraped across the ground and I slid to his side pressing down on him with my chest, pushing the point of my chin as hard as I could into his back while hanging on to his hand trapped underneath him. He twisted toward me and I swung my knee into his face. It didn't feel quite as good as using my fist, but it still felt good feeling my knee flattening his nose. I swung my knee toward his face again, but his free hand partially blocked the blow. I countered by jamming my other knee into his ribs.

Pete grunted rolling toward me and that's when I realized I had swung to the wrong side of Pete. I was holding his pinned arm underneath him from the opposite side Irwin and I had practiced. This allowed Pete to roll toward me. Now instead of having Pete pinned face to the ground, he was on his back looking at me. Blood poured from both of his nostrils and hate from his eyes. He brought a hammer fist down on my thigh, a blow that would have hurt, but on my gunshot wound, it felt like he'd zapped me with an electric cattle prod. His other hand grabbed me by the throat and pinched off my windpipe. I gagged, trying to pull away, but he gripped my other hand keeping me close to him.

I tried to bite him, but with his hand at my throat, I couldn't get my mouth on any part of him to bite. Pete curled his body toward me until we were both on our sides facing each other on the ground and my vision began to fade from lack of oxygen.

Time slowed for me. I can close my eyes to this day and picture that entire scene perfectly. The look on Pete's face, then as I twisted my head away from him I saw two white puffy clouds in the blue sky with the blinding sun to the left of them. My vision faded along with my hopes of winning the fight. I had tried so hard that summer to make something of myself and at the end of it, I would just be the guy who lost his girlfriend to his best friend and got beat up by him.

Anger bloomed out of my despair. I gathered every bit of strength left in me and instead of trying to twist away from Pete's grip on my throat, I screwed my body toward him, my free hand not reaching for Pete's hand at my throat but the one I held with my right hand. The fence building had given me an iron grip and I used it now to roll over the top of Pete, using the weight of my body to twist Pete's hand free of my throat while grabbing his other hand in both of mine. We flopped around and I lost sense of where Pete was in relation to me. All I knew was that my legs were across his body and I had his one wrist gripped in both of my hands. I pulled hard on his arm, flexing my legs against his body.

I felt a jolt go through Pete's body as he grunted involuntarily in pain. Shocked, I let up for an instant, realizing I was hurting Pete bad. Immediately, he tried to free his hand, but I flexed again, pulling down until Pete stopped struggling. "Say uncle," I said, wondering if Pete did say uncle and I let him up, would he then beat my ass?

I didn't have to worry about it because through gritted teeth, he barked, "Never."

I flexed as hard as I could, hugging his arm to my chest and doing my best to straighten my legs out completely by pushing against his body. Then I rolled my shoulders, shoulders that had lifted and pulled down on that heavy fence pounder all summer long. Pete screamed in pain even before I heard the bones in his arm break. I felt it happen. Suddenly, there wasn't any resistance and his hand collapsed into my face. Billy and Bing appeared pulling us apart. Time returned to normal speed when that shithead Bing popped me on the side of the head.

I scrambled to my feet, wondering if the Bee Boys were going to try to kick my ass. I didn't have to worry. They were all staring at Pete writhing around in the dirt. Pete's arm looked normal until about three inches above his wrist where it bent sideways at a ninety-degree angle. One bone stuck completely out of a jagged opening with only a little bit of blood around it, enough to make the bone look, well, bone white. The other bone pushed against the skin, raising a bump the size of a walnut.

Billy yelled at the rest of them to help him get Pete to

the Cadillac. I tried to help, but Bing shoved me out of the way, so I stepped back and watched them carry Pete to the car. They dragged him into the back seat. There was a bit of a fiasco retrieving the keys from Pete's pocket. Bing jumped into the back seat to take care of Pete, Billy took the wheel, and Brian hopped in the front passenger seat as the tires spun. The Caddy bounced over the bridge leaving me standing there with Bob.

We stared at each other for a few seconds then Bob said, "We were going to make the playoffs this year, maybe even go to the state championship."

I didn't say anything. I'd only wanted to smash Pete's nose in, not break his arm.

Bob shook his head. "Shit, Scabs, without Pete as the quarterback, we might even lose to Corvallis."

Now the whole town would have a new reason to dislike my family. I had single handedly ruined football season.

"All this over that princess bitch Jenny. Holy shit." He stared at the blue sky with the thunderheads building in it. "Pussy must be a powerful thing." Bob stopped saying anything other than stringing curse words together.

I'd heard them before and mostly in the same order. The Courier started at the first touch of the key and I stopped by Bob. "Hey, Cowboy, do you need a ride to town?"

Bob stopped cussing, glanced at the road past the bridge toward town, walked around the Courier, and got in. I drove over the bridge enjoying the air cooled by the Bitterroot River. Bob looked at me. "This thing got a radio, or do you want me to sing?"

When I dropped Bob off, Darby resembled a beehive with everybody running around to spread the news. Billy had pulled into the parking lot by the clubhouse and the local EMTs were getting Pete loaded into the ambulance. Bob got out of the Courier but I didn't bother to shut the engine off. I'd already gotten a half dozen dirty looks and knew from experience that not only had the word spread across Darby but phones were ringing in the forks of the Bitterroot. My parents would know what happened before I got home.

Bob studied the crowd gathering at the ambulance then looked back at me. "Sucks to be you, Scabs."

He jogged to the ambulance. I looked at the video store and saw Jenny, looking beautiful in her store shirt and jean skirt, standing on the sidewalk by the front door. She spotted me staring at her and went inside without acknowledging me.

It certainly was going to be a tough senior year for me. Not only didn't I play football when I could have, I had busted the starting quarterback's arm. I hadn't met the deadline for getting the fence put in and the money I made doing the fence would go toward my hospital bill, not college. I tugged the steering wheel around in a hard turn pulling onto Main Street headed south. I pushed the speed limit getting out of town even though I knew the town marshal was a real stickler about it. This summer had been a complete failure. Even kicking Pete's ass hadn't gone right. With my revenge on Pete finished, I considered it was time to finish the fence and implement my backup plan for college.[HL-190]

Chapter Twenty

I walked the now familiar ground along the fence line enjoying the cool morning air. I'd hurt my shoulder fighting with Pete and of all things, my big toe on my right foot hurt like I'd jammed it. The good thing was, I wasn't in any hurry. Today was my last day on the fence. Since I missed my bonus deadline, I'd taken a day off after fighting with Pete before I rolled up the wire from the old fence. I had already picked up all the rolls of wire except for two bundles on the side of Cherylann's property away from the shed.

I'd left the three-wheeler in the shed and hiked the fence line doing one last check that my fence hadn't been knocked down by a herd of elk. Everything looked good except for a couple of spots where I'd missed a few of the metal clips that held the barbwire to the post. I straightened up from attaching the last clip checking the sun for the time. I had a meeting with Cherylann at noon to officially tell her I was done with the fence. Unfortunately, the sun told me I had plenty of time to spare. The last thing I wanted was to be sitting around in Cherylann's kitchen cooling my heels waiting to talk to her.

I turned at the corner posts and meandered downhill along the fresh hundred yards of fence to the last coil of wire. I'd spotted an old Army rucksack in the shed and after strapping the coils on the rucksack, I turned to walk uphill when I realized that wasn't very smart. It would be easier to walk down the fence line until I came out of the trees into the pasture and then I could cut across the open hillside to the shed. That route would save a hundred yards packing the wire uphill with a sore toe. I'd taken the other rolls of wire out that way, but I'd had the three-wheeler at the top. I could sit in the shade of the shed waiting for my meeting time with Cherylann.

I plodded downhill thinking about Jenny and how shitty school would be if I had to see her and Pete holding hands in the hallway. With my mind distracted, I almost missed it. A tree had fallen parallel with the fence and I bumped away from the fence to go around it and noticed the blaze on the tree. A blaze on a tree indicated either a trail or sometimes a property corner nearby. Those trees, called bearing trees, were used to find a property corner marker that was buried in the ground.

I swung the rucksack off my back, happy to give my big toe a break from the weight. I was above Cherylann's pasture just inside the tree line. There were no trails or property corners nearby, so why had someone put a blaze on the tree. I walked to the base of the tree picturing in my mind which direction the blaze faced when the tree had been standing. I tentatively stepped in that direction a half dozen times. I scanned the trees around me and found two more trees with blazes. They weren't easy to find. Someone had painted over the raw white of the blaze with black paint. Anybody hiking past probably wouldn't notice them, but I did since I was looking for them. I positioned myself where I could see all three blazes. As I looked at the ground, an unnatural ring of rocks caught my eye. I pulled the top couple of rocks from the ring and found a three-inch-diameter Forest Service brass cap, which I knew from experience was on top of a three-foot-long steel pipe. The Forest Service set them to denote the Forest Service property line.

My first thought was the Forest Service had screwed up and put the brass cap in the wrong place. I looked at a ninety-degree angle from the fence and could see where an overgrown path ran through the trees. Was this the mix-up in property line Irwin mentioned when he'd shown me the job during my interview? I wasn't sure how that could be since I was over a quarter mile from my new fence line. I ducked between the wires on the fence and followed the brushed trail through the woods.

This line hadn't been brushed out as wide as the trail I had put my fence along. It showed more finesse and precision. Instead of trees cut down, often only the branches had been trimmed off one side of the tree. Definitely, whoever had brushed this property line didn't do the new fence line. The trees ended before I had gone a mile and across the hillside I saw the shed. I took a good back bearing along the trail behind me then scanned the ground near the fence running up the hill by the shed. Carefully, I walked across the open hillside, suddenly aware I was out in the open. Anyone who saw me might wonder what the hell I was doing since I obviously wasn't working on the fence. I found another pile of rocks by the fence about thirty yards uphill from the shed. This rock pile was smaller than the other one and a quick look at the bottom of the rocks revealed another Forest Service brass cap.

If there had been an error on the property line, why hadn't the Forest Service removed the old brass caps? Self-conscious at being in the open, I hurried back the way I had come until I stood by the fence near the fallen tree with the rucksack of coiled wire.

I humped the pack up the fence line despite my hurt toe. About halfway there, I noticed another brushed-out line heading out at ninety degrees from the fence. I slowed my pace, watching my left for more trails. I spotted one more before I reached the fence I had torn down. Following it for two hundred yards into the woods, I found a bent metal fence post stuck in the ground. Not only had there been a fence one hundred yards short of the correct property line, but it looked like there had been another fence two hundred yards short of the correct property line.

I made my way to the fence and then to the corner of my new fence. I cast around in a circular search pattern looking for a brass cap or bearing tree but didn't find any. I counted my steps from my corner post to the old fence then spent ten minutes looking for a brass cap without finding anything.

I walked down the fence, counting my steps, watching for a break in the trees indicating another old fence line. By the time I reached the brass cap, I had counted four old fence lines. I squatted in the shade to think about everything, trying to put on my Pete thinking cap. Pete might be a dickhead, but he was an excellent tracker of human behavior. If the property line had been mixed up, why hadn't the Forest Service removed the brass caps? Why just cover them up? More importantly, the four old fence lines indicated the mistake had occurred over and over again.

I could think of only one plausible solution. The brass caps represented the real property boundary. The precision of that line through the trees indicated the people who had cut that line knew what they were doing. I remembered seeing the old transit mounted to the wooden tripod in the shed and the well-used Stilh chainsaw wrapped in a pair of mangled saw chaps. My guess was a survey crew had put in the original line. Irwin had been creating the new property lines over the years and Cherylann had been hiring high school kids to "fix" the property line error, which was probably why Cherylann didn't want me telling anybody what kind of work I did for her on the ranch. Why would she go to all the work to shift her property line farther onto Forest Service land? It wasn't good pasture and it didn't look like she was logging any of the trees, so she wasn't getting any return on her investment.

Should I tell the Forest Service? The Forest Service hadn't ever been nice to me. They hassled my dad every year about having a wood permit for the exact number of cords of firewood we collected each summer to heat our home in the winter. One summer, they cited my dad for cutting down a "bird" tree when we were getting firewood. They rolled into our backyard one time and forced Dad to put out a campfire we were roasting marshmallows on because they said the fire danger was high, even though the campfire was in a rock-ringed pit surrounded by two feet of dirt and then an acre of wet green grass.

Nope, the Forest Service hadn't ever done anything for me and telling Uncle Sam about the expanding fence line would certainly piss Cherylann off. I decided I didn't feel that big of an urge to report what I thought Cherylann was doing. There was also a chance there really was a property line error and I'd be stirring up trouble for Cherylann for no reason. Sometimes being like Pete might make life more complicated. I decided to accept what Cherylann and Irwin had told me at face value.

My wounded leg ached from squatting and I rose slowly to full height before picking up the rucksack. I didn't want to be late for my meeting with Cherylann. Holding the pack against my lower back with my hands so it wouldn't bounce around, I jogged across the real property line to the shed.

Cherylann was picking beans in her garden and dropping them in a white five-gallon bucket. She rose from her knees, dusting the black dirt off her blue jeans. She wore a light-blue halter top and when she leaned over to dust off her jeans, I remembered how attractive she was even though she was old enough to be my mother. I couldn't figure out what a beautiful woman like Cherylann saw in Irwin. I mean he was a nice guy, but he did drink a lot, and had that funny potbelly beer gut.

"The fence completed?" she asked.

"Yes, ma'am," I replied then wondered if the ma'am would offend her because she might think that meant I thought she was old. "I put in the fence posts, ran the wire, tight but not too tight, and pulled the wire from the old fence."

Irwin came walking from behind the chicken coop pushing a wheelbarrow full of what smelled like chicken shit. "I left the fence posts for Irwin since he needs something to do around here to earn his keep," I added.

Cherylann favored me with a smile and Irwin coughed out "Wise ass" then grinned at me.

"I heard you won the fight with Pete," Irwin said. "Now the whole damn town is pissed they lost their starting quarterback for the year." His grin faded to a soft smile. "At least that's what I heard at the Valley Bar."

I shrugged my shoulders. "Yeah, I can't seem to win even when I do." I grinned at Irwin. "Thanks for the tips on fighting. Worked pretty much the way we practiced. Couldn't have done it without you."

"Well now, you just keep that little slice of news to yourself or they might eighty-six me from the Valley Bar for helping you."

"They can't eighty-six you, Irwin, you're their best customer," Cherylann interjected.

Irwin and I turned to Cherylann. I forced my eyes off her tank top to her face, but I'm sure Irwin didn't even try.

"I'll go with Irwin tonight after we finish our chores and walk the fence to inspect your work. If everything is satisfactory, I'll send you a check in the mail. If it's not done to my satisfaction, I'll give you a call and have you come make it satisfactory."

The smile left my face at the thought of having to return to do more work, but I knew the fence was good. If Cherylann wanted to play games about how well it was done, I'd deal with that when and if it happened. "Sure."

"Just to be clear," she said. "You're late getting the fence done, so you won't be getting the bonus."

I had an impulse right then to say something witty about noticing how the fence line had been moved multiple times and their property line error must be really weird. I'd hint that maybe if I got the bonus I wouldn't need to stop in at the West Fork Ranger Station. Instead, I said, "I got it. No bonus." I cleared my throat. "I just want to say thanks, Cherylann, for giving me the opportunity and to thank Irwin for helping me with Pete."

"Anytime, Scabs," Irwin said.

"You're welcome," Cherylann said then added, "Now that you're no longer an employee, I don't expect to see you on my property. No showing up with buddies to shoot gophers. No turning the shed into a love shack for you and some bubble-gum-snapping teenage hussy."

I gave that some thought then said. "I'd like to come visit with Irwin sometimes, maybe get some more advice on fighting and how to pick up hot chicks."

Cherylann looked at me and it felt like knitting needles poking into my face, but underneath it, I thought I detected a slightly amused frown. "Call first. Don't just show up. Irwin has lots of chores to do. He can't just be playing all the time."

I nodded and turned to head for the door when Cherylann called after me, "Tell your dad I said hello."

I made my way through the front yard to the Courier walking past the spot where Cherylann had me drive the metal fencepost into her lawn. That seemed like so long ago. The Courier started at the flick of the key and I drove down the gravel driveway wondering if my check from Cherylann would be enough to pay for my hospital bill. When I left her driveway for the West Fork Road, I started thinking about plan B. HL-200

Chapter Twenty-One

A few weeks later, I put plan B in motion. I got up early, scraped the frost off the windshield of the Courier and drove to Missoula telling my folks I was going to visit Jenny. I was going to visit Jenny but after I went to Missoula. I'd only spoken to Jenny the one time on the phone after I'd gotten shot. I had thought she might call me after the fight with Pete, but I hadn't heard anything from her.

I didn't want to start school with things unsettled between us. My guess was Jenny had already broken up with me but just didn't have the nerve to tell me to my face. I planned to drop by the video store and confirm it before school started. I didn't want to end up having the breakup conversation in the school hallway with everyone watching.

I made it to Missoula and navigated Malfunction Junction on the first try. I parked in front of a squat building and throwing back my shoulders, I went inside to put plan B into motion. The receptionist gave me a clipboard with a pen attached to it by some paracord. When I finished filling it out, she told me her supervisor would be with me in a few minutes. I waited as patiently as I could keeping my hands in my lap, trying to sit up straight, not my usual slump, until the receptionist told me to take the clipboard into the recruiter's office. She certainly didn't look like she was in the military, more like she was someone's grandma. The kind of grandma who sipped whisky neat and let you smoke in the house.

The recruiter looked just like I had expected him to with close-cropped hair and a large head stuck on top of bigger shoulders. He wore a military uniform with a row of medals across his chest. When I handed him the clipboard, I saw his right hand ended above the wrist and had been replaced with a silver hook. The hook opened like scissors pulling the clipboard from my startled hand. He grunted as he waved toward a wooden chair facing his desk. I again sat quietly, trying not to tap my toe, showing off my best posture.

Was I really ready to spend the next four years of my life taking orders and acting like a petrified hunk of wood? The alternative was spending the next four years trying to save money for college while working in Darby. I knew I could do some odd jobs with my dad, maybe get on the local fire crew if the summer was drier than normal. The lumber mill had announced it was laying off ten workers due to lack of raw material, so it was highly unlikely I could get a job there.

I couldn't escape the fact that, if I stayed, I would spend the money I earned as fast as I made it or almost as fast. At the end of four years, I'd be married, have at least one kid, and be struggling to make house payments, just like my folks had been doing ever since I was born. I didn't see anything wrong with that, especially if Jenny and I were still together. And my guess was that in ten years that was what I would want to be doing. But right now, something inside me wanted to explore, to see more of the world. Darby would always be there when I was done exploring. Nope, being in the Marines might involve a lot of behavioral bullshit, but at the end of four years, I'd have money for college in a savings account. Plus, they might even send me somewhere fun where all the women went topless, like Greece. A year ago, I had believed Pete when he told me women all went topless on the beaches in Greece. Now I thought that might not be true. But it would still be fun to go to the beach and see the ocean.

The plaque on the recruiter's desk read Lt. Ronald Lee. He cleared his throat then asked, "What's the mission of the Corp?"

I decided to go with what I had read on the pamphlet they had distributed at school. "To defend the people of the United States at home and abroad," I quoted.

"That's close enough," he acknowledged. "To quote Lieutenant General Leslie E. Brown, 'our mission is to fight and win, and we must do it better than anyone in the world.'" His hook opened and the clipboard slipped onto the pile of papers on his desk. He brought his hands together like he was crossing his fingers together, but he only had the hook on the one hand making it look like he was thinking of snipping off the tips of his other fingers. "And what role do you want to play in fulfilling that mission?" His black eyes stared at me and I got the sense he didn't think I was going to be good at helping.

I must have taken too long to answer because he gruffly said, "What's the matter, son, cat got your tongue?" He snapped up the clipboard and began thumbing through the pages.

"I get good grades," I said, my voice sounding a little squeaky in my head. I cleared my throat before adding, "I learn fast."

"That is good news," the recruiter boomed, his tone overly sarcastic. "Do you think that's how we beat the Germans? We just let them know real polite like that we were fast learners and they fell over dead. Shit flies in the Air Force, son, but this is the Marines. C'mon, give me something to work with."

I stared at him trying not to flinch from the volume of his words. I fell back on the only thing I did that had any connection to fighting. "I go shoot with my dad, one shot every week, to keep our guns sighted in, and each fall, we hunt deer. I'm a pretty good shot. My dad says I'm better than him."

"Son, it's Montana, everybody hunts. And so your daddy says you're a good shot. What father doesn't tell his little pissant son he's a good shot? Give me some details. What weapon do you shoot?"

Good, a question I actually knew the answer to. I drew in a breath and made sure my voice didn't crack. "A Winchester Model 70 .30-06 loaded with 173-grain match grade bullets."

"All right," he responded. "You got my interest. Most kids only know the caliber of gun they shoot, not the manufacturer, let alone the weight of bullet." His eyes swept over me again as if reappraising my physical appearance. "Why such a heavy bullet? I use 150-grain soft points in my .308."

"Dad says that the extra lead makes the bullet longer, giving it a higher ballistic coefficient, making it inherently more accurate especially at longer ranges." The confidence climbed in my voice and I was able to make steady eye contact through my answer but then dropped my eyes as I finished.

"Ballistic coefficient," the recruiter mumbled, his words coming out as if it was one word broken by syllables. "How far away are these deer you shoot?"

Another easy question. I forced my spine a little straighter before responding. "We go down to my grandpa's ranch on the East Fork below Conner. We shoot out of the hayloft so we have a real-"

"I asked how far, not where," interrupted the recruiter.

"Two hundred fifty to three hundred yards. Dad won't shoot farther than three hundred on game, but in practice, we always shoot at three hundred yards." I sucked in a tight breath.

He looked me in the face and his lips moved even though he didn't speak the words out loud. I didn't catch it all, but I did pick up "Winchester," "173 grains", and "one shot."

His hook gripped the clipboard with a click, and wetting his only thumb with his tongue, he flipped pages on the clipboard. His eyes shifted back and forth as he read through the information. He looked up and studied my face. A change came over him, almost like a relaxing of tension in his body, though his eyes didn't hold any kindness. "Why didn't you tell me you're Archie's son?"

My mind raced. Did he know my dad because somehow they had met in town, or did he know my dad through the Marines? If Pete was right and my dad was a draft dodger, maybe I just landed my dad in some hot water. At the very least, Lieutenant Ron would throw my application in the trash. I should have never come here. My mind raced trying to come up with some answer that didn't end badly for my dad. I tried not to cower or look upset.

"Do you know my dad?" I managed to ask.

The recruiter sat the clipboard on his desk and leaned forward. "Only met your father a couple of times. I doubt he would remember me. I knew about him though. Every Marine in Nam knew about your father. I met him at a forward fire base where he was doing an in-country sniper training."

A puzzled look covered my face and before I could stop my mouth I said. "My dad was never in Vietnam."

The recruiter shook his head. "No son. Name matches and now that I know, I can see him in your looks. He was a little slimmer, but you're definitely his son. Besides, a Winchester Model 70 .30-06 with 173-grain bullets is the exact weapon and bullet your father used as a sniper. And only snipers do a one shot each week sight in."

Disbelief must have been written all over my face because Lieutenant Ron added, "Each week when you shoot, your dad writes down in a notebook the temperature, the wind, the humidity, where the bullet hits, where the shooter felt the shot landed, and any adjustment made to the scope. Only a sniper does that."

That was exactly what my father did.

"Your dad never told you he was a sniper?" the recruiter asked. The look on my face must have been answer enough. "He was one of the best," Lieutenant Ron continued. "I saw him and Carlos Hathcock compete against each other. Three shots at an eight-hundred-yard target, closest to the bull's-eye wins. Archie beat Carlos by half an inch. Carlos wanted a rematch, so they moved the target out to a thousand yards. Carlos won that by an inch, but Archie's shot was within a hand of the center of the target. "

Lieutenant Ron put the clipboard on his desk carefully. "Archie had more kills than Carlos at that time. Then your dad was injured when the Huey carrying him and his spotter went down. I was with the rescue aircraft that went after them. Charlie got to the crash before us and when we arrived, Archie was the only one alive and he was wounded. After that, they sent him back to the world and Carlos went on to become the greatest Marine sniper of all time."

My brain whirled. If Dad was a sniper in Vietnam, why hadn't he told me about it? I felt proud and angry at the same time. It didn't make any sense. One minute, I thought of my Dad as a draft-dodging coward and in the next, I'm told he was an extremely talented sniper. I was beginning to think nothing in my life was what I thought it was.

"My dad told me that during Vietnam he was sent to Canada as a spy to find draft dodgers and bring them back to the US." I gave a slight shrug. "Why wouldn't he tell me about being a sniper?"

Lieutenant Ron pushed back in his chair a little, his rigid bearing relaxing a tiny bit. "Son. I had to kill people in Nam. That's what Marines do. All the people I shot were either getting ready to shoot me, shooting at me, or had just finished shooting at me. But it still rests heavy on my soul. A sniper now. They shoot people from a long ways away. And if you're a good sniper, like your dad was, well, those people are just standing around talking to a friend or hunkering down by a bush to take a shit, or maybe sitting enjoying a cup of coffee. That makes you a hero in the Corp, but to some civilians, that might make you a monster." He paused for a few seconds then added, "As far as catching draft dodgers, I never heard of the Corp doing that, but I don't see why your dad would lie about it."

Lieutenant Ron straightened in his chair, pulling a paper from a folder on his cluttered desk. "You're too young now to join without a parent's signature. Take this home and get one of your parents to sign, then come back. We'll get you set up to leave for basic training as soon as you graduate high school next spring. I'll leave it up to you which parent signs." He paused for a second. "Or just wait until you're eighteen and come back."

He stood up, so I stood up. I wanted to ask more questions about Vietnam, but I could sense Lieutenant Ron was done talking. I also got his point about which parent to have sign my enlistment papers. My dad might not be thrilled about me joining, but then again, I doubted my mom would be delighted either. Next Wednesday, when we went to shoot, I would ask Dad about it. It would certainly make my time in the Marines tougher to have to live up to the notoriety of my father. I cringed inwardly as I realized I had told Lieutenant Ron I was a better shot than my dad. The Marines, instead of an escape from being a draft dodger's son, was starting to feel like living under the shadow of a legend.[HL-210]

I thought a lot on the drive home from Missoula. I barely remembered slowing down as Highway 93 bisected each little town along the way. Lolo, Florence, Stevensville, and Victor slipped past with my thoughts mired in small towns. How everybody knew everything about each other but they really didn't know anything. They only knew what they wanted to know. Or some weird mix-up of that thought. Everyone thought Pete was a cool guy, but he was really a terrible asshole who screwed his best friend's girl. Everyone thought my dad was a draft dodger, but instead, he was a known figure in the Marine Corps while serving in Vietnam. Had he told the story about going to Canada just to manipulate the small-town gossip mill? And what about my mom? What was the truth there?

Woodside Crossing rushed past with the sign pointing east that said Corvallis. On cue, "never, never week," flashed through my brain. Our football coach had drilled that phrase into my head. Whenever we played Corvallis, it was never, never week. We never, never lost to Corvallis. Maybe this year with Pete not playing at quarterback they might lose. I geared down going through Hamilton, glancing over to see if anyone I knew was at A&W.

Pete said my mom was a prostitute who gave handjobs at the end of massages for extra cash. I hadn't believed him at first, but it did make sense of the comments the men made about my mom. Or maybe it wasn't really the truth, just a rumor truth. One person made it up, then another told it like it was the truth, then pretty soon, everyone in town had heard it, and then the snide comments began.

While I could see myself asking Dad about being a sniper, there was no way I could talk to my mom about handjobs. The truth would have to remain a mystery. I decided that I didn't care what the truth was. As far as I was concerned, my mom was just a masseuse and people who made snide comments about it were assholes.

I slowed coming down the hill by the turnoff to Forest Hill Road entering Lick Creek turn while watching for a moose that had been feeding in the cattail ponds by the road for the last month. Hitting a moose in the Courier would probably kill me. Darby rolled up in front of me with its single stoplight that had never been turned on hanging from a wire across Highway 93. I slowed on the opposite side of town and turned right just before Husky gas station and after the laundromat.

I parked on the laundromat side of the street, and taking a deep breath, I climbed out of the Courier. A woman turned the corner of the building with a white laundry basket in her hands. I stepped off the sidewalk between two cars to let her pass.

"Hey, Scabs, long time no seeum."

I looked up at Sally Parker. She looked a lot more like a woman than a high-school girl dressed in a green tube top and a matching pair of shorts.

Chapter Twenty-Two

I stepped back up on the sidewalk by her. "Hey, Sally, haven't seen you since school." I looked at the laundry basket but didn't really look at what was in it. The Parkers had their own washing machine, so I was a little confused why Sally would be in town doing laundry.

She must have caught my look. "The washing machine keeps leaking water out the bottom. Dad's working on it, but I'm waitressing at the Knob tonight and needed a couple of clean things."

"Great." I really didn't know what else to say. Sally's eyes were amazingly blue in the sunshine with a splash of freckles across her nose. I couldn't help but think about what Pete had told me about her. Was that something true, or just rumor true, or Pete trying to get me to leave Jenny for Sally so he could date Jenny?

"I hear you're not playing football."

I nodded. "Yeah." I didn't know what to say when people brought it up. I got kidnapped and shot and had to build fence for Cherylann. It sucks but what you gonna do? People gave me funny looks when I said that. It occurred to me that Sally didn't play girls' basketball or cheerlead for football. It seemed like kids either played all sports in school or played none. Sally was the rare person who only played two sports. She was a cheerleader for boys' basketball in the winter, and she ran the one-hundred-yard dash for track in the spring.

She adjusted the laundry basket to rest on her hip. I reached out and took it from her. "Here, let me carry it to your car." Turned out I was blocking Sally from getting to her Chevrolet Citation. If I hadn't been staring into her eyes, I might have noticed. As I waited for her to open the door to the back seat, I realized the basket held a bunch of women's panties. Picturing Mrs. Parker's ass in my mind, I decided they belonged to Sally and that made me wonder how Sally must look wearing them. I sat the basket in the back seat lengthwise so it wouldn't tip over.

"So, my brother Perry is in town and my folks are letting him take the boat to Painted Rocks on Sunday. You should come up and do some water skiing with us."

Waterskiing indicated that swimsuits would probably be involved. "Sounds awesome."

She smiled. "We'll be at Slate Creek Bay as long as it isn't too crowed. If we're not there, check at the very end of the lake."

I thought fast. "How about you ride up with me and that way, I won't get lost."

Her smile widened. "Great. I'll have Perry drop me at your house around ten in the morning, and we can follow him. We can talk about how you got shot, give me the inside story not just the bullshit floating around town."

My smile faltered. "Sure, sounds like a plan."

Sally gave me a quick hug, her blonde hair smelling like strawberries. I watched her back out and waved as she pulled away. I took a deep breath then let it out slowly. That had been exactly what I needed to give myself the courage to face Jenny. I had a date lined up with Sally, well, sort of a date, and I was not a guy who dated two women at the same time.

I made it to the sidewalk past the laundromat door. A white Toyota pickup headed north with the windows rolled down letting the chunky guitar riff of 38 Special's "Hold on Loosely" jump from the cab into the street. The driver met my gaze, reached over and cranked the volume up, then gave me a thumbs-up as he went by. I paused in front of the door to the video store to square my shoulders. The door pushed forward, smacking into me. I stepped back as none other than Diana walked out the door holding a brown movie case in her hand.

"Scabs," she said. "Nice to"—her face broke into a smile—"see you."

I smiled back, glancing at the sling holding her left arm against her side. She looked different wearing flip-flops, a jean skirt, and a halter top. She still had on her nice sunglasses and an Orvis ball cap.

I nodded at her shoulder. "How's the shoulder?"

Her smile faded. "Everybody asks that. It's just their way of trying to find out what happened." She gave me a quick smile.

I chuckled. "Everybody asked me about my leg for the same reason."

"It's healing up," she answered. "I'll be shipshape in a few weeks." She looked me up and down quickly then stepped out of the way of the door. "Visiting Jenny?"

I nodded, wanting to tell her I was here to end it with Jenny, but I didn't want to tell Diana that before I told

Jenny. Two ladies walked past us then into Honey Hardware. They giggled as they went through the door, casting looks back at us. All the gossip about me around town wasn't anything compared to what was flying around about Diana.

"You hear anything about Seth?" I stepped out of the middle of the sidewalk against the storefront by Diana.

"He's pleading to assault using a deadly weapon to avoid any of the kidnapping charges. His dad's attorney tells him he probably won't do any time in prison, just probation."

"How's Adam?"

"Part of the plea deal was Seth had to give full custody of Adam to his mom." Her voice dropped lower as she spoke. "I wrote him a letter to see how he was doing." She frowned. "The bitch sent it back unopened," she spat.

Before I could stop myself, the question I had wanted to ask Diana ever since the last night at the camp by Myth Lake tumbled over my teeth. "Did you and Seth go all the way?"

She smiled at me patiently, like my mom did sometimes when I asked a stupid question. She stepped closer to me. "Short answer is yes." She reached out and put her good hand on my arm. "Do you want the longer version?"

She stepped across the sidewalk and opened the door to her old truck. She hopped into the truck then gave me the "Are you coming?" look. As I hopped in, she slid over to the middle of the bench seat but not any farther. I slammed the door wondering what kind of looks we would get for sitting along Main Street on just one side of the cab. Probably less looks than talking about Diana's sex life on the sidewalk. Diana started talking in her slow, hesitant way, and I mentally forced myself to adjust my speed of conversation slower.

"Seth and his dad came for an elk hunt two seasons ago. Right after I graduated high school."

I remembered Diana telling me about wanting to fall in love with one of her father's rich dudes.

"He was super nice to me. Telling me how in shape and pretty I was. How good I was in the woods." Her voice caught a little. "I'd never had a guy pay that much attention to me or flatter me like that. It was really nice." She sighed. "I snuck out to the bunkhouse and we made out before he left." Another pause. "Then he came back last spring for a fly-fishing trip without his dad. He told me it was just to see me. He flirted really hard. My dad pulled me aside and told me no fraternizing with our clients. He sent me home but not before I agreed to meet Seth after his fishing trip." She turned on the seat, facing me putting her hand behind me on the seat. "I knew he was divorced and had a kid and was older, but it was so nice to have someone treat you like you were the prettiest girl on earth."

I agreed. "It's nice to be liked."

"We met down at Jackson, south of Wisdom, for a weekend. We had sex. And then he left. He never lied to me or told me he loved me or that he wanted to date after. I knew it was just a wild, fun weekend. I didn't hear from him again until this spring." Her voice hitched and her eyes filled with tears.

I felt a big impulse to find Seth and beat the shit out of him.

"He called this spring saying he was having a custody battle with his ex-wife. He wanted to hide out for a few weeks with Adam. He asked if I had any ideas where he could go. So, I told him about the String of Lakes and Wolverine Creek Campground. He was going to stay at the campground if he thought it was safe then retreat to the lakes if too many people were around the campground. Either way, I was supposed to bring some food for him and Adam, since he didn't have much backpacking food. He didn't want to come into town. He called me from the Sula Store telling me he was heading to the lakes but didn't want to leave his car at the trailhead and really needed the food."

A logging truck went by with a full load and even though he was only doing twenty-five mph, it shook the truck. "You were just trying to help a friend. Anybody would have done it," I said, trying to be comforting.

I didn't have a clue Diana was helping Seth, but Pete seemed to have it figured out right from the start. Maybe I was just too trusting, or maybe people with ulterior motives guiding their actions looked for it in others. I had to ask even though I wasn't sure I was going to like the answer. "So that day by Trout Lake, when you said if I'd made a move you wouldn't have stopped me, was that just to keep me from figuring out you were helping Seth, that's all?"

Diana didn't answer right away and I realized in most people it would be because they were thinking up a lie. But with Diana, I knew she was just trying to organize her words. "I didn't know if Seth and I were going to get back together. I got close to you to keep Pete from hitting on me because I could tell by how he was staring at my tits he was going to. I also thought Seth might be watching and I wanted to make him a little jealous. And I think you're cute, Scabs. I think I might have kissed you, but it wouldn't have been anything more than that." She gave me a sad smile. "Kind of shitty of me, and I'm sorry."

Diana shook her head slightly while dropping her gaze to the floorboards. "Seth never intended to hurt anyone." Her voice completely cracked and tears streamed from both eyes. "Now everybody thinks I'm a slut helping a horrible man kidnap a kid." Her crying became louder, loud enough anyone walking by on the street would hear it. Her arm came off the back of the seat and she buried her face into my shoulder.

I didn't have any idea what I was supposed to do. Diana's body melded into mine, her breasts pressing into my side, as her body shook from the tears. The closeness caused my body to react in a very ungentlemanly way and I tried to focus on what I should say to help Diana. In addition, my brain wanted to drive a steel fence post through Seth's chest and two feet into the ground for hurting Diana. Another part of me wanted to take her into my arms and kiss her.

With so many conflicting thoughts, I didn't do anything. I just sat there saying, "Hey it's okay. I don't think you're a slut." It was probably the dumbest thing I could have said. I focused on different ways to kill Seth in an attempt to control my body.

Diana quit crying after a minute, the flood washing away as quickly as it had come. She got tissues out of her glove box and blew her nose. A couple walked by on the sidewalk, trying not to show they were staring at us.

Diana threw the used tissue to the floorboards. "Dad got hold of Seth and told him that if he ever had any contact with me he'd kill him and bury him in the mountains where no one would find his body."

That sounded like a really good plan to me and while I doubted Diana's dad would need any help, I would be glad to lend a hand if he needed it.

"He told me if I ever contacted Seth he would never speak to me again. Told me I couldn't work for him anymore since he couldn't trust me around his clients." She gave a half snort. "Even my dad thinks I'm some sort of slut."

"So, what are you going to do now?"

Diana wiped her face with another tissue drying the last remnants of tears. "Already doing it. Mom sold the land she inherited from her dad up Dixon Creek. Enough money for me to make it through college if I work part-time during school and full-time in the summers. I enrolled down in Dillon. I just came home this weekend to pick up a few more things for my dorm room."

"College, that's cool. What are you studying?" I asked, happy to turn the subject away from sad things like Seth.

"I'm going to teach grade-schoolers, or at least that's

what Mom signed me up for."

"I'm happy for you Diana." I really was happy for her. I liked the idea of getting away from your past and having the opportunity to explore life while leaving behind all the stupid things you did growing up.

"What about you, Scabs? What are you going to do now? I heard you beat the shit out of Pete. Didn't think you had that in you. Good for you." She gave me a soft punch with her good arm on the chin.

"Yeah, I beat the shit out of Pete and now the whole town is mad at me for taking away the starting quarterback."

Diana held her middle finger up pointing it out the windshield at no one in particular. "Fuck this town's obsession with football."

I didn't dislike the town's obsession with high-school sports. I thought it kind of cool everyone took an interest. If you made a great play, even in a junior varsity game, you were sure to hear about it the next week. The clerk at People's Market might say, "nice catch last weekend," while you were buying groceries. Or at the Knob, the bartender might give you a Roy Rogers on the house because you blocked a punt. I tried to move the conversation on before someone noticed Diana giving the one-finger wave.

"I've been thinking about joining the Marines, you know, get out of town, see the world."

Diana nodded. "Yeah, I think you'd make a great Marine. You've got some good underlying hero qualities."

I smiled at her absurdity and she smiled back at me. It

suddenly felt stifling in the cab of the truck.

"You still going out with Jenny?"

I hadn't wanted to say anything until I was actually sure I was broke up with Jenny, but looking into Diana's eyes I said, "I was just on my way to tell her I'm not interested anymore when I bumped into you."

Diana nodded at the door to the video store. "I've probably kept you long enough. Jenny's probably wondering what you're doing in the slut's truck."

I didn't know how to answer. If anybody was a slut, it was Jenny for screwing Pete, but my guess was Jenny probably did think Diana was a slut. I slid out the passenger door. "I don't think you're a slut." I smiled at Diana as she slipped behind the steering wheel.

She smiled at me holding up the brown rectangular case. "My mom went over to Melrose for the weekend to visit my dad. I've got the house to myself. I could use some company." She wiggled the case. "I rented *Risky Business*. Want to come over tonight and watch it with me? I'll even make popcorn."

My mind drifted back to sitting in the bear grass with Diana wearing just her bra and shorts. "What time does the movie start?"

Diana favored me with a full-blown, teeth-baring smile. "Previews start at eight o'clock sharp."

I closed the truck door. "I'll be there in time for the previews." I turned to face the video store as Diana drove off.[HL-220]

I had a movie date with a hot older chick and a date at the lake with a hot younger chick. So much for me only dating one woman at a time. It was probably time for me to confirm that Jenny, the hot chick my own age, wasn't going out with me anymore. I needed to close the barn door on that whole relationship. The last thing I needed was to be dating three girls at the same time.

Chapter Twenty-Three

The little bell on the door jingled as it swung shut behind me. Keeping my head and determination up, I navigated straight to the checkout counter. Old Man Henderson was renting a VCR and a stack of movies, enough of them I wondered how he could possibly watch all of them in one weekend. I mean, he'd have to watch one movie right after the other in one long gorge of Hollywood. I held back a good six feet not wanting to crowd him as he tended to get perturbed if anyone invaded his personal space. I spotted *The Man from Snowy River* and *Silverado* in his stack of movies. It looked like it was a Wild West weekend at the Hendersons.

Once Old Man Henderson paid for his rental in cash, Jenny helped him carry the VCR out to his truck. When she came back through the door, her face lit up in a gigantic smile.

"Scabs, I am so happy to see you." She called over to her younger sister, "Jessica, watch the register for a minute, would you?"

Jessica sat in the only chair in the store behind the counter watching the movie playing on the big-screen TV. She rolled her eyes at Jenny and made kissing noises with her mouth. Jenny ignored her sister and pulled me by the hand into the little room where they kept all the VCRs and VHS tapes. Once we were out of sight of the customers, she enveloped me in a warm hug. She gave me a kiss on the lips that quickly turned into a French kiss. I pulled back, not sure what in the hell was going on.

Jenny murmured in my ear, "I'm sorry I didn't call sooner, but I was just having so much trouble deciding, and then when I saw you standing in the door, I knew I'd made up my mind."

She pulled back to arm's length, a big smile on her face that flickered for a moment then came back on even stronger. "Was that Diana you were talking with outside?"

Since Diana had just come out of the video store and Jenny had seen me outside, then I was a little confused as to how she didn't know exactly who I was talking with outside. "Yeah, we were comparing hospital stories."

"It doesn't matter," Jenny said as if I had just been caught doing something wrong. "What's important is that I have chosen you."

I blinked, a long blink, while I tried to understand what she was saying. She had chosen me. For what?

Jenny, seeing my confusion, pulled me closer. "I pick you over Pete to be my boyfriend."

She kissed me on the lips, pushing with her face against mine, and I felt her tongue dart into my mouth. I tried to be polite and kiss her back, but I couldn't concentrate on kissing and deciphering what she had said to me. I drew back. "We aren't breaking up?"

She laughed. "Don't get a big head. I mean, it was pretty close, but after you beat Pete up, I had to decide. Did I want to date an offensive lineman or the badass that beat up the starting quarterback?" She gave me a demure giggle. "When I thought of it that way, it was a pretty easy decision."

This breakup was not going at all like I had thought it would. I'd imagined me asking Jenny if we were done, her saying yes, and me heading to Ole's to get three hot dogs for a dollar. Jenny pulled me even closer, her breasts pushing against me. She nuzzled into my neck and began to nibble on my earlobe. There was a part of me that just wanted to keep my mouth shut. Well, not keep my mouth shut, but not say anything at all. From somewhere in my brain, I found my voice. "We're still dating?"

Jenny held me at arm's length and smiled at me, but this time, it began to thin out a little. "We're not dating right now, but I heard you got paid for your summer job. So how about I ask my mom to come in and cover for me and I'll let you treat me to dinner at the Wagon Wheel." She stepped back and pulled up her shirt and bra, flashing me her breasts. "After dinner, I'd say we are dating again."

A mean part of me reared its head on my left shoulder and whispered in my ear that what I should do was play along with Jenny, take her to dinner, then see how far I could go with her, and then, after all that, dump her on her doorstep telling her I didn't ever want to date her.

"What about you screwing Pete? I'm supposed to forget that?"

"In a way, it's kind of your fault."

"How is it my fault?" I kept my voice even, trying to sound like I thought that was a possibility.

"If you hadn't been so stuck on keeping your virginity vow, I'd have been doing it with you. Then you let Pete drive me home from the graduation party after I'd had a couple of beers. I mean, it's almost like you wanted me to sleep with Pete."

My eyelids were pulled back so far in surprise my eyes were on the verge of popping out of my skull. I did a hard blink and then my eyelids fluttered a few times as I tried to comprehend. "Pete said you guys did it a bunch of times." I couldn't quite keep my tone neutral since I had spoken through clenched teeth.

Jenny put her hands on her hips, looking like she might stomp her foot at me. "We didn't do it a bunch of times." She slammed the heel of her left foot into the faded brown carpet. "Why are we talking about this? I told you I picked you to be my boyfriend."

I registered that her denial didn't close the door on her and Pete having done the deed more than once. I didn't know what to say or do at this point. My gut hurt and my hands itched.

Jenny must have sensed I didn't believe her and she stepped forward taking my right hand in both of hers. "Scabs, you need me. My mom is going to buy out the other video store in town, and she's going to let me run that store once I graduate. We even talked about having a store in Conner so people don't have to drive all the way to Darby to rent movies. I'm going to be somebody in town. Once my folks retire, I'll run all three stores and we can do that together. If you stick with me, you can have a job for the rest of your life, and you won't just be the son of the town masseuse."

Jenny said masseuse, but I could tell by her tone she meant whore. Briefly, I pictured a life with Jenny. Always being grateful she picked me over Pete. Always being grateful she gave me a job. Always grateful she overlooked my horrible parents and chose me. Always spending my hard-earned money to take her to dinner. I couldn't put any of that into words, none that would make any sense. I pulled my hand free of her grip. "I don't want to be your boyfriend."

Her eyes flashed with anger and I thought for an instant she might slap me. Instead, she sobbed and reached for me, trying to hug me. "Scabs, don't do this? I think I love you."

I stepped out of her grasp, feeling as if I was treading water in an ocean of feelings. "Sorry, Jenny."

Tears rolled down her red face as she snapped at me, "You don't want to be with me, then who do you want? That slut Diana?"

"I'm not sure," I said. "I just don't want to be with you." I left the room wanting to make a nasty comment over my shoulder about Diana not being a slut like Jenny, but before I could think of anything, I bumped into Mr. Peck standing outside the room.

He looked down at me, his head cocked to the side. "Everything all right?"

I stepped in closer, right up against him, raising my head to look him in the eye. "You should be happy. I just broke up with Jenny." I stepped around him to head for the door pushing my shoulder into him realizing I half hoped he grabbed me. Because if he did I was going to wrap him up just like I did Pete, take him to the floor, and do my best to break his fucking arm.

Mr. Peck didn't grab my shoulder, but as I went out the door, he called after me, "Say hi to your mother for me."

The bell on the door tinkled as it closed behind me. Head down, I made my way around the laundromat to the Courier. I sat behind the wheel for a few minutes letting my anger for the Pecks subsided and the emotion from the breakup fade. I backed out into the street and then turned right heading out of town. HL-230

On the south side of town, I pulled into Ole's Beer Depot and filled the little truck with gas. I went inside and grabbed three hot dogs for a dollar. I felt bad about breaking up with Jenny, but I also knew she wasn't the girl for me. She didn't like camping, didn't like hunting, and didn't go fishing because she didn't even eat fish. We didn't have much in common, other than we both thought she was good-looking. I'd just have to keep dating until I found a woman that liked all those things.

I sat in the Courier eating the hot dogs. I wondered where the evening with Diana would lead. If something happened with Diana, which it probably wouldn't since I still intended to keep my vow to wait until after high school, but if something else happened, I might need to call off my trip to Painted Rocks with Sally. I finished my second dog and took a bite out of the third. Even if Diana and I ended up making out, she was leaving for Dillon and probably thought dating a high-schooler beneath her.

She had been dating an older divorced guy with a kid. Besides, nothing had even happened with Sally. We were just friends. I decided it would be okay if I didn't mention anything to Diana about going to the lake with Sally unless Diana asked me who I was hanging out with on Sunday.

Hot dogs done, I pulled onto Highway 93 and ran through the gears on the Courier, pushing the little engine to fifty-five. The first week of school was going to be interesting. Pete was right. I was naive, but that cocoon had been shed. School without that cocoon might be tough to take. Seeing Jenny in the halls wouldn't be fun. I didn't have any idea how things would go with Pete. Unlike the movies where two guys become best friends after fighting, I didn't think we'd be friends. Mostly because I'd ruined his chance to be the starting quarterback and I thought he was a dick.

I pulled into our driveway and parked alongside the shed. Mom had left the wheelbarrow in the path to the house, so I wheeled it underneath the lean-to on the side of the shed to keep it from filling with water if it rained. Parental consent paper in hand, I walked into the house hoping to slip past my parents and head straight upstairs to my bedroom, but they were waiting for me at the kitchen table.

Chapter Twenty-Four

At Dad's request, I sat at the table opposite them wondering what was going on and if I was in trouble. Had Pete or his parents said something to my folks? Worse, had Jenny's mom told my mom about the breakup? Mom thought the world of Jenny and I was dreading her reaction.

Before I worked up the courage to ask what they wanted, Dad said, "We've got some news for you."

The last time my dad had said that to me, my fake grandmother had died and I wondered if my fake grandpa had passed.

Mom must have read my thoughts. "Nobody died. It's good news, but it might be a little hard on you."

Dad cleared his throat. "I got a job. A good job making decent money, comes with retirement. It's just what we need. Might even be able to help you out with college a little bit."

I clenched my teeth realizing that some sort of terrible additional information was coming. "That's great," I said without any trace of enthusiasm in my voice.

"There's a bit of a downside," he said and my mind raced ahead of him, trying to figure out what he would say next. "The job is with the Alyeska Company."

I'd never heard of Alyeska and my dumbfounded look must have made that obvious. Mom spoke. "The job is in Alaska. Your father would be working for the company that manages the Alaska Pipeline as a security officer."

Well that was going to suck, Dad being away from home all the time. The job must pay an awful lot if he could afford to travel back and forth to Alaska. Another thought hit me. "You two aren't getting a divorce, are you?" I blurted out.

Mom shook her head and I think Dad almost laughed but caught himself. He smiled at me. "No, we are not getting a divorce."

Mom must have realized my confusion. "For the job, we would move to Fairbanks, Alaska." After a pause so she was sure I would understand, she added, "As a family."

Before I could say anything, Dad spoke, and I held my mouth shut. "We know it's your last year of school, so we talked to your fake grandad about you living with him during the school year. He said that would be fine. If you really want to stay here, we understand. But if you want to go with us, well then, we'll try to move as soon as possible so you wouldn't have to switch schools after a few weeks at Darby."

They both looked at me expectantly as I sat dumbfounded. Moving to Alaska. Pictures of jagged granite peaks covered with glaciers rising above miles of open tundra dotted with migrating caribou and rivers packed so full of spawning salmon you could walk across the water on their backs jumped into my head. No having to face Jenny in the hallway or look at Pete's stupid face.

No dumbasses making snide comments about my mom or my dad. And nobody calling me Scabs anymore. Maybe there would be more job opportunities for me. I could do something more than build fence for a summer job. Maybe in Alaska, I could figure out what I was supposed to do with my life.

"That sounds good," I said slowly. "Congratulations on the job, Dad, that's awesome."

"You don't need to decide right now," Mom said. "But we do need to know by tomorrow afternoon. Your father is calling the realtor to talk about renting a house. Housing is a little rough and expensive, so we need to know how many bedrooms."

Dad said, "Sorry for the short notice, but the company is in a hurry to get me there and I only found out a few days ago." School was only a few days away, just how fast could you get to Alaska? Maybe the schools started later there. Maybe I'd have to miss the first few weeks.

"'That's okay." I tried to sound like an adult, like someone who could deal with all these changes calmly. "I don't need any time to think about it. I want to move to Alaska with you."

Big smiles broke out around the table and there were a few more minutes of talk about when we would leave and how we were going to get there. Dad seemed to have everything all figured out for just finding out he got the job. I wondered if he had been looking for a job in Alaska for a while.

The phone rang and Mom went into the living room to answer it. Dad handed me an envelope. "This came for you in the mail. It's from Cherylann."

I waved off the envelope. "That's my check, Dad. I'll sign it, but I want you to take the money and use it for my hospital bill."

"That won't be necessary." Dad gave a half shrug, looking embarrassed. "I stopped by Marcus Daly today to work out a payment plan for your bill. They told me the entire bill had been paid in full."

That set me back on my heels for a few seconds trying to figure out who had paid it. I looked briefly at the envelope in my hand from Cherylann. Had she taken pity on me and paid the bill? That didn't quite seem to fit her. Maybe Pete's father had paid the bill since Pete had been the one who shot me. That wasn't too likely since Pete had his own medical bills to pay because of me. "Who paid it?"

"They said they weren't supposed to tell me, but I'd done a bathroom remodel for the lady in the billing office and she must have liked it because she let me know that Seth Armstrong paid your bill. He also paid Diana's."

That felt a little funny. I wasn't sure if I wanted to take charity from the guy who had kidnapped me. Dad must have read my thoughts. "Maybe he thought it would help him with his sentencing, or maybe he thinks he's atoning for his bad behavior. When people wrong you, often they don't know how to say sorry, so they say it in a way they understand, not always in a way you understand."

I turned that over in my head and it seemed to make sense. I grinned at Dad. "Kinda like don't look a gift horse in the mouth."

I left Dad at the table and headed upstairs to wash for dinner but ended up in my bedroom. I was surprised how small it felt after being out in the woods so much. I spotted my Swiss army knife on my little desk sitting by my Commodore 64. I cut open the envelope from Cherylann with the large blade. A short, handwritten note thanked me for my hard work and discretion. That was an interesting choice of words. She mentioned she needed help harvesting her garden and cleaning up the mess Irwin made in her chicken coop and suggested I could help her since I wasn't playing football and might need something to do with my extra time.

I pulled the consent form from my pocket and stared at it, not really seeing the print on the page, just a blur of words. I slowly tore it in half, then in half again.

Mom called to me from the bottom of the stairs, using my full name. That and her tone of voice indicated I had done something horribly wrong. Shit, the phone call. I dropped the pieces of the consent form in the trash and hurried to the top of the stairs.

Mom started chewing my ass as soon as she saw me. "I just got off the phone with Jenny's mother and she said that you broke up with Jenny."

I wanted to blurt out that she was screwing Pete and ask her what I was supposed to do. Instead, I said, "Mom I have my reasons."

Her icy gray eyes danced with lightning. "PT Thomas, you'd better have a damn good reason for breaking that girl's heart." HL-240

HL Miller Notes

HL-20. I was there that graduation day. I can close my eyes and see my grandfather standing under the smiling tiger painted over the doors to the gym, holding his bible, looking exactly how a man of God should look. Over by the unused tennis courts, sprigs of green grass surrounded the edges of the concrete, and of course, I remember seeing Kristi Harm and Jenny. The perfect day to graduate from high school.

Looking back years later, I'm glad we didn't know what was to come. The government allowed environmentalists to shut down logging, ruining those jobs. After a few years of no logging, the local lumber mills closed adding more folks to the unemployment rolls. Then the government decided that since there wasn't any logging they needed to let wildfires burn. That decision and a little bug called the pine bark beetle destroyed endless miles of pristine forest including a lot of the East Fork. Then the government decided to reintroduce the wolf into Yellowstone National Park and the Selway-Bitterroot Wilderness.

Downtown Darby is less than five miles from the wilderness boundary and lots of ranches with fat cows are even closer. The wolves ate all the elk in the West Fork of the Bitterroot, ending three-generation family outfitting businesses. Then the wolves started eating the ranchers' cows, horses, and dogs, making the survival of the family ranch harder. The only jobs left were being a fly-fishing guide for rich people from out of state, and nobody could feed a family on those tips. One time, someone asked me why people in Darby hated America. I shook my head in disbelief. My generation from Darby loved our country. We just didn't trust a government that kept trying to destroy our way of life.

Back to the story.

HL-30. Most house logs at that time were turned on a giant lathe. This meant the log sagged in the middle and when turned created just enough wobble the logs were narrower in the middle than on the ends. This limited how long house logs could be before the difference in diameter became noticeable and, more importantly, a problem with construction but not for Neville logs. Those logs weren't made with a lathe and they were the exact same diameter the entire length. The only thing limiting the size of a Neville log was the size of the tree.

Back to the story.

HL-31. I tried to make it clear the different types and functions of the various post-hole diggers while cutting out a lot of detailed description from Scabs. Since it is a little confusing, I added this to be double clear about the tools and their functions. The pounder is also known as metal post driver, post rammer, fence driver or

Beelzebub. They weigh twenty to forty pounds and are meant for one person with strong arms and back to use, but I have operated one with me on one handle and another person managing the other.

The post-hole digger with two wooden handles also goes by the name clamshell digger. Think of it as two narrow shovels hinged together that allow you to, when holding the handles together, stab into the ground. Then by spreading the handles apart the shovels come together and you can lift the dirt out of the hole. The key to this tool is the length of the shovel blades. The longer they are the easier it is to dig deep small diameter holes. If you're using one to dig holes for a metal fence post, you're going to want one with long spades.

The other post-hole digger is a long metal bar called lots of names and used for lots of different things other than digging fence post holes. Common names are spud bar, ice spud, hop bar, lining bar, bear spear, or bark spud. The different names generally indicate what the bar is being used for such as peeling up old tile in a bathroom, smashing a hole in the ice, peeling bark off a tree, or lining up railroad tracks.

Back to the story.

HL-40. This was before the days of cable TV and video games. People often visited their friends in the evening to play cards. It was considered okay to drop by unannounced. Since no one had answering machines for their phones, it was hard to contact a friend before stopping by. Whether planned or spontaneous, it was customary at that time to never visit anyone without bringing your favorite adult beverage along with you. Better yet, bring your friend's favorite adult beverage.

The idea was to bring enough for you and your host to drink during your visit. At the end of the evening, if any of the beverages remained, your host was required to offer to get it out of the fridge so you could take it home. At this point, the guest was required to tell the host to keep the beverage for themselves. Scabs' assertion that Mr. Peck would stay until all the beer was gone means that Mr. Peck understood the social construct and knew the only way to get the most beer for his money was to stay until the beer was all gone. It's a small line, but it speaks to what Scabs thought of Mr. Peck.

Back to the story.

HL-50. In high school, you were either a jock or a dirtbag. The line wasn't drawn around popularity but around whether you played school sports or not. Most kids either played all sports or no sports. There were very few in betweeners. Having converted from jock to dirtbag midway through high school, I'm very familiar with both species.

Boy jocks played football in the fall, basketball or wrestling in the winter, and ran track in the spring. Girl jocks played basketball in the fall, volleyball or cheerleading in the winter, and ran track in the spring. Jocks spent their free time going to practice and often left

home before seven in the morning and returned after seven at night. Their Saturdays were filled with games, tournaments or meets. Dirtbags spent their time working at the family business, a part-time job, hunting in the evenings after school, listening to Ozzy, and skipping school on Fridays to go downhill skiing.
Back to the story.

HL-60. My family still had a party line at this time and the rules around the phone at my house were even wackier than Scabs' house. For those who don't know, a party line meant you shared the same phone line with another house. In our case, it was our closest neighbor a mile away. If someone called our number, our phone rang and their phone rang. Our ring was two shorts, ring – ring. The neighbor's was one long, riinnnnnng.

If I was on the phone to a friend, the neighbor could pick up their phone and listen to our conversation. When we called someone with a party line, we didn't let the phone ring more than four times. The conventional wisdom being that was enough time for your friend to answer their phone but not enough time to annoy the party line. We didn't stay on the phone for more than ten minutes because the neighbor might be waiting for an important call. We also had the rule not to call us after nine at night. If the neighbors were in bed, the call would wake them up. If the phone rang at my house after nine and before six, we knew someone had died.
Back to the story.

HL-61. I am not sure which study Irwin is referencing. Scabs talked to me about this study, but I have been unable to track it down to read the results for myself. To the best of my knowledge, this study occurred in the 1970s. A quick internet search of the topic "police shootings stopping power study" will give you plenty of current information on this subject. The few studies I have perused seem to indicate that the .357 is one of the best handgun calibers, but I didn't see any info on bullet type or weight. It also appeared that lots of controversy surrounds any study results.

Personally, when I have carried a handgun, it was for protection from bears and I want penetration then stopping power. In a .357, I use 180-grain Nosler Silhouettes and in the .41 mag, 210-grain Hornady XTP. I don't think Nosler makes the 180-grain Silhouettes anymore. I have shot bears with both weapons, albeit a small bear with the .357. I was less than ten yards from both bears, both bullets penetrated well but if inclined, both bears could have reached me before dying. Thankfully, both bears ran away from me.

Back to the story.

HL-70. I have to interject that I have never seen these petroglyphs. I have heard of them. I always thought they were something you did if you happened to be driving an attractive young lady past the turn to Spring Gulch. You'd ask if she wanted to go see the petroglyphs. Then you could pull off the main road, park in a secluded copse of trees and show the lady some peterglyphs. Back to the story.

HL-80. Some further explaining may be necessary here as I cut a lot of detail from the already long hike into the lake. As you drive into the trailhead for the String of Lakes, the trail winds uphill to your left. Across the large turnaround parking area, the road continues, but it is blocked with a metal Forest Service gate. I'm not sure this is true, but according to Scabs' manuscript, the gated road used to continue wrapping around the east side of the mountain then crossed over a small saddle and ran all the way to the top of the mountain above the lakes.

The current trail joins the old road again at the lower saddle after about three-quarters of a mile. When the Forest Service decided to only allow vehicles to the new trailhead, they gated the road and created the new three-quarters of a mile of trail. While I am not sure this is where the new trail joined the original road, I did stop in this saddle on a recent trip into the lakes. Mostly, I stopped because my old dog was tired from hiking all the way to Rain Lake and back. While the dog rested in the bear grass in the shade under a small fir tree, I spotted a blaze on a tree and large stumps on either side of a band of thirty-foot-tall fir trees running across the saddle. It looked like an old road that made its way across the ridge and down to the gated road.

Back to the story.

HL-81. Including this conversation, in fact, just including the names of the lakes in the narrative, weighed on my mind. Nowadays, the best way to ruin a scenic place is to post pictures of it on social media with a tagline #epicviews , #phenomenalfishing, or #monstertrout. In the short-term, you get many likes. Next weekend, however, the scenic place is ruined by a mass of people seeking their own exciting weekend social media post. Back in the day, word didn't spread quite as fast, but if you mentioned to your cousin Hank that fishing was great at Mash Lake, Hank might not hike into Mash, but he would tell his brother. The brother would mention it in church, and the church members would tell their families, and next month, more people would visit Mash Lake than had been there in the past five years. In order to keep good fishing and hunting spots good, people often stopped telling others where they went fishing or hunting.

"HL, where did you catch that huge trout?"

"In the mouth," is the correct answer to keep that great fishing hole great.

Out of this need for secrecy, many unwritten rules have developed around fishing and hunting spots. If your buddy Tom takes you fishing in his spot, can you go there by yourself? Can you take your cousin Hank with you? The answers to both those question are no, if you want to keep your buddy Tom a buddy.

I've been hiking into these lakes for over forty years and other than a fire that burned in between Mash and Myth, they have remained the same, beautiful beyond words. I decided to obfuscate—there's a word for you—the real names of the lakes in the book for three reasons. First, even though I wanted to use the place names from my childhood to keep the background of the story accurate, I can't stand the thought of seeing trash around any of those lakes. Second, I imagine only about a dozen folks will read this book and they will know what lakes I am talking about regardless of what names I use. Third, even though most people today don't have the gumption to hike twelve miles to go fishing, if they do have the gumption, then they will also have to look at a few maps to figure out the real names. I guess it's my way of adding one more obstacle to keep those places beautiful.

For me, the most beautiful places don't have anyone else there except me. If you do decide to follow in the footsteps of Diana, Pete, and Scabs, enjoy the beauty of these lakes, but please do your best to keep them that way. Don't bother to bring fish poles, most of the lakes don't even have fish in them. The ones that do only have little fish because the wolves ate the big ones. But you don't have to worry about the wolves. The grizzly bears hopped up on goofballs ran them out of the country. And watch out for Bigfoot.

Back to the story.

HL-82. I have camped here before with my dad, and it is easily the best place on the lake. One time, my dad, a friend of his, and I camped kitty-corner on the lake from this campsite. We came early in the year to find Mash

Lake completely frozen over and Trout Lake only open along the shore for ten feet or so in a few places. Snow covered the ground around the lake except for a small area near where the current trail hits the lake. A massive storm dropped lightning on the ridges around the lake all night long. Three people and two dogs spent a wet night huddled in a two-man tent, very similar to the one Pete owned. In the morning, the temperature dropped and the rain turned into snow. It was a long, cold, wet hike through six inches of snow to the truck, with no fish, in a blinding blizzard.

Back to the story.

HL-90. I hate to keep interrupting the story, but I couldn't let this go. The stump that Scab notes on the shore of the lake is very special to me. My dad stood on top of that stump and caught twenty-two fish in the same number of casts. I sat in the sunshine watching him expertly catch each fish. It was a great day, and the last time my dad and I were at the lake. The stump is still there, but all that remains is a crumbled pile of red rotten wood along the shoreline.

Back to the story.

HL-91. I don't know about the veracity of Diana's claim that her uncle caught a fish in Myth Lake, but I know for a fact that my uncle caught a twenty-three-inch trout from Myth Lake way before I went to high school.

We were camped at Mash Lake and my uncle left everyone to try his luck at Myth. I followed a few hours later, and when I reached Myth, I spotted my uncle across the lake. He was fighting a fish and when he saw me, he yelled for me to help. He had apparently hooked the fish thirty minutes prior to my getting to the lake but was unable to land the fish. I hurried around the lake, got my feet wet wading out into the shallows, and scooped the fish out of the water, much like Diana did with Pete's fish.

After we settled down following the excitement of catching the huge fish, my uncle scanned the shore around the lake and asked where my dad was. When I replied he was back at Mash, he then asked who came to the lake with me. Apparently, he was amazed I could navigate the distance between the lakes all by myself. Which I thought was pretty amusing. What ten-year-old couldn't find their way a quarter mile on a trail?

I visited Myth Lake while working on this manuscript to get a feel for the area. As soon as I reached the lake, I immediately spotted the rock my uncle was on when he caught the fish. I hurried around the lake and stood on the hillside watching the surface of the water for any sign of fish rising. I hadn't been to Myth since the day my uncle caught that fish. My mind did the math—forty years ago. Sometimes, time doesn't just fly, it disappears, like the fish in Myth Lake.

Just to be clear, my uncle caught a twenty-three-inch trout on a red and white daredevil in Myth Lake, and that is no legend.

Back to the story.

HL-100. I chuckle every time I read Scabs' description of buying condoms at Bitterroot Drug. Back then, condoms were not readily available, at least in the Darby area, in gas stations or bar bathrooms. The only way to get your hands on a condom was to march into Bitterroot Drug, do a quick sweep through the aisles to make sure none of your aunts were in the store, speed walk down the prophylactic aisle, and quickly grab a box as you went by. No stopping, as that just let everyone in the store know you were looking at the sex stuff.

I half sprinted down the aisle when I saw the checkout clerk didn't have anybody in line, grabbed a box with Trojan written on it, and skidded to a stop at the counter. I paid in cash and as I turned to go, I came face to face with the mother of one of my friends. She smiled at me. "Planning on having a nice prom." I'm not sure I even answered, other than my entire body turning red with embarrassment. I ran outside to my car swearing I would never do that again. Thankfully, I had grabbed the thirty-pack, so I never needed to go back, ever.

Back to the story.

HL-110. True to its nature, the Forest Service would change not only the names of the lakes back to their original names, but they would rework the trail into the String of Lakes ATV trail. Initially, each lake, Trout and Mash, had their own trail leading down from the spring in the high saddle. Trout Lake's trail started before you reached the spring in the saddle and Mash Lake's trail started after you passed the spring. When Uncle Sam decided to let ATVs ride the main trail to the high saddle and on up the ridge above Myth and Rain Lakes, they put in a new trail down the ridge between Trout and Mash then branched the trails into the lakes from that ridge trail.

If you were to hike these new trails from Trout Lake to Mash Lake today, it's pretty much the route Scabs, Pete, and Diana took. ATV riders were only allowed on the main trail to the high saddle, the trails to the lakes you had to hike. That is, until after a decade or so, then the Forest Service had to change things again. They banned ATVs on the main trail, forcing everyone to hump it in the old-fashioned way.

Back to the story.

HL-111. What's really interesting about this fishing story is that it is eerily similar to how I caught a big fish at a lake way up the West Fork of the Bitterroot. I distinctly remember telling Scabs about catching the fish and I don't remember him saying anything about how he had caught a bigger fish in a similar way up the East Fork. He must not have said anything because his fish was bigger and he didn't want to make me feel bad by bringing up his story. Also, it's a pretty common way to catch trout in high mountain lakes. I'm sure many people have had a similar experience.

Back to the story.

HL-120. I know what you're thinking—it's a tired and cheap trick to start the book two-thirds of the way through, then jump back in time, and make the reader wade through page after page of non-action drivel to get back to the exciting point. Please forgive me. It was the only way I could think of to pique the readers' interest in Scabs enough to plow through all that fence building and hiking into the lakes shit. Anyway, for your convenience, I have repeated the start of the book as I imagine by this time you've forgotten all about it. If you haven't forgotten, then skip to the next chapter and keep reading.

Back to the story.

However, if you need a refresher...

I stumbled away from the campfire, leaving its light behind and wiping away the tears in my eyes. I'd never seen my father cry and even here in the middle of nowhere, I didn't want to cry. The branches of a fir tree scratched my face as I blundered into it in the dark. I spun away from the branch blindly fleeing until I tripped and fell, grabbing wildly for anything to help me keep my balance. I slammed into something, not a tree trunk but softer. Arms wrapped around me and slammed me on my butt. I thought Pete had followed me from the campfire and I pushed away from him telling him to leave me alone. A strong hand covered my mouth pushing my head into the bear grass. Whoever I had run into now sat on my chest cutting off my air. The quarter moon waxed, or maybe it waned, in the sky to the left. I could never remember which was which, but the light it gave off was sufficient to tell it wasn't Pete sitting on my chest.

There he was, the fugitive we had been scouring the forest for sat on my chest, clamping my mouth shut with one hand with a pistol in the other. Even in the low light, I could see him forming the shush sign by holding the muzzle perpendicular to his lips.

I guess I should have been scared, but I wasn't, which surprised me. Every Louis L'Amour book I'd read said that the opening in the end of a gun barrel appeared huge when the gun was pointed at you, but I could plainly see the barrel was almost a half an inch in diameter, which meant a .45 was pointed at my head not a 9mm.

After the surprise, shock set in as I realized my life had become a story. Last winter, one of my mom's clients had recommended the book *A River Run's Through It* to her. Mom had told the guy how I always read before going to bed and he suggested Mom buy Norman Maclean's book for me. This was back before Brad Pitt met Louise and Thelma and went on to tell everyone how fly-fishing was for the cool kids. Back when people fly-fished because they wanted to catch more fish to eat, not release.

Besides the fly-fishing story, the book had two more stories in it. I had wondered why the guy recommended the book to my mom because the second story featured a tough logger who liked to screw fat women. What kind of guy recommends that story to a lady's impressionable fifteen-year-old? I'm not sure which story, probably the last story about the Forest Service ranger who played cribbage, but one of the stories talked about how sometimes your life becomes a story.

Well, when I read that, I was disappointed because my life had never been a story and I was eager for the day something would happen to make my life a story. I tried hard to fashion everything I did into a legend, but it wasn't until the kidnapper stuck a gun in my face that I knew, right then, my life had become a story. In fact, my life had been a story for a while, but I just hadn't known it. If this man killed me, then I hadn't figured out I was in a story until the last page of the last chapter.

His hand eased the pressure on my mouth as I quit struggling. He hissed, "Yell, and so help me, I'll put a bullet in your brain."

I wiggled my head against his hand letting him know I wouldn't scream for help. That was the last thing on my mind. When did my life become a story? When did this start? When I agreed to go with Pete to look for the kidnapper? No. Earlier, when I agreed to build the fence for Cherylann?

The fugitive shifted the muzzle of the gun to the side of my head and leaned forward. His black eyes were wide in the pale moonlight and his breath was hot compared to the damp air. "What the fuck are you doing? Why did you run into me?"

I blinked, feeling the dried tears in the corners of my eyes, then looked past the muzzle of the gun at the kidnapper's face. I didn't run into him. He'd tackled me. I tried to speak but only stuttered nonsense about getting away from the fire.

"Did you hurt the girl with you?" His words searing like a hot cast-iron skillet.

I found my voice, replying in a whisper only he and the half-dozen mosquitoes circling our warm breath could hear. "No."

"What was all the yelling?"

How do I explain to a man holding a gun to my head that my best friend had just destroyed my life then tried to kick my ass? "We had an argument."

His leaned back a hair, giving me room to breathe. His whispered voice turned nonchalant as if we were discussing the weather while waiting in the checkout line at People's Market. "Do you have any guns?"

I thought of the revolver buried inside my backpack. If I told the kidnapper about the gun, I would lose the chance to use it. If I didn't tell him and he found it, it would anger him. If only I had it strapped to my belt right now.

That line of thought flitted away like a mosquito, my mind drawn back to the question of when had my life become a story. Graduation day when Jenny, Pete, and I stood around in the parking lot talking after the ceremony sprang to mind.

The gun pushed into the side of my temple. "Boy, you don't answer me, and I may not shoot you, but I will choke the ever-livin' shit out of you." His hand gripped my throat to emphasize his point.

I thought about it. Yeah, that was exactly when my life became a story.

Back to the story.

HL-130. For full disclosure reasons, I feel like this is a good time to let you know I dated Jenny's younger sister my senior year of high school. I had a lot of great times at the Peck residence. I got to know Jenny and her parents really well. I have tried not to let any of my feelings for the Pecks interfere with Scabs' perception of them. However, at this point, I think I can add my own viewpoint without messing up the story.

First, the only girl in Darby at that time hotter than Jenny was her younger sister.

Second, Jenny's sister didn't take any oath about waiting until after high school.

Third, Jenny and Pete had done the sliding thing before, but graduation night was the first time they went all the way.

Fourth, Jenny really regretted how she treated Scabs.

And finally, Mr. Peck is indeed, a giant dickhead.

Back to the story.

HL-140. In case you didn't know, autoerotic asphyxiation is when you choke yourself while you masturbate. Not sure how that became a thing, but it may or may not have given rise to the saying choking the chicken. Sometimes the choking gets too intense and the person accidently strangles themselves to death, resulting in asphyxiation. A circle jerk is a group of guys masturbating together. So, a mutual autoerotic asphyxiation circle jerk is when a group of guys masturbate and choke themselves to death. It's not a real thing, I hope.

Back to the story.

HL-170. I held off on making comments as I didn't want to interrupt the pace of the story since it had finally picked up some speed like it was running downhill. Now that we've hit a little lull, let me add in some comments.

If you do hike into Myth Lake, don't bother trying to find Pete's pack. I scoured the hillside, and while I did find an old rock ring for a campfire, I didn't find any backpacks or other trash in the area. Someone must have come back for the gear Pete and Diana left.

I have no clue if catfish jump, but since they are bottom-feeders, I think it unlikely. More importantly, the lyrics are from the song "Black Water" by the Doobie Brothers, not Steely Dan or Seals and Crofts as Scabs thought. England Dan, partner of John Ford Coley, is also known as the glittery country singer Dan Seals, and the Seals in Seals and Crofts is Dan's brother. Dan Seals isn't related to Steely Dan because Steely Dan isn't a guy, it's the name of the band.

As for me, when I hike I usually have the songs "Cum On Feel The Noize" or "My Heroes Have Always Been Cowboys" stuck in my head.

One of the most important things Scabs taught me was to always have a set of dry clothes waiting in your vehicle. This piece of advice has allowed me to drive home in comfort from numerous hunting trips that have gone wrong. He also taught me that a new roll of duct tape laid on the transmission hump makes a handy beverage holder. Later in life, Scabs would also teach me to leave a half rack of beer at the truck. It's a good idea but a dangerous one. It becomes very tempting after you've drank the beer you packed into camp to think it will be no problem to jog three miles to the truck, grab the half rack, and jog back to hunting camp in the dark. So, use some discretion when leaving beer in your truck.

Fred Wetzsteon International Airport is a form of reverse colloquialism. The straw hat wearing driver of the turd brown truck is talking about a dirt runway on the edge of a cow pasture. To call it an international airport places a grandeur on a common item. It also speaks to how rural the area is. In most places, it would be just a dirt runway, but it is so rural that a dirt runway is considered an international airport. Or maybe, I'm just reading too much into it.

Last, I'm not sure of the size of Scabs' amygdala, but I have been hunting with him when he has made some incredible shots. I saw him shoot a gopher at one hundred fifty yards with an iron-sight Mossberg .22 long rifle. Maybe his overactive amygdala helps him focus on the target better than us normal people.

Back to the story.

HL-190. I did interview Pete. Interview isn't the correct term. I spent two separate evenings bullshitting with him on his back porch drinking the half rack of Keystone Light I brought. Pete didn't disagree on any of the main points. He did say that he didn't break both the bones in his arm, just the one. Pete said the broken arm was a blessing in disguise as the pressure of being the starting quarterback of a team that was supposed to go to state was overwhelming.

When I asked why he had delayed going to look for the kidnapper for a week, he gave me a shit-eating grin as he explained he spent the weekend hanging out with Jenny since Scabs was supposed to stay away. He also admitted to shooting both Scabs and Diana. But he insisted he thought Seth was going to shoot him and that both Diana and Scabs had moved into his line of fire. He expressed regret over the shooting and for being such a dick to Scabs. He agreed with Bob's assessment that pussy is indeed a powerful thing, stating he had been so full of adolescent hormones he let it ruin his friendship with Scabs.

Pete told me his son was visiting next weekend and he was going to have him drive him up to the high saddle in his side by side. Maybe, if his old bones felt good, he might even try to hike down to Trout Lake. I told Pete the Forest Service didn't allow ATVs on the trail to the saddle anymore. His grin in response told me that, at his age, he didn't really care about the Forest Service's rules.

Back to the story.

HL-200. I tried to interview Irwin while working on Scabs' manuscript, but I was unable to locate him. I wanted to get his perspective on teaching Scabs to fight and how well Scabs had built the fence. But I wasn't even able to determine if he was alive or dead. While I was away at college, I remembered Cherylann sold her property up the West Fork, and rumor was, she moved to a ranch in eastern Montana. When I asked around about Irwin, people generally remembered him as a nice guy who moved to Kalispell.

Back to the story.

HL-210. I was unable to determine if anything Lieutenant Ron said about Scabs' dad is true. I did confirm his dad served in the Marines and was in Vietnam, but I couldn't confirm if he was a sniper. I also couldn't determine if he was sent to Canada by the Marines. Apparently, a lot of his military service file is confidential. I did find a lot of information on Carlos Hathcock. His story of being a Marine sniper in Vietnam is incredible and I highly recommend Charles Henderson's book *Marine Sniper*. You know, if you're interested in Vietnam or shooting guns.

Back to the story.

HL-220. I tracked down Diana to interview her while working on the manuscript. I found her in a little town near Dillon, Montana where she lived with her husband. When I sat down with Diana, mother of three, for coffee at The Hitchin' Post, a cafe in Melrose, she had just retired from teaching. Her youth in the outdoors might have weathered her face, but her eyes still held the intensity I remembered from seeing her on the school bus.

When I told her the reason for our meeting, she expressed that Scabs continued to impress her. She never thought he could write a story, let alone a book. She asked lots of questions about Scabs, so much so, most of our time together was spent with her questioning me about Scabs instead of the other way around.

She let me know she never saw Scabs again after watching the movie with him. Diana said getting shot by Pete had been the best thing that ever happened to her. She had graduated from Dillon with her teaching certificate four years later then landed a job teaching at the tiny school in Polaris, Montana. Halfway through the first year of teaching, she noticed that the only senior at school began to be picked up after school by her older brother instead of her mother.

The older brother was everything she wasn't looking for. He didn't hunt, he didn't live in a big city, and other than land, he was dirt-poor. She said it didn't matter because she had fallen for him at first sight. They married within a year of meeting each other. She spent her winters teaching school and her summers teaching her husband how to hike in the Pioneer Mountains. She said it had been a very good life and she couldn't imagine anything better.

She did confirm that she had indeed made a pass at Scabs on the shore of Trout Lake. It wasn't a figment of his teenage imagination as I had suspected. She found it amusing he remembered it. She said Seth had ended up sentenced to five years in prison but only served ninety days before he was paroled. She'd only heard from him once after he went to jail. A late-night phone call in which he apologized for using her. She thought it had been part of a substance abuse treatment program that required him to make amends with everyone he had wronged in his life.

Unknown to Scabs, Diana had been given a deferred sentence of six months in jail for helping Seth. With a wry smile, she explained her first year in college was a very quiet one since any further offense would have landed her in jail and the felony charge would have ruined her teaching career before it started. She shrugged afterward and said in her slow way, "I was young. I've been a model citizen since."

I summoned the courage to ask if Scabs' mom really did give "happy ending" massages. Diana's opinion was that if a man wanted a handjob he could do it himself better than any woman, so she wasn't sure why a man would pay for it. She did acknowledge that Scabs' folks never had much money and sometimes you do what you have to in order for the ends to meet. "No shame in that," she added deliberately.

She left before I wanted her to, but she said she had to pick her grandson up from football practice. She informed me that he started at safety and had made an interception and had seven tackles during his last game. Back to the story.

HL-230. I did attempt to interview Jenny to get her side of the story. When I showed up at her house in Hamilton, her sister Jessica happened to be visiting. Seems they were having a bottle of wine to celebrate Jessica signing her divorce papers. I had a glass of wine with them but sensed that they had a negative mood going about men. I didn't stay long and didn't mention Scabs as I didn't think it would be a good time to bring up past relationships. Back to the story.

HL-240. This seems like a good spot to end the story since everything is going PT's way. There's a chapter on his movie date with Diana, not as long a chapter as you might have expected. Another chapter about water skiing with Sally, not as exciting as you might have expected. But I thought they dragged the ending of the story on longer than needed and didn't add to the core storyline. At this point, his struggle to figure out what he was going to do after high school isn't resolved, but he has met his goal of earning enough money during the summer to keep his dream of going to college alive. Moving to Alaska offers him a new start away from his nickname, gossip about his family, and failed relationships. It seemed like a natural place to stop, and hopefully, it gave you a little jolt when you found out Scabs is actually PT. Even though I dropped hints throughout the story.

There's more in the manuscript after the chapters about Diana and Sally, but it's like a general outline of events that here and there PT dips into and writes in great detail. PT speeds through the move to Alaska, and on the subject of his folks disappearing on the Canning River, he writes only a short paragraph, and the lack of emotion in the words speaks to just how devastating it was for him. A man who writes that can't find the right words indicates a total breakdown.

He writes only a paragraph about his return to Darby to live with his fake grandpa. After his fake grandpa died, the manuscript becomes a list of handwritten dates with short titles to the side. Things like Lake Muncho Lodge - Sheila Mackado / Watson Lake - Packer at Grubstake Outfitters / Tok Alaska – Bartender at Fast Eddy's / Fairbanks Alaska – Clerk at Frontier Sporting Goods. It does have a complete chapter written about his ten-year high-school reunion and meeting Kristi Harm at Bud and Shirley's Motel, but then it goes back to the list of dates. The writing picks up again right after the heading Midnight Mine - Hugh John Bigfoot Hunt.

Sometimes always, I think PT's life has been a story.

The End.

About HL Miller

Thanks for reading *Off to the East Fork*, I hope you enjoyed it. Thank you for going along on the adventure. It's been a long road. I don't write for a living, I write because I love it. Even though I love writing, finding the time to write and being motivated to write becomes a challenge. Any comment or interest in my stories drives me to write. If you liked *Off to the East Fork*, please leave a review where you bought it or on Goodreads, I'd appreciate it.

If you would like to learn more about PT Thomas or me, visit my website - HLMiller.com.

Acknowledgements

Thanks to everyone who, after listening to one of my many stories said, "You should write a book." Those words helped push me down the path of writing. Or was it over a cliff?

Thanks to all those folks that contributed to the book as beta readers and for those who read the books and commented on what they liked, or didn't like. Any and all help has been and will continue to be appreciated.

A special thanks to my family who has put up with PT for most of my life. Writing is a passion and like anything you are passionate about, you sacrifice the opportunity to do other activities, such as spending time with family, in order to engage in your passion. Thanks to my wife and kids for listening patiently to my endless discussions on writing.

All of the PT Thomas Adventure books, including this one, have been reviewed by Kelly Hartigan at XterraWeb. Kelly provides a combination proofreading and copyediting service at a reasonable price. During her review, Kelly caught misspelled place names, which she obviously had to take the time to look up on the web, homophones I didn't even know existed, and noted several point-of-view shifts. I encourage you to check out Kelly's editing services at http://editing.xterraweb.com/.

One of the perks of being an Indie author is that the

final decision of what goes into the book is mine. If you find any mistakes in this book, that is a reflection of the author being old, stubborn, and grumpy. I am sure Kelly caught the error and, because of my previously mentioned character flaws, I chose to ignore her expert guidance.

Made in United States
North Haven, CT
26 September 2022